Bruce began jogging backward into the open clearing that was full of blueberry bushes, his mouth wide open.

Hayley knew he wouldn't stop until he caught one, so she picked one more blueberry and threw it as hard as she could.

It flew right at him, and it looked as if he was poised to finally catch it when suddenly he went down, flat on his back.

Hayley gasped. "Bruce, are you okay?"

"Yeah, I just tripped."

Hayley ran toward him, but didn't see him at first. "Where are you?"

He raised an arm in the air.

As she got closer to him, she suddenly heard him yell, "Oh my God!"

"Bruce, what is it? What's wrong?"

"I just saw what I tripped over . . . I thought it was a log or something . . ."

As Hayley finally reached Bruce, she followed his stunned gaze to the ground, where a body was face-down in a blueberry patch.

Bruce gingerly reached down and turned the body over enough to see that it was a woman, her white summer blouse stained purple by squashed blueberries . . .

Books by Lee Hollis

Hayley Powell Mysteries
DEATH OF A KITCHEN DIVA
DEATH OF A COUNTRY FRIED REDNECK
DEATH OF A COUPON CLIPPER
DEATH OF A CHOCOHOLIC
DEATH OF A CHRISTMAS CATERER
DEATH OF A CUPCAKE QUEEN
DEATH OF A BACON HEIRESS
DEATH OF A PUMPKIN CARVER
DEATH OF A LOBSTER LOVER
DEATH OF A COOKBOOK AUTHOR
DEATH OF A WEDDING CAKE BAKER
DEATH OF A BLUEBERRY TART
EGGNOG MURDER
(with Leslie Meier and Barbara Ross)
YULE LOG MURDER
(with Leslie Meier and Barbara Ross)
HAUNTED HOUSE MURDER
(with Leslie Meier and Barbara Ross)

Poppy Harmon Mysteries
POPPY HARMON INVESTIGATES
POPPY HARMON AND THE HUNG JURY

Maya & Sandra Mysteries
MURDER AT THE PTA

Published by Kensington Publishing Corporation

DEATH of a BLUEBERRY TART

Lee Hollis

KENSINGTON BOOKS
www.kensingtonbooks.com

KENSINGTON BOOKS are published by

Kensington Publishing Corp.
119 West 40th Street
New York, NY 10018

All Kensington titles, imprints, and distributed lines are available at special quantity discounts for bulk purchases for sales promotion, premiums, fund-raising, and educational or institutional use.

Special book excerpts or customized printings can also be created to fit specific needs. For details, write or phone the office of the Kensington Sales Manager: Kensington Publishing Corp., 119 West 40th Street, New York, NY 10018. Attn. Sales Department. Phone: 1-800-221-2647.

Kensington and the K logo Reg. U.S. Pat. & TM Off.

First Kensington Books Mass Market Paperback Printing: April 2020

ISBN-13: 978-1-4967-2493-9
ISBN-10: 1-4967-2493-3

ISBN-13: 978-1-4967-2494-6 (ebook)
ISBN-10: 1-4967-2494-1 (ebook)

10 9 8 7 6 5 4 3 2 1

Printed in the United States of America

For Mom

Chapter 1

Reverend Staples stood before Hayley and Bruce and all the wedding guests filling the pews of the Congregational church and asked, "If anyone here has just cause why these two people should not be married, speak now or forever hold your peace."

He waited a moment, smiled at the happy couple, and then got right to the good part. "By the power vested in me by the state of Maine—"

"Wait! I do! I have just cause!" a man bellowed from the back of the church.

The crowd gasped and whipped around in their seats to see who was rudely interrupting the ceremony.

Hayley's jaw dropped open.

She swooned, fearing she was on the cusp of fainting dead away.

Bruce gripped her hands even tighter to keep her steady as she stared at the intruder standing on the church threshold.

What was *he* doing here?

It was Danny Powell.

Hayley's ex-husband.

Hayley's mind raced. How could he have possibly known she was going to marry Bruce Linney, the crime reporter from the *Island Times* newspaper where she worked? It was Hayley's best friend Liddy Crawford who was supposed to be married today, in this church, at this time. But due to unforeseen circumstances, the wedding had been abruptly called off, leaving Bruce to unexpectedly propose to Hayley, and with Liddy's blessing, the wedding ceremony had resumed with a new bride and groom.

Danny charged down the aisle toward them. Hayley's brother, Randy, who was sitting on the end of a pew, looked as if he might try to intervene and stop Danny en route, but he demurred as Danny blew past him and marched right up to the still-in-shock couple.

"Danny, what's going on? How did you know—?"

He cut her off. "I didn't! Liddy invited me to *her* wedding!"

Hayley glanced at Liddy, who was sitting in the front row with her mother, Celeste. Liddy shrugged. "I never thought in a million years he would actually show up! I mean he lives in Idaho!"

"Iowa," Danny corrected her. "My plane got delayed in Philadelphia and I didn't think I was going to make it, but I got here at the last minute, and imagine my surprise when I walked in here and saw *this*!"

He gestured toward Hayley and Bruce standing numbly at the altar in front of Reverend Staples.

Gemma held up a hand from the middle of the congregation, calling to her father. "Dad, why don't you come here and sit next to me . . ."

Danny shook his head. "I can't, baby girl. Not yet. Not until your mother tells me that she no longer loves me."

"*What?*" Hayley cried.

"I love you, Hayley, I've never stopped loving you. Splitting up with you was the absolute worst decision I ever made in my life, and I will never be at peace until I correct it."

"It's too late," Bruce said sternly, quickly losing patience. "Maybe you ought to listen to your daughter and take a seat."

The two men glared at each other, and Hayley feared a fight might break out so she stepped between them to keep the two men separated.

"I'm not going anywhere, not until Hayley answers my question," Danny said, standing his ground.

Hayley sighed. "Danny, you can't just barge in here and—"

He cut her off again. "Tell me, babe, tell me you don't feel the same way about me that I feel about you. We have always been meant for each other, that's clear to me now, and this time, I'm not going to screw it up!"

"What about Becky?" Hayley asked, suddenly remembering Danny's much younger girlfriend back in Iowa.

"We broke up months ago."

"The kids never said anything . . ." Hayley said, her voice trailing off.

"I didn't tell them. I was embarrassed because it ended badly. I finally told her I didn't love her because my heart belonged to someone else. She didn't have to ask who. She *knew*."

"Oh, Danny . . ."

"Look, buddy, I'm warning you . . ." Bruce interjected, his face reddening.

Danny threw his hands up. "Okay, I'll go. Right after she tells me she no longer loves me."

Bruce shook his head, annoyed. "Fine." Then he turned to Hayley. "Tell him."

Hayley opened her mouth to answer, but no words came out.

The congregation was utterly silent.

"Go on, Hayley, tell him . . ."

Hayley tried to speak, to say the words everyone was expecting to hear, but she couldn't. She couldn't say no.

She was taking so long to answer such a simple question there was now surprised murmuring coming from the pews.

"Hayley?" Bruce asked, his voice cracking.

Danny stood defiantly at her side, feeling emboldened with each passing second.

"Hayley, what's wrong? Tell him!" Bruce demanded, desperately now.

Hayley's eyes filled with tears.

This was the last thing she had ever expected.

Finally, she managed to choke out the words, "I'm sorry, Bruce . . ."

The entire congregation gasped, stunned.

Danny couldn't help but break out into a wide, triumphant smile.

Hayley shook her head, overwhelmed by the enormity of what she was about to do. "I'm so, so sorry . . ."

And then, Danny grabbed her hand, squeezed it lovingly, and pulled her down the aisle behind him and right out of the church.

Chapter 2

Hayley bolted upright in bed. Sweat poured down her face as she breathed heavily, and took in her surroundings. She was in her own bedroom, in her house on Glenmary Road, and her dog, Leroy, was fast asleep at the foot of the bed. There was a lump snoring softly next to her, and it took a moment or two to remember who he was. She gently reached over and pulled down the covers a bit to get a good look at his face.

Hayley sighed with relief.

It was him.

Bruce Linney.

Her husband.

Danny showing up at their last-minute wedding ceremony at the Congregational church two months ago had unfortunately *not* been a dream. Liddy had invited him, never expecting him to actually show up, and he had vociferously objected to Hayley marrying Bruce, mostly because the sight of her at the altar had so surprised him, so shaken him, he had had some kind of involuntary outburst. He had never truly expected Hayley to call the whole thing off and run away with him, and in Hayley's mind, that would have been the second biggest mistake of her life, the first having been marrying Danny in the first place.

But luckily, Hayley was clear-eyed about Bruce, and her feelings for him, and how much she looked forward to starting a new life together, and so it had been an easy choice to make.

She had set Danny straight in front of the church full of wedding guests, reminding him that their time together was squarely and mercifully in the past, and she was now going to marry Bruce. Danny had quietly accepted her wishes, quickly backed off, and left for Des Moines the following day with his tail between his legs.

And that's when she finally got hitched to Bruce.

They had only been married a couple of months now, but it felt as if they had been together for decades. Hayley had initially wondered how they would adjust to married life, what difficulties might lie ahead, but it had been so easy, so natural, so right.

Of course there had been a few bumps along the way. Bruce was an anal-retentive neat freak and Hayley, after having raised two rambunctious, wild, and messy kids, had always struggled to keep a spotless home. Hayley liked to have dinner promptly at six o'clock, again a habit formed with her two hungry kids who had homework to do after dinner, while Bruce, who had never been a parent, preferred a leisurely dinner starting around eight in the evening and lingering with a bottle of wine until well after ten. Bruce was up and at the gym just after dawn, while Hayley hid under the covers until Leroy and her cat, Blueberry, scratched and howled at her until she was forced to drag herself out of bed for their first feeding of the day.

She could write a book about their differences—she and Bruce, not the dog and cat. After a rocky relationship that had begun way back in high school with a disastrous first date, they had managed to avoid each other until fate had brought them back together at the *Island Times* office when the editor-in-chief, Sal Moretti, hired Hayley to be office manager and subsequently the food and cocktails columnist, and where Bruce toiled as the paper's resident crime reporter.

Their work relationship could best be summed up as fractured and contentious, at best they tolerated each other. But then something strange and wonderful happened. The ice melted between them. Some might chalk it up to global warming, but others, especially the romantics among them, like Liddy, or her daughter, Gemma, reasoned it was the spark that had always lain dormant between them, finally reigniting. They fell in love like one usually falls asleep. Slowly and then all at once.

And now, before Hayley even realized what was going on, they were a married couple.

Hayley stared at Bruce's handsome face. She still couldn't believe it. Bruce Linney, the butt of so many of her jokes in the past, now her husband. Whoever said opposites attract had never been so spot-on when it came to Hayley and Bruce. She couldn't help but smile. She had proclaimed on numerous occasions that she would never, ever marry again. And now, here he was, sleeping so sweetly and soundly next to her. It sent a warm feeling throughout her body.

Suddenly her quiet thoughts and reflections were abruptly interrupted by Bruce unleashing a loud sneeze. His whole body jerked and he suddenly sat up, awake, his eyes watering. He looked around, suspicious.

"Where is he?" Bruce growled.

Oh, right, there was one more challenge they were facing now that they were married and living under one roof.

Bruce violently sneezed again.

He wiped his nose with his hand and glowered. "He's in here somewhere!"

Blueberry.

Bruce was allergic to cats, and Blueberry was a big Persian cat with lots of fur and dander.

Hayley had tried all kinds of sprays, a high-efficiency particulate air purifier, and a special vacuum cleaner to suck up all the cat allergens, all to no avail. Bruce was still miserable whenever Blueberry was around, and even when he wasn't. Hayley was at a loss. Blueberry had been a part of the family for years, and she had no idea how she was going to deal with this problem. Bruce tried to be a trouper at first, but it was getting more difficult by the day.

The bedroom door was open a crack, which meant Blueberry had pushed his way through. Hayley jumped out of bed and circled the room, finally spotting Blueberry sitting blissfully by the window that was open a bit, a slight breeze blowing the curtains around as well as Blueberry's small particles of pet dander. It was just light enough outside, with the sun cresting over Cadillac Mountain, bringing daylight to the coastal town of Bar Harbor, that Hayley could make out a slight, almost imperceptible smile on her cat's face, almost has if he was enjoying torturing Bruce.

"Out, Blueberry!" Hayley commanded, clapping her hands loud enough that the sound sent Blueberry scurrying out of the room.

Bruce sneezed one, two, three more times before he crawled out of bed. "My allergies just keep getting worse."

"I know, Bruce, I'm sorry . . ." Hayley said quietly. "We'll think of something."

He didn't believe her.

She had said this so many times.

But nothing seemed to be working.

Bruce slipped on some sweatpants and a tank top, grabbed his gym bag off a chair next to the bed, and headed out the bedroom door. "I'm going to the gym."

"I love you!" Hayley called after him.

"Love you too," Bruce said.

Suddenly she heard a screeching sound.

"What is it?"

"I just stepped on Blueberry's tail. He was on the stairs!" Bruce yelled back.

"Is he all right?" Hayley asked.

"He's fine," Bruce said before mumbling to himself although loud enough for Hayley to hear, "That's one of us."

And then he stomped down the stairs and out the front door to his car.

Hayley threw on a robe and crossed out of the bedroom to see Blueberry huddled near the staircase, staring up at her.

"Wipe that smile off your face," Hayley warned.

Chapter 3

Hayley had breakfast on the table by the time Bruce returned from the gym. She had also placed a brochure next to his plate of scrambled eggs, turkey bacon, and whole wheat toast lightly buttered. Bruce's eyes zeroed right in on the brochure and he picked it up and unfolded it.

"Just six more days," he said with more than just a hint of excitement in his voice.

"I know, I've been counting too," Hayley said.

Bruce scanned the brochure. "They have a *Saturday Night Fever* musical production in the main theater."

"We should definitely go."

"If we ever make it out of our stateroom," Bruce said playfully with a wink.

Because their wedding had been so out-of-the-blue and not planned, the newlyweds had never had the opportunity to book a honeymoon. On the night of their wedding, they had split a pizza and watched a movie, not even a good one, a grade-B disaster movie starring the Rock, which got terrible reviews. Neither of them had even put in for any vacation time at the office, so any kind of romantic excursion had to be postponed until they could work out the details. But now, two months later, they were far more prepared. Sal had approved their vacation time request and they had booked a one-week cruise to the Bahamas, and were scheduled to fly out of Bangor to Fort Lauderdale in less than a week.

The luxury suites had already been booked and there were only a few staterooms left, but Hayley had managed to grab one with a small terrace overlooking an expansive ocean view. Neither she nor Bruce cared about having a lot of space to move around in as long as they were together.

"The food is supposed to be incredible so no dieting, or talking about dieting, okay? This is our honeymoon! We need to indulge," Bruce said, flipping the brochure over to read the back.

"Understood," Hayley agreed, pinching her belly fat and wondering if it would be possible to lose ten pounds before they left Bar Harbor for the airport.

Hayley's cell phone buzzed on the kitchen counter where she had left it so she could scramble Bruce's eggs. She checked the screen.

"She's calling awfully early," Hayley said.

It was her mother, Sheila.

Hayley answered the call. "Hi, Mom."

"Hayley, can you hear me?"

"Yes, I can hear you."

"Hayley?"

"Hi, Mom . . ."

"Hayley?"

"Mom, I'm here. Can you hear me?"

Sheila hung up.

Hayley sighed, waited the five seconds before her phone started buzzing again. She pressed the screen to answer again.

"Mom?"

"Oh, there you are. Can you hear me?"

"I hear you fine, Mom."

"Hold on . . ." There was a rustling sound before Hayley heard her mother's voice again, except she was talking to someone else at the moment. "You put me in the exit row. I can't sit there. If something goes wrong, it will be up to me to open the door, and that's just too much pressure. Do you have another seat? Preferably up front, near a window."

Hayley heard a clicking sound, like someone was typing on a computer.

"Mom, where are you?"

"Philadelphia."

"What are you doing in Philadelphia?"

"I'm on a layover."

"Where are you going?"

"I'm coming to you."

Hayley stared at Bruce, who had just bitten off a piece of turkey bacon and mouthed the words, "What is it?"

Hayley shrugged, having no idea. "You're coming to Bar Harbor?"

"Yes, didn't you get my email?"

"No, when did you send it?"

"This morning. Right before I left Florida."

"Mom, it's eight thirty in the morning. I haven't read my emails."

"Oh, well, basically I just wrote that I'm coming to see you. There, now you don't have to read it."

"Okay, thanks," Hayley said numbly.

"My flight to Bangor gets in at . . . hold on, let me

check the ticket . . . I can't read a thing without my glasses. Excuse me, yes, you . . ." More rustling as she seemed to accost a stranger. "Could you tell me what time it says we get in?"

After a brief pause, a young man's voice answered, "At 1:29 PM, ma'am."

"Thank you, you're a peach." Sheila's voice was faint but got louder as she spoke into the phone again. "I get in at 1:29 PM."

"Do you want me to pick you up?" Hayley asked.

"Of course not. I know you work. I think they have some kind of airport shuttle now between Bangor and the island. I'll look into it when we land. The last thing I want to do is inconvenience you or Bruce, unless one of you just happens to have to drive up to Bangor today."

It was an hour's drive, and Sheila knew the likelihood of either of them taking a trip to Bangor on a workday was remote at best.

Hayley had a worrying suspicion that something was wrong. Her mother always meticulously planned her trips to Maine months in advance. She couldn't understand why her mother would just show up now without any warning.

"Mom, is everything okay?"

There was a long silence on the other end.

Bruce stood up and carried his empty plate and silverware to the sink, glancing at Hayley for some kind of clue as to what was happening.

"Mom?"

"I'm here . . ." Sheila said, her voice cracking.

Hayley heard sniffling.

"Mom, what's wrong?"

"Nothing . . ."

"I can tell there's something wrong . . ."

"It's Lenny . . ."

Lenny was Sheila's longtime boyfriend. They had met playing bingo a few years ago. Lenny was a comfortable companion Sheila could dine with, play golf with, and go on trips with, so, in Hayley's mind, it was a perfectly pleasant match.

Hayley suddenly had a sickening feeling. "Did something happen to him? Is he okay?"

"Oh, he's fine." Sheila sighed. "It's just that . . ." She broke down sobbing. "We split up."

"I did not see that coming," Hayley said absentmindedly before quickly recovering. "I mean . . . I am so sorry to hear that, Mom. What happened?"

"It was so silly. His water heater broke and he ordered a new one, but of course he insisted on installing it himself because he is just so darn cheap. Well, it fell on him and he broke his arm. I took him to the hospital and told him it was stupid of him to try and do it by himself and he got angry and told me I nagged him way too much, can you believe that, Hayley? Me, nag? I mean, have you ever heard anything more ridiculous?"

Hayley bit her tongue. She wasn't going to say a word, but the longer her mother waited for her to respond, she decided to reverse course and just tell a little white lie. "No, I haven't."

"Well, that led to a terrible row, and after the doctor put a cast on his arm, and I dropped him off at his house, he turned to me as he got out of the car and said, 'I'm done.' Then he marched inside his house, and we haven't spoken since. That was two days ago."

"Only two days? Give him some time to cool down."

"No, it's over. He's never talked to me like that before. I was up the whole night and following day crying, and then I said to myself, 'Sheila, you should not have to go through this alone. You need the support of your family in times of crisis.' And so I got online and I booked a flight home to Maine."

"Well, I'm happy to hear you're taking care of yourself. Are you staying with Jane while you're here?"

Jane was Hayley's BFF Mona's mother, who had remained close to Hayley's mother ever since they had met in kindergarten back in the 1950s.

"No . . ."

"Celeste?"

Celeste was Liddy's mother, another longtime pal of Sheila's.

"Uh . . . no . . ."

"Did you book a hotel or a bed-and-breakfast?"

"I guess I didn't think that far ahead. I just needed to get out of Florida . . ."

Hayley gripped her cell phone. She knew what she had to do, and steeled herself to finally say it. "Well, you're welcome to stay with Bruce and me."

There was an audible sigh on the other end of the line. "Thank you, Hayley. I appreciate that."

"How long must you stay . . . ?" Hayley couldn't believe her Freudian slip, and tried to quickly correct herself before her mother noticed. "I mean, how long *can* you stay?"

"I didn't book a return ticket yet. I was just going to play it by ear, see how I feel . . ."

"Perfectly understandable," Hayley said, looking to Bruce apologetically as he slowly figured out they were about to be hosting an unexpected houseguest. "The thing is, Mom, Bruce and I are leaving for our honeymoon in less than a week."

"Oh, that's wonderful. I still can't believe you didn't invite me to the wedding!"

"Well, as I've explained a hundred times, we didn't plan on getting married, it just happened in the moment."

"Where are you going?"

"A cruise to the Bahamas."

"How romantic. And where do you leave from?"

"Fort Lauderdale."

As soon as it came out of her mouth, Hayley prayed there was a bad connection again and her mother had not heard her.

"I beg your pardon?"

Nope. She heard her. Sheila just wanted her to repeat it.

"Fort Lauderdale," Hayley mumbled.

"You're coming to Florida and you didn't tell me? That's only a two-hour drive from me. Were you going to sneak in and sneak out, hoping I wouldn't find out?"

"We're only in Fort Lauderdale one night before the boat leaves, so I didn't think—"

"That's fine. You don't have to come up with excuses."

"I was going to tell you, it's just—"

Before Hayley had to grovel for forgiveness, Sheila was already on to another train of thought. "You know, I could housesit for you while you're gone. Feed the pets, take Leroy out for his walks, this could work out perfectly."

"That's so nice of you, Mom, but Mona has already volunteered—"

Sheila wasn't interested in hearing what Hayley had to say at this point. She was too busy mapping out her extended stay in Bar Harbor. "You know, this could be really good for me, emotionally I mean. I'm happy to be away from Florida for a while."

"A while? How long do you mean when you say *a while*?"

Sheila ignored the question. "The memories of Lenny and that whole traumatic affair are just too vivid."

Traumatic affair? They had had an argument about a water heater. But Hayley refrained from making any comments out loud.

"Thank you for the kind invitation, Hayley."

"You're welcome?"

What invitation?

"Oh, I have to go. They're boarding my flight!" Sheila chirped. "Did you say Bruce will pick me up at the airport in Bangor?"

"No, I don't think I did—"

"Tell him I can't wait to see him! It will be the first time as my son-in-law!"

And then she hung up.

Bruce stood by the sink, staring down at the floor, resigned to the imminent arrival of his brand-new mother-in-law. "How long is she coming for?"

"Not long," Hayley lied.

Chapter 4

When Hayley walked through the back door into the kitchen, she found it odd that Leroy was not racing to greet her, jumping up and down excitedly. In fact, there was no sign of him or Blueberry, who was usually perched under the kitchen table with a perpetual grumpy look on his face. Upstairs she could hear the vacuum running. Hayley sighed. She knew exactly what was happening. Her mother, Sheila, was cleaning the house. Anyone else would find this a kind gesture, but not Hayley. Especially since she had already thoroughly vacuumed the upstairs bedrooms the night before. No, her mother was sending her a very clear message: Her cleaning skills were just not good enough.

A beef stew was bubbling in a pot on top of the stove and the warm scent of some kind of freshly made bread or rolls wafted out from the oven. Hayley knew her mother had done her homework. Beef stew was one of Bruce's favorite comfort foods and she was out to impress him. The vacuum noise stopped and she could hear her mother cross into the bathroom. Of course she was going to start scrubbing the toilets because Hayley had also done that the night before as well.

Hayley walked down the hall, veering right into the living room to find Bruce in his recliner, eyes closed, snoring softly. A half-empty beer bottle was sitting next to him along with a plate of crumbs, probably the last bits of cheese and crackers Sheila had prepared for him as a pre-dinner snack. Hayley gently nudged Bruce awake, and he sat up with a start.

"What? What's happening?" he asked groggily.

"Nothing. You never came back to the office after you picked my mother up at the airport in Bangor," Hayley said.

"We didn't get back to town until almost four, so I decided to work at home for the rest of the day," Bruce said.

"Yes, I can see you've been working very hard," Hayley cracked.

"Your mother's been spoiling me. Man, that beef stew sure smells delicious, doesn't it?"

"Where is Leroy?" Hayley asked.

"Probably upstairs with Sheila. She's been giving him a lot of treats, so his loyalties have shifted. We're not his favorites anymore."

"He shouldn't have too many treats. He'll get sick."

"Too late. But your mother cleaned it up."

"And Blueberry?"

"Probably rubbing up against Sheila's leg as we speak. I thought that cat hated everybody, but he seems to adore your mother."

They heard the toilet flush.

"She's done scrubbing the toilet bowl, which means she'll be down here any second," Hayley warned.

"She's a very nice woman," Bruce remarked. "We had a really good chat on the car ride home."

"Yes, she's working hard to win your favor so when she and I have a disagreement, you'll side with her."

"Don't be so cynical," Bruce said, grinning.

Sheila called down from the top of the stairs. "Hayley, is that you?"

"Yes, Mom. I just walked in."

Sheila pounded down the stairs with Leroy and Blueberry on her heels. Hayley's jaw dropped at the sight of her two pets together. Usually they kept a safe distance between them.

Sheila threw open her arms and hugged her daughter tightly. "Thank you so much for opening up your home to me. I can't tell you how much I needed to get away!"

Bruce threw Hayley a look as if to say, "See? She's lovely!" But Hayley wasn't falling for it. It was only a matter of time before . . .

"I thought I would help out and clean your house since I know you're so busy writing your columns that you just don't have the time," Sheila said brightly.

"I cleaned the whole house last night, Mother," Hayley said through gritted teeth.

"Oh, you did?" Sheila asked innocently, looking around, zeroing in on a dust ball near one of the couch legs.

"I hope you don't mind me making dinner. I just didn't want you to have to worry about it. I went through your cupboards and figured you didn't have time to go grocery shopping because all I could find was junk food. But not to worry, Bruce was kind enough to drive me to the store so I could pick up a few things. Wasn't that sweet of him?"

Bruce beamed like a boy who had just received a gold star sticker on his homework.

Hayley took a deep breath. "Mom, thank you for making us dinner."

"Well, Bruce works so hard he deserves a proper meal waiting for him when he gets home from work."

The insinuation was clear.

Hayley wasn't looking after her husband.

The fact that she worked full time too was willfully ignored.

"Unfortunately, I didn't have time to make a home-made dessert. I just picked up some ice cream at the store and some fudge brownies at that new bakery on Cottage Street," Sheila said.

"Bruce and I love the fudge brownies there," Hayley commented.

Sheila lightly patted Hayley on her stomach. "I bet you do."

Hayley bristled, but held her tongue.

"By the way, Mom, please don't give Leroy too many treats. The vet says he needs to lose some weight."

"He's such a little sweetheart. It's so hard for Grandma to say no to him. And Blueberry, what a treasure."

This stymied both Hayley and Bruce. Of all the words in the English vocabulary, "treasure" would probably be the last word either would use to describe their ornery, obstinate Persian cat.

"I'm going to go upstairs and change into something more comfortable," Hayley said.

She caught her mother giving her the once-over.

Hayley sighed. "What?"

"Nothing," Sheila said with a smile.

"Go on, you know you want to . . ."

"I was just noticing your outfit . . ."

Hayley paused, debating whether she really wanted to know, but she couldn't help herself. "What about it?"

"It's very cute," Sheila said.

"Thank you."

Hayley turned to go upstairs when she heard her mother chirp, "It must have come from the back of your closet, judging by the amount of laundry I saw piled up next to the washing machine."

"I was going to do a load tonight," Hayley said defensively.

"No worries, I already started one," Sheila said.

"That was so thoughtful of you, Sheila," Bruce said. "Can you stay forever?"

It was an innocent remark, but when Bruce noticed Hayley staring daggers at him, he quickly retracted it. "Just kidding," he managed to choke out.

Hayley marched up the stairs. She loved her mother and was happy to see her, but the little digs were sometimes just too much to handle. Hayley confronted her about it the last time she had seen her in Florida after she had begun dating Bruce. Sheila had looked so surprised and stricken, she almost melted into a puddle of tears. Hayley had to quickly apologize, and when her mother had finally been able to collect herself enough, she had given Hayley a hug and told her that all was forgiven. And then she had commented, "You look so tired, Hayley. You should really try to get up a little earlier in the morning to put yourself together. Especially now that you're seeing someone."

At least the Caribbean cruise was just five days away.

Chapter 5

Hayley relished in witnessing the long anticipated reunion of her mother with the mothers of her own two best friends, Liddy and Mona, when Mona threw an impromptu barbecue in her backyard the following late summer evening.

Mona's couch-potato husband, Dennis, even managed to drag himself away from ESPN long enough to man the burgers and breasts of chicken sizzling on the grill. Mona had pots of lobsters boiling in the kitchen and side dishes laid out on a picnic table. A few hand-picked baby boomers from their mothers' high school graduating class had also been invited, and everyone showed up with six-packs of beer and bottles of wine. Randy arrived to tend bar. However, his husband, Sergio, the local police chief, was a no-show because he had to work since the summer tourist season was in full swing and the busiest time of the year for law enforcement.

Sheila had been gushing all day about how excited

she was to see Liddy's mother, Celeste, and Mona's mother, Jane, her two partners in crime since middle school. In fact, their tight circle mirrored the close friendship Hayley shared with Liddy and Mona a generation later. When Hayley and her mother, along with Bruce, first arrived, the shrieks and cackles as the older ladies jumped up and down, hugging each other, was downright deafening. Hayley marveled how much Liddy and Mona so closely resembled their mothers, Celeste being a highly opinionated, well-traveled fashionista like Liddy, and Jane being plain-spoken, salt-of-the-earth-but-just-don't-cross-her kind of woman just like Mona. Hayley couldn't understand why her friends could be mirror images of their mothers, but Hayley was the exact opposite of her own mother. When Hayley mentioned this to Bruce, he promptly spit out the beer he was guzzling and guffawed. She rather irritably asked him if he had anything to say, and he quickly shook his head no and announced he was going to grab some potato chips before skedaddling the hell out of there to avoid any further discussion.

Hayley suspected Bruce might not agree with her assessment that she was *nothing* like her mother, but was not about to engage in an argument at Mona's barbecue. It could wait until they got home and Sheila was safely ensconced in her daughter Gemma's old room, well out of earshot.

Hayley wandered over to the bar and had Randy pour her a glass of red wine. "Do you think I take after Mom?"

"In what way?" Randy asked, eyeing her carefully.

"I don't know. Personality-wise, I guess. I tried talking to Bruce about it, and he just took off like he was outrunning the plague."

"Smart man," Randy said under his breath as he handed Hayley her wine.

"*What* did you say?" Hayley asked pointedly.

"Nothing," Randy said, almost too quickly. "I have nothing to say on that subject at all."

Hayley grimaced and then her eyes fell upon Sheila, Celeste, and Jane chattering away incessantly, catching up, belly-laughing at old memories.

"It's like watching me, Liddy, and Mona twenty years from now," Hayley remarked to no one in particular.

"Except that you and Mona are spitting images of your mothers, but I couldn't be more different from mine!" Liddy roared from behind her.

Hayley spun around to see Liddy and Mona approaching. Mona, studying her mother's pageboy haircut and bulky, shapeless, dull gray sweater and torn blue jeans, raised an eyebrow. "Do I really dress like her?"

Liddy put a comforting hand on Mona's shoulder. "Of course you don't, Mona . . ."

"Thank you, Liddy," Mona said, not used to hearing a compliment come out of her mouth.

Liddy folded her arms and gave Mona the once-over. "You look worse."

Mona shook away Liddy's hand and glowered at her.

They all turned back around to stare at their mothers, who were no longer laughing and were now laser-focused on someone who was just arriving at the barbecue. The new unannounced guest was a tall, bony woman with teased-out hair dyed blond and leathery skin tanned a tad too dark. She wore a red polo pullover and a jean skirt with brown sandals. Her toes were painted to match her red shirt. She carried a pink box with her. She stopped to kiss Dennis, who seemed startled by this woman invading his personal space. He held up the spatula he was using to flip the burgers almost as a weapon to defend himself, but couldn't stop her from planting her lips on his sweaty, scruffy cheeks.

"I didn't know you and Caskie Lemon-Hogg were friends, Mona," Liddy said, confused.

"We're not," Mona snapped.

"Then what's she doing here?" Hayley asked.

"Beats me. I didn't invite her," Mona said.

After mauling Dennis, and then moving on to Bruce, who tried to get away but wasn't fast enough, Caskie hooked an arm around Bruce's neck and smashed her lips against his face. She aimed for his lips, but he managed to duck enough so that she smacked his forehead. This didn't deter her at all, and after releasing Bruce, she carried her pink box right over to the makeshift bar to assault Randy. Randy was quick enough to hand her a stiff drink, a martini with two olives, Caskie's cocktail of choice apparently. Caskie was so grateful to have a martini in her hand that the gesture saved Randy from having to suffer through the same public display of affection as Dennis and Bruce had just endured.

Caskie, still balancing the pink box in one hand as she gripped the stem of her martini glass with the other, glanced around at the other people at the barbecue. Sheila, Celeste, and Jane all turned their backs on her before she had a chance to greet them. So instead, Caskie made her way over to Hayley, Liddy, and Mona.

"Mona, there you are. I am super embarrassed to be crashing your party like this. I just stopped by to give you this," Caskie said, handing her the pink box.

"What is it?" Mona asked, staring at it, confused.

"One of my homemade blueberry pies," Caskie chirped.

"That's so sweet of you," Hayley said because she knew Mona probably wouldn't bother with any further pleasantries.

"Well, Mona gave me a steep discount on a lobster order last month when I had some family in town and so I wanted to repay her kindness," Caskie said, smiling sweetly.

Caskie Lemon-Hogg was a local eccentric, widowed for over two decades. Some say her husband, a retired Air Force major, took his own life rather than face the prospect of spending the rest of his life with his overbearing, obnoxious wife, but that was just a cruel rumor. Although her husband, Max, did die of a self-inflicted gunshot wound, the coroner ruled it was an accident when the gun unexpectedly discharged while he was cleaning it. Since then, Caskie had lived off her husband's pension and several property rentals they had together, and basically spent her time driving around town poking her nose in other people's business and flirting with men of all ages. Her one hobby was picking blueberries in the summer months. She also crocheted Christmas stockings in the winter, which she donated to needy families, but blueberry picking was her true passion. Every year by Labor Day she had so many Tupperware containers of blueberries, she had an extra freezer installed in her garage to store them all. Then she would spend the rest of the year baking pies, muffins, cakes, any recipe that required blueberries. She was described by a few gossipy locals as the Blueberry Queen. After a well-documented scandal that involved the wife of a town council member walking in on her husband in bed with Caskie, Mrs. Lemon-Hogg was renamed the Blueberry Tart.

Mona reluctantly flipped the pink box open to re- veal a delectable-looking blueberry pie. "Looks deli- cious," she said, trying to muster a slight bit of enthusiasm, but sadly failing.

"Is that your father over there, Mona?" Caskie asked, her eyes brightening at the sight of Mona's white-haired, crotchety, stout, seventy-something-year-old father, Sid.

"Yeah, that's him." Mona shrugged.

"I haven't seen him in ages! He still looks so hand- some!" Caskie cooed, dashing off.

"Better get to him while he's still coherent. He's on his fifth bourbon," Mona called after her.

Once Caskie was off to accost another unsuspecting victim, Sheila, Celeste, and Jane marched over to join their daughters.

"What the hell were you thinking, inviting that woman to this barbecue, Mona?" Jane barked.

"She didn't, Mrs. Butler," Liddy said. "Caskie just came by to give Mona one of her blueberry pies. As a thank-you."

"I don't believe that for a second," Sheila said sharply. "I'm sure she heard I was in town and decided to come over to see how much I've aged!"

"I'm sure that's not true, Mom," Hayley said.

"I can't stand her!" Celeste cried.

"Why? What did she ever do to you, Mother?" Liddy asked, curious.

"She was always such a fake and an opportunist, ever since we were teenagers back in high school. She pretended to be so smart and superior, but then I would catch her cheating off my paper in history class. Can you believe that?" Celeste huffed.

Sheila gasped. "She cheated off *me* in biology!"

"She never cheated off me, but I never got higher than a D-plus in any class," Jane grumbled.

"There was also a rumor going around that she was having an affair with our history teacher Mr. Cadwell," Celeste said. "At first I refused to believe it, mostly because *I* had a huge crush on Mr. Cadwell myself and wrote short stories in my diary about the two of us running away together to Portsmouth . . ."

"That was your fantasy getaway? *New Hampshire?*" Liddy asked, laughing.

"Your grandparents never took me past the Trenton Bridge, so anywhere over the state line was exotic!" Celeste snapped defensively. "Anyway, one day after school I walked into the classroom because I had forgotten my notebook and I saw the two of them about to kiss. Caskie claimed she had something in her eye and Mr. Cadwell was just trying to help her get it out, but I didn't believe her!"

Jane piped in, arms folded. "What about Sheila's boyfriend, that exchange student from Santorini, the olive-skinned hunk with the wavy black hair who played on the soccer team?"

"Dimitri!" Sheila sighed. "That's right. He was going to ask me to prom, but then that awful Caskie Lemon heard about it, and told him I was already dating your father so she could snag the hot Greek for herself!"

"But you and Dad *did* date in high school!" Hayley cried.

"That's not the point! I wasn't ready to settle down my senior year, and I was weighing my options. I had gone out with Dimitri twice to the movies and was considering going steady with him until Caskie intervened. I heard he became a stock trader for a company in Düsseldorf. I could have lived in Europe!" Sheila wailed.

"That's all ancient history now, Mom. I think it's time to let it go," Hayley said. "I'm sure Caskie is a different person now."

"I wouldn't be too sure," Mona said, glancing over at Caskie, who was hanging off Mona's father, Sid, smiling seductively as he told one of his dumb jokes.

"Would you look at that? Now she's making a play for *my* husband!" Jane bellowed.

"Mom, you and Dad have been divorced for over fifteen years!" Mona reminded her.

"You know what they say," Sheila remarked. "A leopard can never change his spots. Or *her* spots."

Caskie was in no rush to leave, and stayed at the barbecue another hour, much to the chagrin of her former high school classmates, Sheila, Celeste, and Jane. After cutting her pie into pieces and serving all of Mona's guests, Caskie eventually flitted away. Mona had to physically stop her father, who was now apparently smitten, from following her out as if she was the Pied Piper.

However, despite the ruckus Caskie had caused by her unexpected appearance, the reminiscing did result in one good idea. With Sheila back in town, Hayley suggested it might be fun for her mother, Celeste, and Jane to organize a last-minute high school reunion for their classmates who were in town and still living. Randy even offered to hold it at his bar, Drinks Like a Fish. The mothers quickly jumped on board, and Sheila gratefully thanked her boy for coming up with such a brilliant idea.

She turned to everyone at the barbecue and asked,

"What on earth did I do to deserve such a loving and wonderful and brainy son?"

Randy basked in the glow of his mother's adoration and Hayley gamely went along, biting her tongue, resisting the urge to remind her mother that the reunion, in fact, had been *her* idea.

Chapter 6

The Class of 1968 was the last graduating class of Bar Harbor High School, which opened in 1908 on Cottage Street and closed its doors to merge with Pemetic and Mount Desert high schools in order to form the regional Mount Desert Island High School in the fall of 1968. Sheila, Celeste, and Jane had the distinction of being among the last students to attend Bar Harbor High, and of all the members in their graduating class, eleven had died, sixteen had moved away, and the rest still resided in town. So Hayley was surprised that twenty-two people, including spouses, attended their last-minute Class of '68 reunion at Randy's bar, which in her mind, was a rather large number considering the small class size of just over forty students.

A couple of old yearbooks were laid out on the bar for the attendees to peruse and laugh at, especially the 1960s fashion choices they had made, including velvet bell-bottoms, psychedelic tie-dyed shirts, furry vests à la Sonny Bono, midi skirts that never caught on, flower-power dresses, and Beatles-inspired long hair and beards. It was a year of political unrest and upheaval for the country, with several of the boys from their class quickly drafted into Vietnam after graduation, two never to return. Still, on this night, the memories were more lighthearted and festive as the group fell back into their friendships as if over a half century had never even passed.

Hayley, Liddy, and Mona watched as their mothers and their classmates got rowdier as the night wore on, due mostly to Randy offering happy-hour prices on all his beer and booze. Some tables were pushed aside to form a makeshift dance floor, and it didn't take long for everyone to be bopping and swaying to Sly and the Family Stone's "Dance to the Music," and "Love Child" by Diana Ross and the Supremes.

"I feel like we're in *The Twilight Zone*," Mona said. "We're chaperoning a high school dance but all the kids are way older than us."

"At least everyone seems to be having fun," Hayley said.

"Who's that trying to dance with your mother, Mona?" Liddy asked.

They all looked over to see a wiry old man with a long white beard and pock-marked skin, who appeared disheveled in his ill-fitting clothes, staggering around the dance floor, bumping into people, hanging off Jane, who was trying to ignore him.

"That's Rupert Stiles, some old geezer from their class. Now he's the town curmudgeon and resident drunk. Look at him. He can barely keep his balance," Mona growled, shaking her head, disgusted.

Rupert's watery eyes were fixed on Jane, who was trying to pretend he wasn't there, but he refused to take no for an answer and kept tapping her on the shoulder, trying to get her attention.

"I think she needs my help," Mona said, rolling up the sleeves on her sweatshirt, spoiling for a fight. But before she could come to her mother's rescue, Jane finally had had enough. She spun around, planted both hands on Rupert's scrawny chest, and pushed him away from her. Rupert went flying across the room and crashed into a couple of people. Trying to act as if nothing had happened, he politely excused himself and then staggered over to a floor plant and threw up in the pot.

Randy arrived with a new bottle of beer for Mona and sighed. "Did he just do what I think he did?"

"He sure did," Hayley said, scrunching up her nose. "I think you better cut him off."

"This is worse than that University of Maine fraternity party I hosted here a few years back," Randy said, shaking his head.

"Should I kick his butt out of here, Randy?" Mona asked, almost excited to serve as a bouncer.

"No, it's okay, Mona, I was going to get rid of that plant anyway," Randy said as he moved off to wait on another guest at the other end of the bar, who was waving a twenty-dollar bill.

Sheila ambled over to them, escorted by a distinguished older man with a handsome face and perfect teeth. He was the only man in the place wearing a sports jacket, but with no tie to keep it casual.

"Hayley, do you know Carl Flippen?"

"Yes, nice to see you, Carl," Hayley said, smiling.

Carl Flippen owned an auto repair shop in town and was the go-to guy when you needed a tow truck. Hayley was used to seeing him in greasy jeans and a mechanic's shirt so she was impressed by his efforts to clean himself up for the reunion.

"Carl and I dated in high school a few times, long before your father mind you, may he rest in peace," Sheila spouted, giggling, like she was still back in 1968.

Hayley had to wonder just how many boyfriends her mother had back in the day "before her father" came along her senior year.

"Your mother is still as beautiful as she was the day I first laid eyes on her in civics class," Carl said with a wink to Sheila. "I remember you always smelled so good."

"It was Yves Saint Laurent Rive Gauche. I wore it all the time because I loved everything French after studying the language in high school. I wanted to go to Paris and study at the Sorbonne after graduation," Sheila said wistfully.

"What stopped you?" Carl asked.

Sheila sighed. "Hayley's father. He rode a motorcycle and had a tattoo. I always was a sucker for the bad-boy type."

Liddy snorted. "Like mother like daughter."

Carl chuckled and said, "Well, I got busted for jaywalking once, so does that make me a bad boy?"

Hayley smiled and looked at her mother. "I like him."

Carl turned to Sheila and smiled. "I'm going to flag down Randy and get us a couple more drinks. Same thing?"

Sheila nodded, her eyes sparkling. "Vodka martini, two olives."

"You got it, beautiful," Carl said, kissing Sheila lightly on the cheek and ambling away.

Sheila grinned from ear to ear and said almost breathlessly, "Carl is recently widowed."

"You probably shouldn't sound so happy about it," Hayley remarked.

Sheila glared at her.

"Sorry, Mom, that just came out," Hayley said sheepishly.

Hayley touched her mother's arm to show her that she was indeed sorry. No more sarcastic comments. The fact was, she had her fingers crossed, hoping that perhaps her mother would quickly find herself a new beau after being dumped by Lenny in Florida. Carl had always seemed to her to be a kind, thoughtful man. He had his own business, and the fact that he had bothered to dress up for this occasion spoke volumes. And she had always heard Carl was a loyal, loving husband to his wife, Bev, when she was alive. Bev had not been gone for very long, so Carl might need more time before opening himself up to find someone else, but perhaps that someone else eventually could be . . .

"Caskie!"

Hayley snapped out of her thoughts and turned to Sheila.

"Caskie? What about her?" Hayley asked.

"She's doing it again!" Sheila cried.

"Doing what?"

"Look over there!"

Hayley turned to see Caskie, who had just arrived in a colorful floral lace fit-and-flare dress, standing at the other end of the bar, her hand clutching Carl Flippen's thick bicep, laughing uproariously over something charming he had just said.

Liddy joined Hayley and her mother. "What's going on?"

Hayley glanced over at her distraught mother, whose eyes were glued to the opportunistic Caskie flirting shamelessly with the hapless Carl, who was fast succumbing to her bewitchery, then turned to Liddy. "I'm afraid history might be repeating itself."

Chapter 7

At the sight of their dear friend Sheila in obvious distress, Celeste and Jane swooped in for support, buzzing around her like a pair of hummingbirds around a Brazilian verbena.

"What is it, honey? What's wrong?" Celeste asked, her face full of concern as she patted Sheila gently on the back.

Sheila finally took a deep breath and exhaled and then shook her head. "It's nothing. I'm just being overly sensitive."

"About what?" Celeste demanded to know.

"I was just having a conversation with Carl Flippen, I mean we haven't seen each other in years, and there was a nice connection between us. But when he went to get us another drink at the bar . . ."

Celeste and Jane whipped around to see Carl still chatting with Caskie.

"That hussy decided she wanted him all for herself and is now trying to get her claws into him," Jane grumbled. "I've had it with her!"

"Jane, what are you going to do?" Sheila gasped.

Hayley stepped forward, not wanting Mona's mother to cause a scene in Randy's bar. "Jane, everyone's having such a nice time . . ."

"I'm sorry, but I'm sick and tired of that woman getting away with her bad behavior for the last fifty years! Someone should finally stand up to her and give her a piece of their mind, and it might as well be me!"

Mona had always complained that her mother tended to get confrontational after a few beers.

Like mother like daughter.

Hayley speedily stepped in front of Jane before she had a chance to march over to Caskie. "To be fair, Jane, Caskie just arrived and ran into Carl at the bar, so there is no way she could have known that he and Mom had been talking . . ."

"Are you taking *her* side, Hayley?" Sheila asked in a rigid tone.

Hayley groaned. "I'm not taking anyone's side. I just think we should give the poor woman the benefit of the doubt."

"*Poor woman?*" Celeste cried. "It's funny, Hayley, I don't remember you being around in high school to witness firsthand Caskie Lemon's shenanigans. Oh, that's right. You weren't even born yet so how could you?"

"You're right, Celeste, I wasn't there, and you probably have every right to harbor resentment against her after all these years, but I just don't see how now is the best time and place to confront her about it."

Liddy and Mona suddenly appeared at Hayley's side to assist in defusing the situation.

"Hayley's right, Mother, there is no reason to ruin the reunion," Liddy said.

"Caskie already has just by showing up!" Celeste argued.

"I really just want to punch her in the face and then I can go home happy!" Jane growled.

Mona took her mother by the arm forcefully. "I'm not going to let you do that, Mom. You've already been arrested once in your life for starting a bar brawl."

"Only because that man cut in front of me in line while I was trying to order a cosmopolitan!" Jane bellowed.

"It was Reverend Staples! You cold-cocked a man of the cloth!"

"Just because he knows important people like God doesn't give him the right to be rude!" Jane argued.

"What are we talking about?"

They all suddenly fell silent.

Hayley instantly recognized the voice.

It was Caskie Lemon-Hogg.

Everyone slowly turned around to see Caskie in her brightly colored dress and with a big smile on her face. In the background, Carl Flippen was still at the bar waiting for his drinks from Randy.

Hayley was the first to speak. "Nothing, really. We were just—"

"You!" Sheila snapped.

Caskie's smile faded slightly. "*Me?*"

"Yes, you," Sheila said. "How you acted back in high school and how it seems you haven't changed a bit in all these years and—"

"Mom, please . . ." Hayley begged.

"Don't interrupt your mother," Jane barked. "She's been waiting decades to get this off her chest."

"I'm sorry, did I do or say something to offend you?" Caskie asked warily, sensing something was seriously wrong.

Sheila, Celeste, and Jane all laughed derisively, which made Caskie even more nervous.

"Where do we start?" Celeste asked.

"I know," Sheila said, staring at Caskie. "How about we start with how Caskie cheated off our papers back in high school? You always pretended to be so smart, and you did your best to make the rest of us feel stupid, but you never bothered to study for any tests . . ."

"I studied *all* the time . . ." Caskie whispered, humiliated.

"I guess not enough, because you had to copy all our answers!" Shcila snarled.

"I did study . . . day and night . . . my parents even hired a tutor to help me, but it didn't do any good because I had undiagnosed dyslexia. I've had it my whole life and can deal with it now. But back then, nobody knew what it was and I felt like the dumbest person in the world. I was so desperate. I was afraid I would fail all my classes, and so yes, I sat next to you and Celeste during every test so I could get a passing grade."

"Like I said before, she never cheated off me," Jane said.

"I wanted to get into a good college," Caskie whispered.

Jane opened her mouth to protest, but realized in this instance, Caskie was right.

Hayley felt terrible for Caskie in this moment. The woman had never expected to come to the reunion tonight and face the wrath of Hayley's mother and her friends, who were so full of animosity and resentment.

But Caskie's admission of battling dyslexia did seem to stymie the women, at least for a minute, as they regrouped and considered this new revelation.

"I went home and cried every day after school because I just couldn't understand why I was such a dummy who couldn't pass a simple math test," Caskie said, choking back tears.

Hayley could see Sheila softening, just a little, but Celeste was more hard-hearted and wasn't about to let Caskie off the hook completely.

"That doesn't excuse all the other manipulative, mean things you did back in high school, like steal Sheila's boyfriend so you had someone to take you to prom!"

"Dimitri? I had no idea you were interested in him. I thought you were already dating Al, the man you married, Hayley's father . . ." Caskie said.

Hayley refrained from confirming Caskie's version of events. Her mother was angry enough.

"We weren't exclusive at that time . . ." Sheila cried.

Caskie was near tears. "I didn't know that . . . I never would have . . ."

Her voice trailed off. She could see that she wasn't convincing any of them.

"It wasn't just Dimitri. You were constantly eyeing all the boys, especially the ones who were already taken! And apparently you haven't changed one bit!" Celeste roared, gesturing toward the bar.

Caskie turned around to see Carl paying for two drinks. She turned back around, mortified. "Carl? Sheila, are you and Carl . . . ?"

Sheila sniffed but didn't answer.

"How long have you two been together?"

Hayley couldn't help herself. "Ten minutes."

Sheila threw Hayley an annoyed look.

Celeste was quick to come to her friend's defense. "It doesn't matter how long. It's like you have some kind of radar. If another woman is interested in a man, suddenly there you are ready to mess it all up. You've been doing it your whole life!"

Jane was eager to jump in and join the fray. "It's no wonder everyone in town calls you the Blueberry Tart!"

"They *what*—?" Caskie gasped.

The mothers realized they had probably gone too far.

Hayley knew they had, and was about to demand they all apologize when a man's voice stopped her.

"Am I interrupting something?"

It was Carl Flippen, who had returned with Sheila's martini, stopping short of handing it to her when he sensed the obvious friction.

They all froze.

There was a long uncomfortable silence until Sheila finally slapped on a smile and reached out to take her cocktail from him. "Thank you, Carl."

That's when Caskie Lemon-Hogg raced out of the bar, sobbing.

Island Food & Spirits
BY HAYLEY POWELL

Back when I was a rambunctious twelve-year-old palling around in the summer with my besties Liddy and Mona, our mothers, who also were tight friends, would sometimes force us to accompany them when they would go blueberry picking. It was usually in August when it was hot and humid, and so we never wanted to go, but that's when the bushes were ripe and ready with big, bright, juicy, purple and blue berries just waiting to be picked.

We would moan and groan about how sweaty we got and how the humidity frizzed our hair, and so our moms promised that if we spent a couple hours filling our buckets with blueberries, they would pack a picnic and take us to Lakewood to swim and cool off after we were done. Well, that was a sweet enough offer, so we grabbed our bathing suits and towels as our mothers loaded Jane's van with the necessary supplies, and off we went.

After what felt like twelve hours of hard labor picking blueberries, our mothers drove us to the lake as promised, and we dashed down the dirt path, jumping into the cool water, splashing and playing around. Meanwhile, our moms would set up a couple of blankets and put out a cold supper of my mom's chicken salad sandwiches, Jane's delicious blueberry scones made with fresh blueberries from a previous trip, and Celeste's blueberry lemonade, which she kept cold in a big thermos filled with ice.

I used to find it odd that our mothers brought a separate thermos for themselves, which they did not share with us. When we would run out of lemonade and ask for some of theirs, they would adamantly refuse, admonishing us that we needed to learn to make our lemonade last. Then they would look at each other and laugh. By the time we got to our dessert of scones, our mothers would be howling uproariously. Then they would take off down to the lake, and sit in the shallow water and laugh and chat, getting louder and louder as they polished off their "special" lemonade. Years later, we finally figured out that our moms had spiked theirs for an adult beverage, which would explain why Liddy and Mona's fathers had to come together to the lake so one of them could drive us home in the van because our moms were too buzzed.

Anyway, on this particular day, while our mothers splashed around giggling uncontrollably, Mona had an idea that if we found some good sticks we could make fishing poles before the next time we came so we could fish after our supper. We set off in search of sticks, spreading out in the woods right by a small beach. Liddy was about ten feet away from us when she waved us over in her direction. When we got close enough, she put a finger to her lips, signaling us to be quiet and then whispered, "I thought I heard a kitten crying." We listened for a few moments, but didn't hear anything. Mona was getting impatient and wanted to get back to finding our sticks, and we were about to leave, when suddenly we all heard a mewling sound coming from somewhere in front of us. We heard it again, and followed it, and when we seemed to be right on top of it, Liddy crouched down and parted the bushes and there was a litter of the most adorable black and white baby kittens. We barely had time to take in the adorable sight when Mona suddenly gasped and cried, "They're not kittens!"

That's when our eyes fell upon the biggest, fattest, angriest momma skunk we had ever seen. Before any of us had a chance to move, she turned her back to us and raised her tail and sprayed all three of us. The next thing we knew, we all were running as fast as we could, screeching and crying, straight out of the woods back toward our mothers, who were now startled by our screams and worriedly calling our names.

I wish I could say at this point that we all three ran into the loving open arms of our mothers, but unfortunately as soon as they got a whiff of us and the horrid skunk spray, they sidestepped us, waving and hollering at us to go jump into the lake while they stared helplessly at each other, trying to figure out how to get us home without being overcome by the rancid stench.

When the lake did very little to wash off our horrible scent, the moms finally had us pile into the back of the van as they all crammed up front and rolled down the windows and drove as fast as the law would allow them, straight to the Shop 'n Save where they proceeded to fill their cart with every last can of tomato soup so they could take us home and give us tomato soup baths to try and get rid of the horrid odor.

It ended up being a great story for our mothers to tell over and over again, much to the embarrassment of us three girls. But with the passage of time, even we found the humor in the story and nowadays it's always a hit when we retell it at parties.

Now I'm in the mood for some blueberry lemonade and blueberry scones, so I'm going to have to whip up both for when the girls drop by tonight for a visit. Oh, and I'll be sure to add a little something to the blueberry lemonade to make it adult friendly.

BLUEBERRY LEMONADE

SIMPLE SYRUP
INGREDIENTS
2 cups sugar
2 cups water
1 cup blueberries

ADDITIONAL INGREDIENTS
2 cups fresh squeezed lemon juice
6 cups water
Blueberries for garnish (optional)

Place simple syrup ingredients in a saucepan and bring to a boil, stirring occasionally. Remove from heat and puree with an immersion blender or food processor. Strain the mixture into a large pitcher.

Add the 2 cups lemon juice, 6 cups water, and mix well.

Fill glasses with ice and pour the blueberry lemonade into them, top with additional blueberries and enjoy.

Blueberry Lemon Scones

Ingredients
1¼ cup fresh or frozen blueberries
Zest from one lemon
1 egg
2 cups flour
¼ cup plus 2 tablespoon sugar
½ teaspoon salt
2 teaspoons baking powder
1 stick of butter, sliced and cold
½ cup heavy cream
1 teaspoon vanilla

Glaze
Ingredients
1 cup powdered sugar
3 tablespoons lemon juice

Preheat your oven to 400 degrees F. Line your baking sheet with parchment paper and set aside.

In a large bowl, mix together the flour, sugar, baking powder, salt, and lemon zest.

Add your cold butter and using a pastry cutter mix until you have the consistency of wet sand.

In a small bowl, mix your egg, cream, and vanilla together.

Pour the egg mixture into the flour mixture and mix together but do not overmix—just until it comes together. Now add your blueberries, quickly folding in and don't overmix.

Dump your mixed flour onto your parchment paper, add a little flour to the top, and begin patting your dough into an 8-inch circle. Slice it into 8 wedges.

Arrange the wedges on the parchment so they are not touching.

Bake in the preheated oven for 20 minutes or until golden brown.

Remove from oven and cool. Prepare your glaze for the cooled scones by mixing the powdered sugar and lemon juice and drizzling all over the scones.

Serve and enjoy!

Chapter 8

Hayley popped open one eye. She took in the inviting smell of bacon wafting up to her bedroom from the kitchen. She reached out from underneath the covers to grab her phone, which sat on the nightstand next to the bed. She looked at the time. It was just past seven in the morning. The class reunion at the bar had not broken up until after midnight, and she and Bruce had stayed behind after everyone left, until almost one in the morning, to help Randy with the cleanup.

Hayley turned over. Bruce was not in bed next to her. She knew why. He was already downstairs being spoiled by her mother with a full breakfast. Usually on a workday, it was every man for himself and that usually meant coffee and a plastic-wrapped pastry at the Big Apple convenience store on the way to the office. But with Sheila fully settled in at Hayley's house, the routine had abruptly changed, and Bruce was on track to gain at least ten pounds during her visit.

The pets were nowhere to be found either. Typically they were all over the bed at this point, trying to prod

Hayley out from under the comforter, so she could only assume they had already been fed and were now parked near the kitchen table anticipating someone dropping a piece of bacon or egg they could quickly hoover up before anyone had a chance to stop them.

Hayley forced herself out of the warm, comfy bed and threw on a sweater over her T-shirt and cotton shorts since it was unusually cold this morning, and then she dragged herself down the stairs to the kitchen, where, as expected, Bruce was sitting at the table as Sheila served him another helping of scrambled eggs and bacon. Bruce merrily scarfed it down as Sheila buttered some more toast for him at the counter.

"Good morning," Hayley grumbled.

"Oh, good morning," Sheila chirped. "Sit down and I'll get you a plate."

"It's really delicious." Bruce moaned. "Her scrambled eggs are the best I've ever had."

"I just doll them up with a few herbs and spices, nothing too fancy," Sheila cooed modestly. "But I'm so glad you like them."

Sheila moved to the stove, where she flipped over some sizzling bacon in the frying pan. "Bacon will be just another minute. I know you like yours extra crispy, Hayley."

"Thank you," Hayley mumbled, looking down to see both Leroy and Blueberry exactly where she had expected them to be, perched nearby, ready to pounce on any stray food crumbs.

"Well, I, for one, had a wonderful time last night," Sheila said even though no one asked. "That was so kind of Randy to do that for us. It was such a treat seeing all of my old high school classmates and sharing memories and seeing how they're all doing."

"Most of them anyway," Bruce cracked.

"Let's not get into that. If I never hear the name Caskie Lemon-Hogg again in my lifetime, it will still be too soon," Sheila groaned.

The doorbell rang.

Hayley, who was hungrily eyeing the bacon frying a few feet away, sat up, surprised. "Who's at the door at this hour?"

She glanced over at Bruce, who had no interest in finding out as he scraped the last of his eggs onto a fork and shoved them into his mouth.

"Just enjoy your breakfast, Bruce, I'll get it," Hayley said with as much sarcasm as she could muster this early in the morning.

"Thanks," Bruce said with his mouth full.

Sheila was busy preparing Hayley's breakfast plate.

Hayley stood up and ambled down the hall to answer the door.

On the front porch stood Police Chief Sergio Alvarez, the handsome Brazilian always dashing in his crisp, pressed uniform.

"Sergio, what brings you here so early? Did Mom invite you for breakfast too?"

"No, I'm afraid I'm here on business," Sergio said.

Hayley's heart skipped a beat.

Based on his serious expression and somber tone, something was definitely wrong.

She opened the door wider. "Come in."

Sergio stepped into the foyer as Hayley closed the door behind him. He spotted Sheila in the kitchen salting Hayley's eggs before she set the plate down on the table.

"Your breakfast's ready, Hayley!" Sheila called to her.

Hayley leaned in closer to Sergio. "What's going on? Did I do something?"

"I'm not here for you. I'm here for your mother," Sergio said, a pained look on his face.

"Oh . . ." Hayley whispered before leading Sergio down the hall to the kitchen.

Sheila brightened at the sight of Sergio. "Well, if it isn't my strapping son-in-law Sergio! Look at that gorgeous face! I always said, my son, Randy, got his taste in men from me!"

She dropped her spatula, raced over, and threw her arms around him. He forced a smile and drew her in. Sheila reached up and patted his hard chest. "Feel these pecs . . ." She then moved to his upper arm. "And those biceps . . ."

She pulled back from the hug and spun Sergio around so his back was to everybody. Then she slapped his behind. "And that butt! Talk about a work of art."

"Mom, stop objectifying Sergio," Hayley scolded.

"I don't mind . . . really . . ." Sergio said.

Sheila guided him to the kitchen table. "Sit down and have some breakfast."

"I can't," Sergio said quietly. "Like I told Hayley, I'm here on business."

Bruce, who was now stuffing buttered toast into his mouth, suddenly dropped the crust on his plate. "Police business? What's happened?"

"Whatever it is, I'm sure it can wait until everyone has a full stomach," Sheila said, pulling out a chair. "Go on, Sergio, sit down."

"I'm sorry, Sheila, this can't wait," Sergio said, struggling to just get it out.

Hayley finally decided to help him. "Mom, Sergio is here to see you about something."

"*Me?*" Sheila laughed, genuinely surprised. "What on earth could I have possibly done?"

Sergio sighed. "When I got to the station this morning, there was a lady there waiting to see me. Do you know a Caskie Lemon-Hogg?"

Sheila grunted. "See, it's been two minutes and her name has come up again. There is no getting away from her!"

"What did she want?" Bruce asked, now curious.

Sergio paused. This was not easy for him. But then he took a breath and soldiered on. "She has taken out a restraining order."

"A restraining order? Against who?" Sheila asked.

"You," Sergio said softly.

Sheila gasped. "*Me?*"

Sergio nodded. "You, Celeste, and Jane. She says you threatened her last night and she is in fear for her life!"

There was a long silence.

And then Sheila cackled. "That is the most ridiculous thing I've ever heard! We did no such thing! She's making the whole thing up, isn't she, Hayley?"

Hayley stood frozen by the kitchen counter. She picked up a glass of orange juice her mother had poured for her and downed it.

Sheila turned to her. "*Hayley?*"

"What?"

"Tell Sergio that Caskie is lying," Sheila said.

Hayley set the glass back down on the counter. "It's just that . . ."

Sergio's eyes narrowed. "It's just that what?"

"At the reunion, I remember Mom saying something like if Caskie didn't stop behaving badly, she'd regret it," Hayley muttered.

Sheila threw her head back and laughed. "Oh, please. That is *not* a threat! I was just speaking my mind!"

"I'm sorry, Sheila, but actually it is, and Mrs. Lemon-Hogg gave me a list of six witnesses who were nearby and heard you say it."

"Please tell me you are not going to take this woman seriously!" Sheila scoffed.

"It's already done! She wasted no time. Apparently she has friends in high places. She called Judge Larkin at five this morning. By the time she showed up at my office at six thirty, the judge had already granted the protection order. If you go anywhere near her, I'm going to have to place you under arrest."

Sheila's mouth dropped open in shock as she processed this information and then her face reddened with anger. "This is just a desperate cry for attention and an attempt to embarrass me for calling her out at the reunion!"

"Look on the bright side, Mom. Now you have a reason to avoid her! It's actually a win-win!" Hayley said.

Sheila gave her daughter a withering look.

And Hayley decided it was best to just stop talking and eat a piece of the now burnt bacon in the frying pan.

Chapter 9

Julio's Salon was the most popular hair salon in Bar Harbor, most notably due to its charming, swoon-worthy namesake and owner, Julio Garcia. Many of his loyal customers were more than happy to pay the fifty bucks for a wash and style from the lead stylist, Julio himself, especially since the service included the sexy Argentinean seductively running his strong, manly fingers through one's hair, which was known to cause heart palpitations on more than one occasion.

Julio had immigrated to the United States from Buenos Aires when he was in his early twenties, already a trained hairdresser, and was drawn to Maine by an old friend, Betsy Calhoun, whom he had met while she was on vacation in South America. Betsy was a local stylist with her own shop in Bar Harbor, and she gave Julio a job sweeping hair off the floor and running errands. It didn't take long for him to graduate to cutting hair, and then after only a few months, most of Betsy's customers were requesting Julio. It was only natural for Julio to ultimately strike out on his own and open his own salon. He got the necessary funds from a rich girl he was dating at the time, Jeanette Stout, whom he later married. This new venture—the salon, not his relationship with Jeanette—did not sit very well with Betsy, who felt betrayed and never spoke to him again.

As Julio's business took off, Betsy's faltered, and she finally moved to Scarborough to live with a new boyfriend and cut hair there. That's when Julio's inevitable domination of the Bar Harbor beauty business was finally complete. Now, he was in constant demand for bridal parties the day of the weddings as well as the first choice of many of the celebrities who summered on the island, and all the rich folks attending private functions and special events.

Julio was now in his early forties, still drop-dead gorgeous, with a silky smooth deep voice that continued to send ripples through the bodies of most of his female customers, not to mention a few males who reliably wandered in for a quick trim and shave. And even though Julio was still married to Jeanette, who was rarely seen in public, many people assumed he was single and ready to mingle by the way he flirted shamelessly with his clientele, especially his older, attractive female customers, even the ones who were not drowning in money. If a woman was younger than forty-five, then Julio never really seemed to appear to be interested in anything but her hair.

Sheila had made an appointment for both her and Hayley today during Hayley's lunch hour because, in her words, "You really need to do something about that wild frizzy mess on top of your head, Hayley."

Hayley bit her tongue and agreed to accompany her mother, mostly because Sheila had offered to pay the fifty bucks it would take to get Hayley's uncooperative hair under control.

Julio had often cut and styled Sheila's hair in the years before she permanently moved to Florida for a warmer climate, and so he knew just how to treat her when she swept into his shop with Hayley lagging behind her. He hugged Sheila tightly, making sure she got a good whiff of his masculine-scented cologne. In one of his more over-the-top gestures, he kissed her hand, and then led her over to a black leather salon chair, whipped open a black bib with all the focus and precision of a matador waving a red cape in front of a snorting bull, and then draped it around her and whispered in her ear as he tied it gently around her neck, "What can I do for you today, beautiful?"

After giggling like a schoolgirl who just got asked to the prom by the high school quarterback, Sheila requested a bit of color to wash out the gray and a blowdry. Julio was more than willing to accommodate her.

Meanwhile, Hayley was approached by one of "Julio's Angels," the three girls who usually picked up the slack when Julio was fully booked and unavailable. Kathy was a pert, short, lively redhead who guided Hayley over to a free chair where another drop-dead gorgeous South American man with a wide smile waited to greet her.

"This is Julio's cousin Juan. He's just moved to Maine from Mendoza, Argentina, to work with us. He's in training, so I hope you don't mind him observing," Kathy said.

Hayley gave him the once-over, wondering why every Argentinean man she came in contact with was a bona fide hunk, and said happily, "I've always wanted to travel to Mendoza."

"It is a beautiful place to see," Juan said warmly, touching Hayley's shoulder gently as Kathy left to retrieve a bib for her to wear.

"I'm sure it is, but I'm more interested in the wine," Hayley cracked.

Juan laughed. "Yes, Mendoza is the world's premier wine capital with the best vineyards!"

"Well, I'm not sure when I can afford to go, so the next time you visit your family there, be sure to bring plenty of bottles back for me to try," Hayley said.

"It would be my pleasure," Juan said, standing close behind her and locking eyes with her through the giant wall mirror in front of them.

God, he was handsome.

His piercing eyes were a deep, earthy brown, almost like dark chocolate, which, Hayley reminded herself, would go great with an Argentinean Malbec. He stared at her so intensely, she finally had to look away.

"Juan . . ." Julio said.

Juan ignored him, still smiling at Hayley.

Julio sighed. "Juan!"

Juan glanced over at his cousin, annoyed. "Yes?"

"Have you fixed the lock on the back window yet?"

"No, I forgot my tool belt at home. I will do it tomorrow."

"You said that yesterday and the day before that. Would you please get it done before someone lets themselves in and robs me blind?"

"I know what I'm doing tonight," Sheila joked.

The other ladies laughed.

"Well, sorry to burst your bubble, Sheila, but I never keep cash here at night and I lock most of the equipment and products in the supply closet, so the only things here to steal are a few teasing combs and a couple of bottles of champagne I serve the customers who are waiting."

"I'll take it!" Sheila shouted.

More laughs from the customers and staff.

Julio turned to his cousin. "Juan, I'm running low on curlers. Go and pick some up at the drug store, please."

Juan nodded and shot out the door, all the women in the shop staring lustfully at his perfect behind as he left.

Hayley looked toward the reception desk, where Kathy was on the phone, the bib hanging over her free arm.

"I'm afraid we charge a twenty-five-dollar fee for cancellations within twenty-four hours of the appointment . . . Okay, I'll tell Julio," Kathy said before hanging up and crossing over to the sink where Julio was shampooing Sheila's hair. "That was Caskie Lemon-Hogg. She can't make her appointment today. She said she will call tomorrow to reschedule."

"That's fine," Julio said as he massaged Sheila's scalp, which caused her to moan slightly with pleasure. "Don't charge Mrs. Hogg for canceling. She's a loyal customer and rarely cancels at the last minute. I'm sure it's for something important."

"I wouldn't be surprised if she has some salacious tête-à-tête planned with somebody else's husband!" Sheila announced loud enough for everyone in the salon to hear.

The whole room fell silent. The only sound came from a whirring hair dryer perched over a sixty-something still rather sexy woman in curlers, who was flipping through a *People* magazine.

Hayley sighed, "Mom, please!"

Sheila threw up her hands as she relaxed in her reclined chair and Julio rinsed the shampoo out of her hair with a sprayer. "Never mind! Pretend I didn't say a word!"

The woman under the hair dryer reached up and flipped the switch, shutting it off. Then she tossed her magazine down on the floor and shot up out of her chair. "I'll have you know, Caskie Lemon-Hogg is my best friend!"

"Oh, hello, Regina, we missed you at the reunion last night," Sheila said with a nervous laugh.

"I had more important things to do! And I do not appreciate you bad-mouthing Caskie when she is not here to defend herself!"

Sheila sat up as Julio patted her hair with a towel. "You're right, I'm sorry. I shouldn't talk about people behind their backs."

Hayley was surprised her mother appeared so contrite. The woman who had decided to confront her was Regina Knoxville, a local who had served on the school board and town council at one time, but Hayley did not know a lot about her except that she looked extraordinarily good for her age but was married to a rather plain-looking, dull, colorless husband whose name she could never remember. Hayley had always thought Regina might have married him for his money.

There was more awkward silence.

Regina seemed satisfied with Sheila's apology.

But then Sheila couldn't resist adding, "I would be happy to say it to her face the next chance I get!"

Kathy, who was brushing out Hayley's frizzy mop of hair, was so startled, she dropped her hairbrush and it clattered to the floor.

Hayley closed her eyes, wishing she was anywhere else but here.

Regina marched over to the reception desk and threw three twenty-dollar bills down. "I am not going to stay here and listen to that woman accuse my friend with her bald-faced lies! I'll come back another time!"

Regina stormed out of the salon.

"She's still wearing our curlers. Should I go after her and get them back since we're running low?" Kathy asked.

"No," Julio said with a grin. "Let her keep them. I'm more interested in knowing if what Sheila said is true."

Sheila suddenly demurred. "I really shouldn't say . . ."

"Because you don't know!" Hayley chimed in. "Stop making things up just because you don't like her!"

"History is on my side, Hayley," Sheila argued. "And if Caskie Lemon-Hogg has one thing, it's a sordid history!"

Julio and Kathy and the rest of his staff were eager to hear more, but Sheila mercifully decided to take the high road and not speculate anymore, at least while she was getting her hair done, much to Hayley's relief.

Chapter 10

Hayley followed Sheila into the kitchen as she crossed to the refrigerator and pulled out a brown bag. "I made you lunch since I knew we wouldn't have time to eat because of our hair appointments."

Hayley took the bag and peered inside it. "Thanks."

It was a tuna sandwich on whole wheat and a green apple.

Pretty boring.

Sheila noticed Hayley's slight frown. "I just thought you might appreciate a healthier option than what you normally have for lunch."

Hayley bit her tongue, not wanting to start an argument. "That's very thoughtful. I really should be getting back to the office."

"I'll drop you off if you don't mind. I'd like to take your car to Ellsworth and do a little shopping. Just hang on while I run upstairs and freshen up."

Before Hayley had the chance to respond, Sheila spun around and flew down the hall and up the staircase.

Hayley bent down to pet Leroy, who excitedly wagged his tail and licked her hand. Blueberry was nowhere to be seen, not even bothering to make an appearance to acknowledge Hayley's presence.

Standing back up, Hayley reached in the bag, grabbed the apple and took a bite. Suddenly she heard a blood-curdling scream from upstairs.

"Mom!"

Hayley dashed past Leroy and raced upstairs to the bathroom, where she found her mother with her back pressed against the open door, a hand to her mouth and her eyes widened in shock as she stared at Bruce, who was stark naked and dripping wet, a towel held in front of his midsection in order to give himself a modicum of cover.

"Bruce, what's going on?" Hayley gasped.

"I was taking a shower and your mother just barged in as I was getting out and—"

Hayley turned to Sheila. "Did you see—?"

"*Everything!*" Sheila wailed, now covering her eyes. "I will never be able to *unsee* it!"

"Bruce, what are you doing home?" Hayley asked as he hurriedly wrapped the towel around himself.

"I've been putting off cleaning the gutters and it's supposed to rain this weekend, and so I came home during my lunch hour to get it done. I got all grimy and so I decided to take a shower before heading back to the office . . ."

"I had no idea he was in here, let alone in his birthday suit!" Sheila cried defensively.

"It's okay, Mom, why don't you go downstairs?" Hayley said.

"The reason I came up here is because I need to use the bathroom!" Sheila barked.

Hayley nodded and turned to Bruce. "Are you done?"

"No, but I can wait in the bedroom!" Bruce snapped, charging past Sheila and Hayley and disappearing into the master bedroom.

"I'll just be a minute," Sheila said, closing the door.

Hayley followed Bruce into the bedroom and shut the door for some privacy.

"I'm sorry about that," Hayley said softly.

Bruce sighed. "Hayley, I'll never understand how you raised two kids in this tiny house!"

"Three, if you count my ex-husband."

"It's too crowded, especially with her staying here!"

"Shhh, keep your voice down. She'll hear you."

"I'm sorry, I don't mean to flip out, but I'm a little disturbed by the fact that I just flashed your mother!"

"Calm down, I know it's been a little stressful having her here, but remember, we are leaving in three days for our honeymoon, an all-inclusive cruise where we won't have to worry about anything. And it's a big ship, huge in fact, where we'll have lots of room to move about and not feel crowded!"

This seemed to placate him momentarily. He took a deep breath and exhaled. He looked Hayley in the eyes. "And you promise she'll leave when we get home?"

"I promise," Hayley reassured him.

He kissed her softly on the lips. "It's ten minutes to one. We could do a lot in the time before we have to be back to the office from lunch." He pulled her closer and went to drop his towel. She hooked an arm around his neck and they were about to fall back on the bed when there was a loud knock on the door.

"I'm done, Bruce! Bathroom's all yours!" Sheila yelled.

Hayley grabbed Bruce's towel before it fell to the floor and kept it wrapped around him. "She's right outside."

Bruce sighed again. "Three days . . . three days . . ."

Chapter 11

Sheila sullenly twirled her spaghetti onto her fork, stared at it listlessly for a few seconds, and then with a heavy sigh, shoveled it into her mouth. The tension in the air was palpable and Hayley and Bruce exchanged furtive glances, not quite sure what the problem was. After sitting down at the table for dinner and thanking her mother profusely for the Italian meal she had whipped together before both of them had arrived home from the office, Hayley quickly sensed that something was off. There was a profound, obvious sadness about her mother, who shuffled around the kitchen, shoulders slumped, half-heartedly stirring the marinara sauce, which included her homemade meatballs, and checking on the garlic bread baking in the oven. Hayley had asked several times what was bothering her, but Sheila had simply shrugged and said under her breath, "Nothing."

But now, the silent treatment was reaching a boiling point and Hayley had suffered enough. She slammed down her utensils and cried, "I can't take this any-more! Something has upset you and I want to know what it is, and please do not say 'nothing' again, because it is so clearly *something*!"

Sheila stared at Hayley, then at Bruce, and then back down at the pile of spaghetti on her plate. "I really don't want to get into this right now!"

"Well, I'm sorry, Mom, but you are just going to have to because you are a guest in our house and Bruce and I deserve to know if there is a problem!"

Hayley watched her mother, who sat up in her chair, mustering up her courage, and then announced, "I heard everything."

"Heard what?" Bruce asked.

"Everything you two said about me," Sheila mumbled. "How you hate having me here and how much you want me to leave."

"How could you have heard us? We were in the bedroom with the door closed," Hayley said.

"The walls in this house are very thin," Sheila said quietly.

"No, you had your ear pressed up against our door, and neither of us ever said we hated having you here," Hayley argued.

"Well, you might as well have," Sheila snorted. "I had no idea what a burden and an intrusion it is having me here, and what a pain I am to have around."

Hayley grabbed her glass of merlot and chugged it down.

She needed it now more than ever.

Bruce leaned forward. "Sheila, I am so sorry you got that impression. I never meant to imply I don't like having you around. I was just surprised when you walked in on me in the bathroom, and I probably over-reacted. This is a small house, even for just Hayley and me. But you are family, and you are always welcome here."

Hayley set down her wineglass and looked at Bruce, more in love than ever. She marveled at how he had just expertly and shrewdly brought the temperature down on the situation.

Sheila nodded and then reached over and took his hand. "I like you."

"So do I," Hayley said with a smile.

"I accept your apology," Sheila said before picking up her fork and cutting into one of her jumbo meatballs.

Bruce opened his mouth to correct the record that he did not exactly apologize, but then snapped his mouth shut again, thinking better of it.

Sheila ate the piece of her meatball and then wiped the sides of her mouth with her gray cloth napkin as she chewed and swallowed. "You're a thousand times better than the last one."

Hayley eyed her mother warily. "I beg your pardon?"

Sheila was twirling more spaghetti onto her fork and smiled innocently at Hayley. "What?"

"The last one?" Hayley asked. "What last one?"

Sheila, who Hayley could sense suddenly regretted the comment, decided to focus on her pasta dish. "I made the meatballs with beef, pork, and chicken. Do you like them, Bruce?"

"They're delicious," Bruce said, looking at Hayley nervously.

"What last one?" Hayley asked again.

Sheila sighed. "I was just trying to pay Bruce a compliment. Am I not allowed to say nice things about your latest husband?"

"*Latest* husband?" Hayley asked. "You make it sound like I've been married more times than Elizabeth Taylor! Twice, Mom! I've only been married twice!"

"I know that! I was talking about Danny. He was never a reliable husband, always had some scheme up his sleeve," Sheila said before turning to Bruce. "I tried to warn her, but she was young and rebellious and was not going to listen to anything her mother had to say."

Hayley popped the last piece of her garlic bread in her mouth and said, "Danny had many faults, but we made two great kids, and for that I'll always be grateful to him."

"Don't talk with your mouth full," Sheila said absentmindedly.

Hayley swallowed, grimacing. Then looked at Bruce and smiled. "But this time I got it right."

"You did indeed. And it was worth taking a few swings and misses before the home run . . ."

"What do you mean by *that*?" Hayley asked, stiffening.

"Just that it took a few tries to find Mr. Right. Like that veterinarian you dated for five minutes . . ."

"You mean Aaron, and we dated for a while . . ."

"Not a *long* while. I never met him in person. You two broke up before I even had the chance."

Hayley bit her tongue, trying to ignore the comment. "Bruce, could you pass the garlic bread?"

Bruce reached for the basket and handed it to her, studying her face to see if she was about to explode.

Hayley saw her mother open her mouth to speak but cut her off. "If you say anything about me eating too many carbs, I will leave this table."

"I was not going to say anything like that," Sheila said, obviously lying. "I was just going to mention the man you dated that I did manage to meet . . . but just once in passing when I was in town one summer. The handyman. What was his name? Lou?"

"Lex, and he was not a handyman, he was a care-taker on the Hollingsworth estate in town . . ."

"Yes, Lex, that's right. He seemed nice."

Hayley seethed, but decided to just let it go.

"Didn't he serve time in prison at some point?"

Hayley threw her fork down. "Yes, he did! Is this your way of saying you don't approve of my past choices in men?"

"I just asked a question!" Sheila gasped. "Why are you attacking me?"

"Because you keep finding little ways to belittle me and criticize me, and I'm getting sick and tired of it!" Hayley shouted.

Sheila sat back in her chair, stunned. "Is that what you think I'm doing?"

"Yes!" Hayley yelled.

"What kind of monster do you think I am?" Sheila cried, her eyes welling up with tears. "All I was trying to do is tell you how much I love your new husband! I'm sorry if you think I'm being cruel and heartless!"

This stopped Hayley in her tracks.

She began to question if she was getting too far in-side her own head. She turned to Bruce, who was laser focused on his empty plate, scraping the last of the marinara sauce onto his spoon and eating it, hoping they would not draw him back into the conversation.

Hayley glanced back at her mother. "Mom, I'm sorry . . ."

Sheila was using her napkin to dab away her tears. Then she tossed it down on the table and stood up. "I think it would be better if I just left."

"Back to Florida?" Hayley asked.

"No, I made a commitment to feed your pets while you're away on your honeymoon, and so I will stick around until you come back, but I am not staying here."

"Mom, don't be ridiculous . . ."

"I wouldn't feel comfortable . . ."

Bruce also stood up, crossed around the table and put an arm around Sheila. "Please, we don't want you to leave . . ."

"I think it's best . . ." Sheila said, sniffing.

"We'll feel awful if you go," Bruce said.

"I saw a vacancy sign outside that new inn on Mount Desert. I can go there. I can pack my things and be out of your hair in an hour, let me just clear the dishes first."

"No, Sheila, we can do it," Bruce said. "But I wish you'd reconsider . . ."

"Thank you, Bruce, but I've made up my mind," Sheila said before fleeing the dining room and going up the stairs.

Bruce turned to Hayley. "We can't just let her leave like this . . ."

"You heard her. She's made up her mind. There is nothing we can do. She is so stubborn!"

"Now I know where you get it from."

Hayley glared at him.

Bruce's eyes widened. "Did I just say that out loud?"

Chapter 12

"Mom, please call me back. I want to apologize for last night," Hayley said as she sat behind her desk at the *Island Times* office the following day. "And I want you to come home. I hate the idea of you sleeping at a B and B when you should be staying with us. Okay, I know I've already left you a few messages, but I hope you get in touch with me soon."

Bruce wandered in from the back bull pen and poured himself a cup of coffee from the pot sitting in the maker on top of a small mini fridge next to the supply room. "Still no answer?"

Hayley shook her head. "No, and I called the inn and the receptionist told me she doesn't want to be disturbed."

"Maybe you should just go on over there and bang on the door until she answers," Bruce suggested.

"No, I know my mother. She will call me back once she feels I've been punished enough and have suffered the appropriate amount of guilt. That could be today, tomorrow, or after we return from the cruise. I just have to let her work through her anger, but she'll come around. She always does."

"It may take her a while. She looked pretty hurt when she left last night," Bruce commented, taking a sip of his coffee.

Hayley raised an eyebrow. "Are you saying I was too hard on her?"

Bruce realized his mistake. He clutched his coffee like a lifesaver as he nervously contemplated his next move. "No . . . ?"

Hayley sat back in her chair and folded her arms, waiting to hear more.

He was really sweating now. "I'm just saying . . ."

"Yes?"

"I'm saying . . . mothers are going to be mothers. It's in their DNA to nag their daughters about everything. Sheila is no exception. But she obviously loves you."

Hayley wanted to lay into Bruce and berate him for taking her mother's side, but deep down she knew he was right. Despite the sometimes combative nature of their relationship, she really did care deeply about her mother and felt bad with how the dinner had so quickly devolved into a heated argument the night before.

Hayley reached for the phone. "I'm going to call her again."

Before she had the chance, the front door flew open and Caskie Lemon-Hogg flew into the office. She looked harried and tired and her usually perfectly coiffured hair was a bit of a mess. She obviously had not been to Julio's hair salon in a while.

Caskie's tense face melted into a look of relief. "Hayley, I'm so glad I found you here . . ."

"I'm right here every day from eight to five, five

days a week, forty-nine weeks a year . . ." Hayley said, then hoped she had not sounded bitter about it.

Bruce excitedly chimed in. "Not next week! Next week we'll be tanned from the scorching Caribbean sun and buzzed on fruity drinks that come with our all-inclusive cruise package!"

Caskie stared at Bruce for a moment, not quite comprehending, then quickly turned back to Hayley, and with a fiercely determined look, said, "I've done something I regret and I want to try and make things right."

Hayley suspected she knew what this was about. "The restraining order?"

Caskie's face fell. "Oh, you already know about that?"

"The police chief is my brother-in-law . . ."

"I see . . ." Caskie mumbled. "I feel terrible about it . . ."

"Caskie, I was at the bar the night of the reunion, and although I admit my mother, Jane, and Celeste said some cruel things that may have upset you, they in no way were physically threatening to you . . ."

"I know that. I shouldn't have done it. It was in the heat of the moment . . . I've already been to the town hall and put in a request to cancel it. I wanted to tell Sheila myself and apologize for overreacting," Caskie said, appearing genuinely remorseful. "I just stopped by your house and she wasn't there."

"She left . . ."

"Back to Florida?" Caskie gasped.

"No, we had a disagreement . . . actually it was more of a fight . . . and, well, she packed up and left and has checked in at that new inn on Mount Desert."

"Oh, I'm sorry to hear that . . ."

Bruce set his coffee cup down and circled around behind Hayley and gently put his hands on her shoulders. "Once Sheila has a chance to cool down, I'm sure they will work everything out."

"Yes, let's hope so . . ." Caskie said. "Do you think she's over there now?"

"I've been trying to call her, but the desk clerk says she doesn't want to be disturbed, so I'm assuming she's hiding out in her room," Hayley said.

"Thank you, Hayley, thank you," Caskie blurted out before blowing her a kiss. "I'm going to head over there right away."

And then she flew back out the door as a gusty wind blew her hair into even more of a mess. If she had been holding an umbrella she probably would have lifted off the ground like Mary Poppins.

Hayley turned her head and reached down and softly kissed Bruce's hand, which rested on her shoulder. "We better make up with Mom before we leave, or there will be no living with me on the cruise."

"I know . . ." Bruce said absentmindedly before catching himself. "I mean . . . as I said, I'm sure it will sort itself out soon."

Chapter 13

Ten minutes later it was finally quitting time, and Hayley and Bruce drove home from the office to finish packing for their long-awaited trip. Hayley couldn't believe their honeymoon had finally arrived after such a long wait. It had been a busy summer season at the paper and Bruce had been putting in longer than usual hours covering the spike in local crimes due to the influx of tourists. But now, in less than twenty-four hours, they would be on a plane to Florida, where they would meet the ship and set off to the Bahamas.

Hayley had already packed one suitcase with her dressier clothing items for the dinners on board, and also a brand-new shimmering silver party dress for the *Dancing with the Stars* themed event scheduled for one night while at sea. She had no plans to participate since she was basically an incompetent hoofer, but she at least didn't want to look out of place. Her small suitcase was reserved for her bathing suits and casual wear for the day trips. That's what she began working on as well as assembling her myriad of toiletry items that cluttered the bathroom sink. Bruce had already squeezed in a couple of pairs of shorts and a small stack of T-shirts. He was far less concerned with his wardrobe, as he planned to spend most of the cruise in his one blue pair of swimming trunks with little anchors on them. Hayley tried convincing him to pack a skimpy red Speedo she had bought for him on Amazon, but he adamantly refused, even though she knew he would look hot wearing one.

Hayley picked it up, fantasizing him in it, and decided to slip it in the suitcase just in case. Bruce emerged from the bathroom and saw what she was doing.

"I told you, there's no way I'm putting that thing on," he said.

Hayley giggled. "I suppose I shouldn't push it. I don't want to have to be compcting with all the other women on the cruise who'd be vying for your attention."

"Oh, you think so . . ." Bruce laughed, shaking his head.

"You're a sexy man, and if you've got it, you should flaunt it, I always say."

"Really? *You* said that?"

"Somebody said it. I don't remember who. I just adopted it," Hayley said before picking up the Speedo and swinging it around on her finger. "Come on, just try it on."

"No way!"

"But the suit you're taking is so boring. I think my son Dustin wore those exact same swimming trunks when he was eight."

"Not a chance," Bruce scoffed.

"Not even for *me*?" Hayley begged. "I promise, if you just try it on so I can see, I won't sneak it in the suitcase."

Bruce sighed and, resigned, snatched the Speedo from her and disappeared into the bathroom. He emerged a minute later and Hayley gasped at just how sexy he looked. "Oh my God . . ."

"Okay, out with it. How ridiculous do I look?"

"You look amazing . . ."

Hayley studied her husband's muscular frame. If anything, Bruce had a rocking body. He worked out at the gym more than any other man she had ever been with, certainly a lot more than she did.

She slowly lowered her eyes to his nether regions.

"And, yeah, baby, it leaves *nothing* to the imagination!"

"Now you're just making fun of me," Bruce said, cupping his crotch, and spinning around to scoot back into the bathroom to change.

"I'm not! And look at that butt! So firm and perky!"

Bruce poked his head out of the bathroom. "If you ever describe my buttocks as perky again, I swear I will file for divorce!"

Hayley laughed. Her cell phone buzzed on the night table next to her. She glanced at the screen. "It's my mother!"

"See, I knew she'd forgive you once she had the chance to cool off," Bruce called from the bathroom.

Hayley quickly picked up the phone to answer the call. "Mom?"

She heard heavy breathing.

"Mom, are you there?"

More heavy breathing.

"Hello?"

Hayley began to suspect an obscene caller had somehow gotten ahold of her mother's phone, but then she heard a familiar voice choke out, "Hayley . . ."

She knew it was her mother.

"Mom, what's wrong?"

"Oh God, Hayley, it's awful!" Sheila cried.

"Mom, what is it? What's happened?"

Sheila began to sob uncontrollably.

"Mom . . . Mom . . . talk to me . . ."

After a few more seconds, Hayley heard Sheila whisper, "I think she might be . . ."

Her mother suddenly screamed bloody murder.

And the phone went dead.

Island Food & Spirits
BY HAYLEY POWELL

One of the best things about growing up in a small town in the 1980s was the freedom we had to roam around on those long, hot summer days once the school year was over. Our parents basically let us loose in our neighborhoods with the surrounding natural beauty of Acadia National Park as our playground. We played on the rocky shores of the Atlantic Ocean, took long strolls on park roads or the carriage path that ran along the edge of Frenchman Bay. Sometimes we would even bike the five miles to Sand Beach to swim in the unforgiving cold water, even in the dog days of August. We would build forts and camps in the thick woods behind our house or even climb one of the many steep mountain trails. Along with my best friends Liddy and Mona, we would be gone for hours, but we always made it home by five o'clock to wash up for supper, which our mothers insisted upon.

With all of this freedom that we were given during our summer vacation, I found it astounding that there was one hard-and-fast rule we were warned never to break. Our mothers had gotten together and decided until we all turned thirteen, we were not allowed to go into town without adult supervision. Okay, I understand if we were six or seven years old, but this one particular summer, we were all twelve and felt strongly that we were now far too old to be banned from walking downtown. What did they expect to happen? Did they think we would knock over a bank or get kidnapped by a marauding gang of Canadian tourists? It made no sense that we could run around the entire island unsupervised where there was a good chance we might encounter a Maine black bear, but we were strictly forbidden to have any human contact on Main Street! As much as we all tried to reason with our mothers, they were adamant that we obey their orders.

Well, that summer I had already turned thirteen and Liddy and Mona were mere months away from the big one-three. It was time our mothers stopped treating us like babies! Besides, all of our friends were already allowed to roam all over town. It was embarrassing that we still couldn't. We confronted our mothers, arguing that we just wanted to pop into the summer shops, or maybe get an ice cream cone, but it was still a firm no go. They absolutely refused, and that was the end of it. We were prisoners for one more summer.

About a week later everything changed.

Mona had come up with a brilliant solution to our problem. She pointed out that it was entirely possible for us to sneak into town, just once. If we left at ten in the morning and were home by two, our mothers would never know. She explained that her mother worked at the Jackson Lab all day and could not keep tabs on us. My mother collected rent part-time at the housing authority a few days a week and stayed home the other days to watch my little brother, Randy, who, unlike me, preferred staying indoors to watch soap operas and game shows on TV. My mother gave him a video recorder for his birthday, and that finally got him out of the house. He spent a lot more time in the backyard making his homemade James Bond spy movies. As for Liddy's mom, well, she sold real estate and was all over the island every day, and so she was the one mother we would have to be extra careful to avoid. But we were confident we could pull it off, just once, and no one would be the wiser.

The following day our plan went off without a hitch. We had a blast hanging out with friends, people-watching on the town pier, drinking milk shakes. It had been so easy, we did it again the next day. And the next day. And the next day after that.

Before we knew it, half the summer was gone. We did have a couple of close calls. Mona's mom drove right by us on Cottage Street one day as we were coming out of Epi's sub shop after splitting a large hero. She parked across the street, and she and another woman got out and headed our way. We frantically dashed back inside, ran to the far end of the shop, crawled into a booth, and sank way down in the seats, peeking out to see the ladies pick up a lunch order and turn to go. We all looked at each other, relieved, when suddenly Mona's mother stopped, said something to her friend, turned back around, and walked straight for us. The three of us were shaking because we knew we were caught and would probably never see the light of day again. But miraculously, she just walked to the counter, grabbed some packaged condiments, and then turned back around to where her friend was waiting, and they left. We were so scared we practically ran the whole way back to my house, swearing we were never going into town again!

Well, that pact lasted until the next day. The many pleasures of downtown Bar Harbor were just too tempting. Another time we almost ran into my mother, who was walking into West End Drug with my brother in tow. I swear Randy looked right at us. I was so worried he would narc on me, but that night at dinner he never said a word, so I assumed we were in the clear.

However, as the summer wore on, I began to get the feeling we were being watched and I just couldn't shake it. I mentioned this to Mona and Liddy as we were strolling up Roberts Avenue heading back to my house one day, and much to my surprise, they both admitted that sometimes they had the same feeling that we were being followed! We ultimately decided to chalk it up to feeling a little guilty about deceiving our parents.

As we passed one of the beautiful three-story homes that lined the street, the front door opened and Liddy's mother stepped outside, followed by a young couple carrying a baby. Liddy's mother began motioning and talking about the large front porch with the comfortable rocking chairs for a warm summer night. Mona, Liddy, and I turned and raced up the driveway to hide behind the house next door, but not before I spotted someone down the street watching us. However, the stalker dashed out of sight before I could get a good look at who it was.

It was that day we decided we were done. No more going into town. It was getting too risky.

About a month later, just before Labor Day, my mom invited Mona's mom and her family, along with Celeste and Liddy, over to our house for her annual "We Made It Through the Summer Barbecue." After chowing down on burgers and hot dogs right off the grill, Mom ushered us all inside for some homemade blueberry ice cream for us kids and some more of her famous blueberry mint gin cocktails for the adults. It was time for us to watch the world premiere of Randy's latest spy movie he had been working on all summer.

Randy, who was dressed up in a suit like his

hero James Bond, popped the VHS tape into the VCR, lowered the lights, and gave a brief introduction hinting at some special guest stars who would be making an appearance in the film.

The opening credits came up.

"Randy Powell Presents . . . A Randy Powell Production . . . Starring Randy Powell in . . . They Almost Got Away With It!"

Weird title, I thought, but okay.

And then the film started and there we were, Mona, Liddy, and I smack dab in the middle of the Village Green, eyeing some cute high school boys passing by wearing those tight bike pants. It got worse from there. There was scene after scene of us in town living it up, and even at one point, giving some lost tourists fake directions and laughing about it. I knew we never should have done that! Luckily Randy was far enough away, the microphone barely picked up the audio. When the film was finally over, you could hear a pin drop. Our mothers were furious. Needless to say, the party broke up pretty quickly after that, and everyone went home.

I braced myself for some yelling, and my mom did not disappoint. When she was finally done, I turned and gave Randy one of my "wait until I get you alone" looks as he stood safely behind our mother and stuck out his tongue at me. I stomped up the stairs, but not before I heard my mother say to Randy, "And now I will deal with you, young man!" Randy began to cry because the one thing he hadn't thought of when he decided to bust us three girls was that he would also get busted for going into town unsupervised! And he was way younger than we were! He lost his video camera and VCR for a month! That sure made me feel a whole lot better, that and another scoop or two of homemade blueberry ice cream.

BLUEBERRY MINT GIN COCKTAIL

INGREDIENTS
1 ounce gin
1 ounce blueberry simple syrup
4 ounces sparkling water
Ice and mint leaves for garnish

BLUEBERRY SIMPLE SYRUP
INGREDIENTS
1 cup blueberries
¼ cup sugar
½ cup water

In a saucepan, bring the simple syrup ingredients to a simmer and cook over medium low heat, stirring occasionally for 30 minutes, until jelly-like.

Mix all your ingredients in a cocktail glass with ice and garnish with a mint leaf. If you like it a bit sweeter, add some more simple syrup.

Easy Homemade Blueberry Ice Cream

Ingredients
4 cups fresh blueberries
¼ cup sugar
Juice and zest of 1 lemon
3 cups heavy cream
1 can sweetened condensed milk

In a food processor puree your blueberries, then pour them into a saucepan. Over medium heat add your sugar, lemon juice, and lemon zest and bring the mixture to a boil, then reduce the heat and simmer for 15 minutes until reduced slightly. Pour into a bowl and place in the refrigerator to chill.

In a stand mixer or large bowl with a hand mixer, beat cream until stiff peaks form and then fold in the sweetened condensed milk until combined. Fold in the blueberry puree. Transfer to a clean container and freeze until firm, about 6 hours.

Serve and enjoy!

Chapter 14

Bruce hastily threw on his clothes and drove himself and Hayley over to the inn on Mount Desert. Two police cars with flashing blue lights were already parked out front on the street. On the lawn outside, just under the soaring oak trees that shaded the property, a small gathering of guests mingled and gossiped about what was happening inside the large colonial-style inn that was just a five-minute walk from the Village Green in Bar Harbor's historic corridor. After parking behind one of the police cruisers, Hayley and Bruce jumped out and raced over to Sheila, who was spotted leaning against one of the oak trees as if she was trying to catch her breath. When they reached her, Sheila reacted with a start as Hayley touched her arm, and then she burst into tears and threw her arms around her daughter.

"Oh, Hayley, it was horrible . . ." Sheila moaned.

Hayley lightly patted her mother on the back. "It's going to be okay . . ."

"Can you tell us what happened?" Bruce asked quietly so the other guests who had been evacuated from the inn and were now loitering nearby could not hear their conversation.

Sheila kept her head buried in Hayley's chest for a few more moments before finally letting her go and stepping back. She was wearing a bulky gray wool sweater because the sun had already gone down and there was a sharp chill in the air as darkness began setting in. She hugged herself as she spoke. "I . . . I walked down to the Big Apple to pick up some bottled water and a few snacks to keep in my room for later, and when I got back and was fumbling for the key I noticed the door to the room next door to my room was slightly ajar. I remember it was room six, which I thought was weird because I'm in room nine. The rooms are not numbered sequentially for some reason. Seven and eight are down another hall. Anyway, I didn't think much of it at first, but as I passed by, I thought I saw someone lying on the floor. Well, I knocked on the door and when there was no answer . . . I pushed it open just a crack so I could get a better look, and that's when I saw her . . ."

Hayley gripped her mother's arm. "Who?"

"Her head was turned away so I couldn't tell at first . . . that's when I called you . . . but while we were on the phone, I walked around the body and I saw her as clear as a summer's day . . . it was Caskie . . . Caskie Lemon-Hogg . . ."

Sheila broke down again, sobbing.

Hayley and Bruce exchanged stunned looks.

They had just seen her less than a half hour earlier.

She was on her way over to the inn to apologize to Sheila.

How did she end up dead in another room?

Chief Sergio Alvarez, flanked by two of his officers, Donnie and Earl, emerged from the inn and met with a team of crime scene investigators who had just arrived at the scene.

Bruce turned to Hayley. "If they've called in forensics, that must mean one thing . . ."

Hayley nodded. "They think it's a homicide."

Hayley left Bruce to comfort her mother and briskly crossed the lawn over to Sergio, who was directing his officers to string up some yellow police tape to keep the guests and growing number of rubbernecking locals a safe distance from the building.

Sergio spotted Hayley approaching. "Not now, Hayley."

"Just tell me one thing and I promise not to bother you anymore," Hayley begged. "How did she die?"

Sergio exhaled, glanced around to make sure no one could overhear him doling out confidential information to a civilian, and then whispered under his breath, "Somebody strangled her."

And then he quickly walked away, pretending he had not said a word. Hayley just stood there, dismayed, before running back to Bruce and her mother. She decided to keep the cause of death to herself, at least for now.

Bruce kicked into crime-reporter mode and began questioning the guests outside, asking if they had seen anything suspicious, as Hayley quietly comforted her mother. About twenty minutes later, Officer Donnie ambled out of the hotel and over to one of the cruisers to make a call. Hayley left her mother and dashed over to him, hovering behind him until he finished talking to his girlfriend, who seemed more concerned with Donnie picking up a few items on her grocery list at the Shop 'n Save than she did about the apparent murder at the inn on Mount Desert.

"I know my shift ends at seven, but I'm probably going to have to work late . . . I'm at a murder scene, Sally! It's kind of serious . . ."

Sally appeared to cut him off and he stood there, shoulders slumped, listening. "Okay, heavy cream, a dozen eggs, vanilla extract . . . Any particular brand? Uh-huh . . ."

Donnie turned to glance back at the inn to make sure his boss, Sergio, wasn't looking for him, and instantly noticed Hayley eavesdropping on his conversation. "Sally, I have to go! I'll go to the store just as soon as I can get out of here and then I'll come right home."

Hayley could hear Sally still talking as Donnie ended the call and pocketed his phone. "What's the word, Donnie?"

"I'm not supposed to talk to any reporters about what's going on in there!" Donnie barked.

"Well, then it's a good thing I'm not a reporter. I'm just a food columnist for the paper. It's not my job to cover the police beat."

Donnie pointed a shaky finger at her. "Yeah, well, it's common knowledge that's never stopped you before!"

"What's Sally making?"

This seemed to confuse him. He hadn't expected that to be her first question.

"She's making a blueberry cake for dessert tonight."

"Sounds yummy!"

He eyed her suspiciously. "I'm sure you would think so. The recipe came from one of your columns."

"Did she get the fresh blueberries from Caskie Lemon-Hogg?"

Donnie gulped, shifting nervously from one foot to the other. "I don't know . . ."

"Poor Caskie . . . I heard she was strangled . . ." Hayley whispered.

Donnie's eyes widened. "Where did you hear that?"

"I have my sources," Hayley said coyly. "I know she was found in one of the rooms and I also heard there was no sign of forced entry."

"Well, then your source is not a reliable one because there was a door adjoining the room next door, and the lock looks like it was broken!"

Donnie immediately knew that he had just shared way too much information.

"The room next door? Where my mother was staying?"

"I can't say!"

"Donnie, tell me!"

"No!"

"I already know about the broken lock. I'd hate for Sergio to find out that it was you who told me about it."

Donnie's mouth dropped open. "Are you blackmailing me? Is that what you're doing? Are you really going to tell Sergio what I said?"

Hayley didn't want to torture the poor boy any further and so she decided to put his mind at ease. "Of course not. You know me better than that. I was just trying to scare you into telling me."

She could see the relief on his face. He believed her.

"I appreciate your honesty," he said.

Hayley turned to leave.

"Yes . . ." Donnie said in a low voice.

Hayley spun back around.

"Yes, what?"

"Yes, it was your mother's room. But if you say it was me who told you, I'll deny it."

"Does that make her a—"

Donnie cut her off. "Yup. A suspect. And not only just a suspect. Your mother's our number-one suspect."

Hayley heard a loud gasp behind her.

Donnie peered over Hayley's right shoulder and his eyes suddenly popped wide open.

Hayley knew who it was.

She slowly turned around to see her mother, clutching her chest, a panicked look on her face. "You think *I* did it?"

"No!" Donnie cried. "I didn't say that! I didn't say anything! Leave me alone!"

Donnie bolted away, back toward the inn.

Hayley rushed over to hug her mother again, who was on the verge of a full-blown meltdown.

"Are they going to arrest me?"

"No one's arresting you, Mom!"

"I swear I had nothing to do with what happened to Caskie! I may not have liked her, and she may have taken out a restraining order against me, but that doesn't mean . . . Oh dear Lord, it looks really bad, doesn't it?"

"Mom, did you notice when you were in your room that the door that connected to the room next door had a broken lock?"

"What? No! I had no idea there was even someone checked in to the room next door! I didn't see or hear anything!"

Hayley nodded, then saw Bruce, who had just finished questioning the other guests, walking toward them.

"Am I going to jail?" Sheila sputtered.

"You're not going to jail! I promise!" Hayley assured her.

But Hayley was not entirely sure that was a promise that she could keep, especially given the circumstantial evidence.

In fact, there was only one thing she was sure of at the moment, and it was time to tell Bruce.

Bruce approached with a puzzled look. "What's going on?"

"Mom's moving back to our house and we're canceling our honeymoon."

Bruce's face blanched. "What? Why?"

"I think we may have to prove that my mother is not a murderer."

Chapter 15

"According to Andy Shackelford, who owns the inn, the guest registered in the room where Caskie Lemon-Hogg's body was discovered was Rupert Stiles," Sergio said as he sat behind his desk at the Bar Harbor Police Station, perusing the bed-and-breakfast records that had been printed out for him.

"Rupert Stiles?" Bruce asked, surprised. "But that doesn't make any sense. Why would he book a room at the inn? He's a local. Last I heard, he rents an apartment down on lower Rodick Street."

Hayley didn't buy it either. Something else had to be going on here. The last time she had seen the gruff curmudgeon with his long gray beard was at her mother's high school reunion at Randy's bar a few nights earlier, where he unsuccessfully tried to pick up Mona's mother while heavily intoxicated. He didn't seem capable of walking in a straight line, let alone strangling an able-bodied woman.

"Have you spoken to Rupert about this?" Hayley asked.

Sergio nodded. "He claims his credit card was stolen and that it wasn't him who booked the room. The thing is, the desk clerk says that the man who checked in with the card had a long beard, just like Rupert's. I sent Donnie and Earl over to Rupert's apartment to pick him up and bring him down here so we can put him in a lineup. The clerk is waiting in a room down the hall."

Bruce furiously jotted down notes on his pad, making sure to get every detail right for his next column. It was not often that the police chief was willing to dole out information to them about an ongoing investigation, so he was not about to let this rare opportunity pass. He finally finished and looked up.

"It just doesn't add up. I'm having a tough time believing that Caskie and Rupert Stiles could have had any kind of relationship given the vastly different social circles they traveled in. If they were having some kind of an affair, which strikes me as totally implausible, why plan a clandestine meeting at a bed-and-breakfast where lots of people can see you coming and going, and why use your credit card so there is a clear record?"

Hayley quickly jumped in. "Plus, Caskie showed up at our house looking for my mother. That was the reason she was going over to the inn, to apologize for taking out the restraining order against her. How did she wind up in the room next door, strangled to death?"

"Maybe Rupert lured her into the room somehow, and tried to take advantage of her, and she resisted and things just got out of hand," Bruce suggested.

Hayley shook her head. She still could not wrap her head around the fact that Rupert Stiles might be some kind of a violent predator.

"The desk clerk also claims that he saw the bearded

man running out of the inn shortly before your mother stumbled across the victim's body," Sergio said.

It did not look too good for Rupert.

But at least there was another suspect besides Sheila.

Officer Earl rapped on the door to Sergio's office. "We're ready."

Sergio stood up from his desk. "I'll be right there."

Hayley half expected Sergio to bar them from observing the police lineup, but he didn't and so she and Bruce quietly followed behind him, hoping he wouldn't notice them and order them out. Donnie was escorting the desk clerk out of a nearby office, and Hayley recognized him as Petey Shackelford, the inn owner's son, who had been in Gemma's class all through high school. He was awkward and agitated, not at all comfortable at being at a police station, let alone serving as a witness.

He noticed Hayley and gave her a half smile. "Hi, Mrs. Powell."

Hayley, who desperately wanted to not be noticed so she and Bruce could stay for the lineup, gave him a quick wave and mouthed "Hello."

Sergio excused Donnie and shook Petey's hand. "Thank you for doing this, Petey."

Petey mumbled something, but Hayley couldn't make out what he had said. Then he turned to Hayley again. "How's Gemma doing?"

The question startled her. His attention was back on her. Sergio didn't appear annoyed that his witness was more focused on talking to Hayley than preparing to pick out a potential murderer, and so Hayley decided to answer his question. "She's in New York, studying at a culinary institute, doing quite well. She wants to be a caterer or maybe a food critic."

"That's so cool," Petey said wistfully, with a hint of envy. Right now, the poor kid probably wished he had gotten out of Bar Harbor after high school when he had the chance, instead of being here at the police station.

"Petey, if you don't mind . . ." Sergio said patiently, redirecting his attention to the large one-way mirror that gave a full view of a long room where Officer Earl led in four men, all dressed similarly, all with some type of facial hair. Rupert was second from the left, holding a sign in front of him with a number two on it. He was a bundle of nerves and tugged on his long gray beard, his eyes darting back and forth. He could not have looked more guilty if he tried. The other three men appeared relaxed and calm. None of them sported beards that came even close to being as long as Rupert's. The lineup struck Hayley as a bit unfair, since Rupert stood out so much from the others. It would be hard *not* to pick him. But still, Petey studied all four men carefully before speaking.

"Do you see the man you checked into the B and B, Petey?" Sergio asked gently.

Petey nodded. "I think so."

"Can you point him out?"

Petey nodded again. "Number two . . . I think . . ."

"You *think*? You're not sure?" Sergio asked.

Petey sighed, looked at all four men again, and then resolutely turned to Sergio. "Number two. I'm sure. One hundred percent."

"Okay, thank you, Petey," Sergio said as Officer Earl escorted the four men back out of the room.

Sergio turned to Donnie. "Go ahead and place Rupert under arrest."

"Sure thing, boss," Donnie said, unhooking a pair of handcuffs from his belt and dashing off down the hall.

Hayley turned to Bruce. "I am still not convinced he did it."

"Neither am I," Bruce said. "But Sergio's got an eyewitness and I suppose we should be grateful."

"Grateful? For what?" Hayley asked, confused.

"Grateful he didn't arrest your mother. She's the one with the clear motive."

Chapter 16

"I didn't kill nobody, Hayley, you have to believe me!" Rupert cried, his bony fingers clutching the bars of his jail cell. After the lineup, Officer Donnie wasted no time in booking and processing Rupert and tossing him in one of the three jail cells located in the back of the police station. Bruce wanted to get back to the office to file his scoop on the arrest of a suspect in the Caskie Lemon-Hogg murder, but Hayley chose not to go with him, telling him she had an errand to run, but neglecting to mention it was sneaking back to the jail cells to talk to Rupert.

The poor old coot seemed genuinely relieved that someone, anyone, was interested in getting his side of the story at this point, especially Hayley, whose reputation for digging until she unearthed the truth preceded her.

"I believe you, Rupert, but the desk clerk identified you in the lineup," Hayley said, studying Rupert's face on the other side of the bars, which was panic-stricken and confused.

"It wasn't me, I swear on my life!" Rupert wailed.

You just may have to, Hayley thought to herself.

Rupert reached his arm through the bars of the cell and grabbed Hayley's hand. "I like you, Hayley, I always have. You've always been nice to me when you didn't have to be, and I appreciate that. You're one of the few good ones in town."

"Thank you, Rupert," Hayley said, feeling sorry for him.

"One of the few I can tolerate sober, to be honest!"

Hayley's reputation may have preceded her, but so did Rupert's, as a loud, sometimes disruptive drunk.

He squeezed her hand so tightly she winced.

"Please, Hayley, you have to help me. Somebody is setting me up for this murder!"

"Do you have any idea who would want to do that?"

Rupert shook his head. "Not a clue."

"Where were you last night?"

Rupert let go of Hayley's hand and stared at the floor intently. Hayley waited patiently for him to say something.

A minute went by.

"Rupert?"

"I'm thinking . . ."

"You don't remember?"

"I may have had a couple of bourbons yesterday afternoon at your brother's bar . . ."

Hayley didn't need a translation. A couple of bourbons most likely meant a full bottle downed throughout the afternoon until he was so blitzed he couldn't remember anything after sundown. "What time did you leave?"

"I remember leaving when it was still light out . . ."

That wasn't good, not in Hayley's mind. If Rupert couldn't remember where he went and couldn't provide a rock-solid alibi, then there was no way he could prove he didn't strangle Caskie.

"Think, Rupert, think. Where did you go?"

Rupert was trying real hard, but his memory just wasn't helping him out. "I remember thumbing a ride on route three . . . a pickup truck pulled over . . ."

"Do you remember where you were going or who was driving the truck?"

Rupert concentrated for a few more moments, but then let out a frustrated sigh and mumbled, "No . . ."

"Who in town drives a pickup truck?"

"Just about everybody . . ."

"Mona drives a pickup. Was it Mona?"

"No, I don't recall it being a woman."

"Was it a man?"

"Don't recall that either . . ."

This was not going to be easy.

"Rupert, you live on Rodick Street here in town, is that right?"

"Yup."

"Then what were you doing hitchhiking on route three?"

Rupert shrugged. "I don't know, Hayley . . . I can't remember . . . It looks bad for me, doesn't it?"

"Just stay calm, Rupert, we'll figure this out."

"I had nothing against Caskie. Hell, I barely knew her. But nobody's going to listen to an old drunk. They're going to pin this on me and send me away for the rest of my life, aren't they?"

Rupert was shaking now as the reality of his grim situation sunk in and there was very little Hayley could do to keep him from spiraling. He reached back through the bars again to grab her arm. "Please, help me clear my name, Hayley! Don't let them blame me for this!"

Hayley found herself saying, "I'll do my best, Rupert . . ."

She knew with a positive identification from the desk clerk and Rupert's fuzzy memory, most people in town would automatically assume he was guilty. She also knew that if by some miracle she was able to prove Rupert's innocence, that would probably leave her own mother as the last suspect standing.

Which meant she had to find the real killer and fast.

Chapter 17

Sheila was not happy when Hayley returned home later that evening and announced that in her mind Rupert Stiles was innocent of the murder of Caskie Lemon-Hogg. Because Sheila knew if that was true, then the police just might start focusing on her again.

"Who are we to question the police?" Sheila snapped, hoping Hayley might drop the whole matter, as she stirred a pot of chili on the stove, which she was preparing for their dinner when Bruce finally got home from the office.

"I just don't believe he did it," Hayley said. "He told me he barely knew her."

"That's what he *claims*, but how can we really be sure? We don't know what kind of history they may have had, or how he felt about her, or what kind of bad blood there might have been between them."

"His alibi is a little shaky, I admit, but I got the feeling he was telling me the truth," Hayley said.

"Well, I got a feeling that your father would always

be faithful to me and I was wrong about that, so you can't always trust all of the *feelings* you get!"

Hayley didn't want to argue with her mother. She could tell she was nervous about being on a list of murder suspects and still traumatized by the ordeal of discovering Caskie's body. She decided to drop the whole matter and instead talk about Sheila's grandchildren: Gemma, who was thriving in New York, and Dustin, who was studying film animation in California. That lasted two minutes until a pickup truck pulled into the driveway and Mona barreled into the house and announced, "I know who killed Caskie Lemon-Hogg!"

"Rupert Stiles, that's who has been arrested and charged with the crime, so there is no need for us to get involved any further!" Sheila exclaimed.

Hayley, who was grating cheddar cheese to throw on top of the chili, threw her mother an annoyed look before turning back to Mona. "What are you talking about?"

"I can't believe I didn't remember this until today when I heard they arrested Rupert. I saw Caskie yesterday before she was killed!" Mona said matter-of-factly before peering into the pot of chili. "Oh, man, that smells delicious."

"You're welcome to stay for dinner, Mona," Sheila said brightly.

"I wish I could, but I got my rug rats waiting for me at home to scrounge up something for them to eat. They're like feral animals and can get really dangerous when they're hungry."

Hayley set the grater down and wiped her hands on a towel. "What about Caskie?"

Mona blinked at Hayley a couple of times as if she had lost her train of thought, but then the train finally got moving again. "Oh, right. You know how Owen

Meyers buys lobsters from my shop for his restaurant?"

"Yes," Hayley said.

Owen Meyers owned a place called The Shack, which was fancier than it sounded and was popular with the summer tourists, and featured a few signature dishes including Owen's lobster rolls, fried clams, and homemade blueberry pies.

"Well, I stopped by The Shack yesterday to make a delivery, and guess who was there—!"

"Caskie," Hayley answered.

"Yeah, how did you know?" Mona asked, perplexed.

"Because you just came in here with the news that you know who killed Caskie, so I just assumed . . ."

"Oh, right. Anyway, you know how she spends all summer picking blueberries and selling them? Well, I guess Owen was a customer because she was there with a big load of them. About two dozen boxes of blueberries wrapped in plastic. Anyway, the restaurant wasn't open yet so there were no customers, but when I came in the two of them were in the middle of a huge argument!"

Sheila gasped. "What about?"

Mona shrugged. "Beats me. They stopped when they saw me. And then they both pretended everything was fine. But I could tell Owen was madder than a man with no legs in a shoe store! His face was beet red and I could see the veins popping out of his neck!"

"Then what happened?" Hayley asked.

Mona shrugged again. "Nothing. I dropped off the cooler with the lobsters in it, Owen paid me, and I left."

"So how do you know who killed Caskie?" Hayley asked.

"Owen did it," Mona said, as if stating the obvious. "Didn't you hear me? I saw them fighting."

"That doesn't at all mean he killed her!" Hayley argued, throwing her hands up, frustrated.

"Looked pretty suspicious to me," Mona spit out defensively.

"Hayley's right," Sheila said, surprising Hayley by coming to her defense. "I had my issues with Caskie, the woman took a restraining order out on me, but I did not kill her even though it could look like I did to some people."

Mona nodded. "I know you didn't kill her because I've known you since I was seven years old and came over to play with Hayley after school. But Owen's only been on the island a few years and he has bad breath and once cut me off in the parking lot of the Shop 'n Save to get the only available parking space, so clearly he has no conscience and could be a malicious killer for all I know!"

"Thank you, Miss Marple," Hayley said, sighing.

"Hayley, watch the chili while I go upstairs to change," Sheila said, scurrying out of the kitchen.

Hayley was certain Sheila was lying. She didn't have to change. She was already in some comfortable clothes for the evening. It's not like she had to dress up for dinner with her and Bruce. As Mona picked up a wooden spoon off the counter to try the chili, Hayley could hear her mother upstairs in Gemma's room, talking to someone on the phone.

Hayley turned to Mona. "What are you doing for lunch tomorrow?"

Mona didn't have to think about it. "Nothing."

"How about you, me, and Liddy have lunch?"

"Sounds good to me. Where do you want to go?"

"I have a craving for a piece of homemade blueberry pie at The Shack."

Mona raised an eyebrow, knowing she was now officially a part of Hayley's independent investigation
into the murder of Caskie Lemon-Hogg. "See? I knew
you'd want me to tell you."

"Just don't mention to my mother what we're doing
tomorrow. She'll want to come along. She's going to
be a basket case until Caskie's murder is solved, and I
don't want to be saddled with all that baggage," Hayley whispered.

It didn't take much to convince Liddy to join them
the next day at noon. She was already a fan of The
Shack, stopping by at least twice a week for one of
Owen's delectable lobster rolls.

When the three of them convened outside the
restaurant at the far end of Cottage Street across from
the Tailgate Sports & Pizza, Hayley was ravenous. She
had skipped breakfast and had only had three cups of
coffee all morning. Liddy also was starving, having
just come from an open house she had worked all
morning. Mona was the only one who wasn't hungry,
because she had just stuffed herself with a cheese-
burger and onion rings at the Side Street Cafe an hour
earlier because noon was too late to eat lunch, in her
opinion. Mona ate breakfast at five, lunch at eleven,
and dinner at four thirty. She was usually in bed by
seven.

They entered through the door and a bell rang. The
restaurant was surprisingly empty except for a few pa-
trons, and Hayley noticed that Owen, a short, squat
man with a big belly and bushy mustache, was waiting
tables. What was even more surprising were the three
women he was currently waiting on—their mothers,

Sheila, Celeste, and Jane, seated at a corner table with menus in front of them.

"What are *they* doing here?" Liddy asked.

"I'm afraid to ask," Hayley said, marching over to their table, followed by Liddy and Mona.

Owen was clutching a pad of paper and a pencil and appeared tense and aggravated.

"It's a simple question," Celeste cooed. "I don't understand why you are getting so upset."

"I'm not upset! I'm just trying to take your order!" Owen snapped.

"Mom, what's going on here?" Hayley asked.

"We're just ordering lunch," Sheila said with a tight smile.

Jane casually perused the menu. "I just can't decide what I want . . ."

Owen, suddenly feeling crowded by Hayley, Liddy, and Mona, practically elbowed his way out, and as he fled to the kitchen, called out, "I'll come back to take your order in a few minutes!"

Sheila, Celeste, and Jane then dropped their menus and leaned in to each other. "Did you see that? He's definitely hiding something."

"Mother, I asked you what you were doing today and you said nothing," Liddy said, glaring at her mother.

"I'm sorry, I didn't realize I had to keep you abreast of my daily schedule. It's not like you took the time to inform me that you would be coming here for lunch with your friends too," Celeste said, playfully eyeing Sheila and Jane.

Mona looked as if she felt like she should say something to her mother too, but wasn't sure what. "Don't order the fried clams. My deadbeat husband, Dennis, ate them here once and got sick. We couldn't prove it was the clams but he said they tasted funny."

"Good to know, dear," Jane said.

Hayley put her hands down on the table and hovered over Sheila. "What did you mean when you said Owen is hiding something? What did you ask him?"

"I simply asked what he and Caskie were fighting about on the day of the murder, and suddenly he wasn't so welcoming and friendly, which I find highly suspicious, don't you, ladies?"

"Extremely so," Celeste added. "Did you see how fast he ran back to the kitchen to get out of answering the question?"

Jane just nodded as she studied the menu. She seemed to be more interested in what she was going to order for lunch. "Has anyone tried the seafood bisque here?"

Like mother like daughter.

"So *that's* what's going on here," Hayley said. "You're afraid if Rupert Stiles is released, you'll be arrested, so you three are investigating to find out who killed Caskie. That's why you ran upstairs last night, not to change, but to call Celeste and Jane to meet you here for lunch today."

"Yes," Sheila admitted. "We're working as a team to clear my good name. To clear all our names. Isn't that what you three are doing here as well?"

"We're just having lunch together!" Liddy insisted.

"Not me. I already ate. I just want to know why Owen killed Caskie," Mona said.

Sheila sat back in her chair and gave Hayley a knowing smile.

"Mom, this is ludicrous. You have no experience in this kind of thing," Hayley said with a worried look.

"You three aren't exactly trained policewomen like Angie Dickinson," Celeste cooed.

"Oh, I loved her in that show," Sheila said.

"What show?" Liddy asked.

"The one where she played the policewoman," Sheila said. "What was it called, Celeste?"

"*Police Woman*."

"Right. She was so good in that," Sheila said, nodding.

"Mom, focus," Hayley admonished. "I don't want you snooping around. If the killer is still out there, you might spook him, or her, and there's no telling what kind of danger you could be in."

"That's a chance I'm willing to take, Hayley," Sheila said stubbornly. "I refuse to go to prison for a crime I did not commit!"

"Nobody's arresting you!" Hayley wailed.

"Yet," Celeste quickly added.

There was an uncomfortable silence, which Mona finally broke. "Mom, what are you doing here? You hate watching detective shows because of the violence. Why are you involved in this too?"

"Because Celeste offered to pay for lunch," Jane mumbled.

Celeste stared at Hayley, Liddy, and Mona and pointed a fork in their direction. "You three are obviously here for the same reason we are. Why should we stop investigating if you three don't?"

"Because you're too old for this," Liddy said.

More uncomfortable silence.

Even more uncomfortable than the last time.

And for good reason.

The three mothers were terribly insulted.

Hayley knew there was no coming back from that one.

Even Liddy, who rarely regretted anything she said, knew she had gone too far. "I'm sorry . . . I didn't mean to imply . . ."

Celeste bristled. "You didn't imply anything. You were quite plain about it."

"You enjoy your lunch. We're going to go sit down at a table over there," Hayley said quietly.

"That one's free," Sheila said, gesturing toward the table farthest away from them.

Hayley, Liddy, and Mona took the hint and retreated, sitting down at a table on the far side of the restaurant. They quietly picked up their menus to peruse the lunch selections. Owen had yet to emerge from the kitchen, and Hayley wondered if he ever would, given how flustered he had become when asked about his argument with Caskie Lemon-Hogg. But he did. For a short time, just to take their orders and deliver their food and to clear their plates when they were finished. He never spoke or answered any questions, especially about the murder victim, which only fueled Hayley's suspicions about him. Their mothers finally gave up and paid their bill and left the restaurant, not bothering to stop and say goodbye to their daughters on their way out.

It looked as if some kind of competition between mothers and daughters was brewing. Who would solve the murder first? Hayley found the whole idea of a race to be childish and utterly ridiculous. And yet, deep down, Hayley knew she couldn't let her mother show her up. She had to solve this crime first.

Chapter 18

The turnout for Caskie Lemon-Hogg's funeral service at the Congregational church was much larger than Hayley had expected. Hayley's party alone was made up of seven people including herself, Bruce, Liddy, Mona, and their three mothers. There had been a long, drawn out discussion on whether or not it was appropriate for Sheila, Celeste, and Jane to attend given the ugly scene that had transpired between them and Caskie at the high school reunion party at Drinks Like a Fish, but in the end, it was decided that they should at least have the opportunity to pay their respects despite the bad blood.

Although her mother would never admit it, Hayley also suspected that Sheila was worried about optics. She clearly did not want to be perceived as a heartless enemy of the deceased, thereby fueling speculation that she had been the one who strangled poor Caskie, and so Hayley could tell her mother was working hard as they entered the church to give the impression that she was genuinely grieving over the loss of a dear classmate by mustering up some tears and needing the support of her daughter as she made her way down the aisle to a pew in the middle, not too close to the front. Celeste and Jane, who feared guilt by association, also put on a good show, holding on to each other and bowing their heads solemnly.

Bruce turned to Hayley and whispered in her ear, "You didn't tell me it was an open casket funeral."

"I didn't know," Hayley whispered back.

"Seeing a dead body freaks me out," Bruce said, averting his eyes from Caskie's corpse, which was laid out down in the front of the church.

"How can that be? You're a crime reporter! You must have seen dozens of them in your long career," Hayley said, incredulous.

Bruce shook his head. "I've always managed to steer clear unless they were already covered up by a sheet. I had this dream as a kid that my grandfather kept looking at me while lying in his casket at his own funeral, and I woke up in a cold sweat. It stuck with me and I haven't felt comfortable around dead bodies ever since."

They took their seats in the middle of a pew just past Liddy and Mona while Sheila, Celeste, and Jane sat down at the end of the pew across the aisle from them. Hayley was now between Bruce and Edie Staples, wife of Reverend Staples, the man who would be delivering the sermon.

Edie clutched a Bible and leaned in to Hayley. "Your mother looks wonderful. She hasn't aged a bit. What's her secret?"

"I wish I knew. I'd bottle it," Hayley joked.

"She must be so relieved that the police have arrested

Caskie's killer," Edie said. "Before they caught Rupert and got him to confess, there was a rumor going around that Sheila might have been the one who—"

Hayley interrupted her. "Rupert didn't confess."

"I'm sorry, what did you say, dear?"

"Rupert says he didn't do it."

"Oh, well, of course he would say that. Murderers always claim to be innocent . . ." Edie said, shaking her head. "Until the evidence inevitably proves they're lying . . ."

"What evidence?" Hayley asked.

"I'm sure the police would not have arrested a suspect unless they had enough evidence to make a case in court . . ."

"I haven't seen any evidence that would convince me beyond a reasonable doubt that Rupert hurt anyone . . ."

Edie was not about to back down from her position. "I heard they have an eyewitness . . ."

"Yes, but witnesses can sometimes be mistaken, and from what I know, there is no physical evidence tying Rupert to the murder . . ."

"Ruth Farrell at the Ladies Auxiliary told me Rupert can't remember where he was or what he was doing on the night Caskie was strangled!"

"Yes, Rupert tends to drink too much and that makes his memory fuzzy, but that's not exactly concrete proof that he's a cold-blooded killer."

Edie was getting a little miffed that Hayley was so argumentative, especially on this somber occasion. "Well, if you are so certain Rupert has been falsely accused, then who do you think did it? Your *mother*?"

"I didn't say that . . ." Hayley sputtered.

Edie gave her a look that said, *You might as well have.*

Bruce clutched Hayley's arm and hissed in Hayley's ear. "She won't stop staring at me."

"Who?"

"Caskie!" Bruce said, panicking.

Hayley looked up front at the casket. She had a clear view of Caskie faceup, lying in repose. She turned back to her husband. "Her eyes are closed, Bruce . . ."

"They weren't a minute ago! Her head was turned this way and she was looking straight at me!"

"You really do have a problem being in the same room as a dead body, don't you?"

"I told you, it's like a horror movie, you know, *Night of the Living Dead* . . . and they keep staring at me like they're going to jump out of the coffin and come after me . . ."

Edie, who had been eavesdropping, reached over and patted Bruce's hand. "I hear that new psychiatrist in town, Dr. Hishmeh, is quite good. I certainly have no reason to see him, but you might want to consider it."

Bruce scowled at her. "Thank you, Edie . . ."

"By the way, I hope you stay for the reception after the service. I made blueberry tarts using Caskie's recipe as sort of a tribute to her . . ."

"How nice," Hayley said, having no intention of trying one since Edie Staples was a terrible baker and had proven it time and time again at every one of her husband's church service receptions.

Bruce gripped Hayley's hand again, so hard Hayley winced in pain. He looked down at his shoes and said in a hushed tone, "Look, look, look, she's doing it again!"

Hayley glanced up front to see Caskie in the same position as she was before, as still as a, well, corpse.

Hayley leaned over and whispered in Bruce's ear, "Maybe you *should* talk to someone about this."

Owen Meyers, the owner of The Shack, arrived with his wife, Peggy, and marched down the aisle on the far right of the church, turning into the pew where Hayley was seated and plopping down next to Edie Staples. Edie made small talk with Peggy as Owen nervously looked around at the crowd of mourners that filled the room. He hadn't noticed Hayley yet, but when she leaned forward and offered him a welcoming smile, he reacted with a start.

"Hello, Owen, it's nice to see you . . ."

Owen, suddenly flustered, tugged on his wife's sleeve. "I want to go sit further down front."

Peggy gave him a confused look. "Why? I'm fine right here."

"Why do you have to constantly argue with me? Can't you just do what I want this *one* time?"

Edie reared back, her eyebrows raised, thrilled to be smack in the middle of a couple's abrupt spat.

Peggy turned to Edie. "Excuse us, Edie, I'm going to be the dutiful wife and adhere to my crazy husband's wishes."

"I understand. Be sure to stick around after the service. I made blueberry tarts."

"Yummy . . . see you later," Peggy said, smiling, nodding to Hayley as she stood up and followed her husband.

There was no doubt in her mind that Owen did not want to sit anywhere near Hayley out of fear she might try to question him about that mysterious fight between him and Caskie on the day she was killed.

Hayley watched Owen drag Peggy all the way down to the front pew and sit down on the end. He cranked his head around and glared at Hayley for a few seconds before spinning back around so he could blatantly ignore her.

Hayley checked her watch. The service was scheduled to begin in two minutes. Reverend Staples emerged from a side door and took his place at the podium off to the left of the coffin. Edie sat upright at the sight of her husband, a big smile plastered on her face, excited, almost ready to applaud wildly as if she was at a Tom Jones concert.

Reverend Staples shuffled his index cards, studying them, and then looked out at the crowd, ready to begin, when the door to the church slammed open and two more mourners shuffled in.

It was Regina Knoxville, Caskie's best friend, and her husband, Albert.

Reverend Staples allowed them time to find some seats before launching into his prepared spiel.

Regina, clutching her purse like a lifeline, wearing a tight-fitting sexy black dress with a plunging neckline arguably inappropriate for church let alone a funeral, clung to her short, wiry husband, who was holding her up with a supportive hand underneath her elbow. They made their way down the aisle, stopping at the pew where Sheila, Celeste, and Jane were seated. There was absolute silence in the entire church as the three women locked eyes with Regina.

Regina's nostrils flared and she stumbled a bit, her anger almost overwhelming her. Albert slid a bony arm around her tiny waist, steadying her. Regina then focused her attention on Celeste, and for a moment, Hayley thought Regina might spit at her. It was no secret to everyone in the room of a certain age that back in the day, after high school and before Celeste married Liddy's father, she and Albert had been an item. Like Regina, Celeste had actually been more interested in Albert's family money than crushingly boring Albert himself. This history obviously did not sit well with his first and only wife, Regina, and she made no bones about it.

There were a few intermittent hushed whispers from surrounding mourners watching the friction between Caskie Lemon-Hogg's best friend and her three unambiguous enemies. Sheila, Celeste, and Jane had no choice but to acknowledge Regina with polite nods, but Regina was having none of it. She slowly, intentionally turned her back on them, as if she couldn't stomach looking at them anymore. This dramatic move caused some more murmuring.

Reverend Staples, who did not like to be upstaged, tapped his foot, impatiently waiting for Regina to stop stealing focus. With her devoted husband's help, Regina finally moved to the opposite side of the aisle and excused herself as she pushed her way to the middle of the pew directly in front of Hayley. Regina sat down at the first open space, forcing Albert to practically crawl over her to get to the other side of her and sit down. Reverend Staples finally began, welcoming everyone. Hayley debated with herself briefly on whether or not she should say something to Regina, and then decided to err on the side of caution and at least be polite. She tapped Regina gently on the shoulder. Regina slowly turned around, nostrils still flaring as her angry eyes fell upon Hayley.

"I'm so sorry for your loss . . ." Hayley whispered.

Regina never deigned to even bother with a response. Hayley was Sheila's daughter after all, and in her mind, the apple did not fall far from the tree. She simply gave Hayley an irritated look and turned back around.

Edie, who had been transfixed listening to her husband speak from the podium, suddenly snapped out of it and glared at Hayley. She was not amused in the slightest that Hayley was talking during her husband's sermon. "Shhhh . . ."

Hayley gave her an apologetic look and then redirected her attention toward Reverend Staples.

"It is with great sadness that today we say goodbye to one of our own . . . Caskie Lemon-Hogg was a resident of Bar Harbor her entire life . . ."

"Oh my God! Not again!" a man screamed.

Everyone in the church jumped with a start. Heads swiveled around to see who was the source of such a sudden outburst.

Hayley knew exactly who was responsible because the man who had shouted and interrupted the sermon was sitting right next to her and he had nearly busted her eardrum.

It was Bruce.

His head was down and he was nervously knocking his knees together and ringing his hands. His eyes were squeezed shut and he said in a low voice, "Is she still looking at me, Hayley?"

Hayley sighed and glanced at the prone body of the deceased, still lying in the coffin with her eyes closed, just as she had been the whole time. Hayley put a hand on Bruce's hunched back. "No, sweetheart, she's not."

Edie stared at both of them and then leaned over closer to Hayley and whispered, "I'll get you Dr. Hishmeh's number."

Chapter 19

When it was time for Regina Knoxville to deliver her eulogy there was a palpable tension in the air as she clutched a tissue in her fingers and made her way to the front of the church. Reverend Staples stepped aside, giving her a wide berth.

When Regina took her place behind the podium and adjusted the microphone downward because she was a foot shorter than the towering minister, it caused some loud feedback that startled the gathered mourners. Then, Regina blew her nose into the tissue and stuffed it down her cleavage. She cleared her throat and looked out into the audience, her eyes watery and bloodshot, her bottom lip quivering.

"Let me tell you something about Caskie Lemon-Hogg, a wonderful, kind, generous woman, who also happened to be my best friend . . ." Regina paused. "One night, about four or five years ago, we talked about when the day came that one of us passed on to the other side . . . what type of service we would like to have, what kind of arrangements we'd like made . . . and Caskie told me she wanted to be cremated . . . because it would be her last chance to have, in her words, a 'smoking-hot body just like yours, Regina . . .'"

There was silence throughout the church as everyone took this in, followed by some titters, then outright, raucous laughter. Hayley quickly joined in, appreciative of the fact that Regina had alleviated some of the tension with a joke.

Regina waited for the laughter to die down before continuing. "Of course, later on, Caskie changed her mind and decided it would be best if she was buried in a plot reserved for her next to her loving parents in the Ledgelawn Cemetery, and that's where we will say our final goodbyes later today. Caskie lived in Bar Harbor her whole life, and for those of us who knew her, *really* knew her," Regina said, pointedly glaring at Sheila, Celeste, and Jane, who all stared down at their shoes, trying not to make eye contact with her, "we saw the goodness in her. Caskie never had children of her own, but she volunteered as a chaperone at school dances and on class trips. She struggled with dyslexia her whole life and started a scholarship fund for students with learning disabilities. She was known around town for tirelessly picking blueberries every summer, and yes, she would sell some to local businesses, but she would also generously donate many more to the Sonogee assisted living facility for the elderly, before it closed, so the kitchen staff could make the residents blueberry muffins and pies and pancakes. Did you know that about her?"

There was silence in the church as Regina paused.

She fixed her eyes on Sheila, Celeste, and Jane again. "Did *any* of you know that about Caskie?"

More uncomfortable silence.

Regina's eyes narrowed. "Sheila, would you like to say something?"

Hayley watched her mother squirm for a few seconds before she vigorously shook her head.

But Regina was on a mission and not about to let her off the hook. "I'm sorry, I didn't hear you . . ."

Sheila looked up, embarrassed and croaked, "No . . ."

"That's a shame. You knew Caskie most of your life, so I thought you might have a memory you'd like to share. What about you, Celeste?"

Liddy's mother looked around, mortified to be called out like this. "No, thank you . . ."

"That's a shame. You're such a good public speaker, especially at town council meetings when you're talking about a zoning law that's in your best interest . . ."

Celeste waved her off, looking down at the floor.

"Jane? You like to express your opinion, whether anyone asks for it or not. What about you? Would you like to say something about Caskie?"

Jane shook her head, looking around for any means of escape.

"No? *Nothing?* You three are here because I assume you considered Caskie your friend, correct?"

Nothing from the mothers. Their eyes were all now glued back to the floor. Hayley felt terrible for them.

"The circumstances surrounding Caskie's death are no secret," Regina said, speaking into the microphone so her words echoed throughout the church even louder. "Our dear friend was *murdered*!"

Bruce leaned into Hayley and whispered, "Oh boy, here we go . . ."

"Someone strangled her!"

Revered Staples began to sweat. A memorial service

was not the occasion to discuss the unpleasant details of Caskie's early demise. He started to stand up, but Regina fired him a fierce look, warning him to back off, and he quickly sat down in his chair without incident.

"Luckily the police have arrested a suspect. A man we all know, Rupert Stiles. Rupert too has lived in Bar Harbor his whole life. He has never caused any trouble, and yes, he is awfully fond of the sauce, and has been known to mouth off when he shouldn't. But does that make him a violent man? Not in my mind. In fact, the Rupert Stiles I have known since kindergarten has never had a violent bone in his body. I know this is probably not an appropriate time to discuss this, but I knew Caskie, and how she always stood up for those who were treated unfairly, and I know she would never want the wrong person to go to prison. No, the Caskie I know is right now screaming for justice, and I feel it is my responsibility to take up the mantle and see that justice is *done*!"

Hayley noticed Regina's husband, Albert, desperately trying to signal his wife to wrap it up before things got too out of hand, but Regina was not about to be stopped now. Hayley suddenly felt a wave of nausea over so adamantly defending Rupert to Edie Staples, because now it appeared as if she was squarely on Regina's side. And nothing could be worse because Hayley knew what was coming next.

Regina gripped the sides of the podium like a Baptist minister preaching the gospel and screamed into the microphone, "Rupert Stiles is innocent! We all know it!"

There was more feedback, so loud many people had to cover their ears.

Regina threw her arms up in the air. "He had nothing against Caskie! They were friends! Which begs the question, who were Caskie's *enemies*?"

Stunned silence.

Everyone seemed to brace themselves.

Regina pointed a finger at Sheila, Celeste, and Jane. "Right there! In this room! *They* were her enemies! They made it crystal clear they hated her, and I find it offensive and disgustingly hypocritical that they dare to show their faces here in this church, on this day, when we are gathered here to pay our love and respect for Caskie! You ladies don't belong here!"

Edie gasped next to Hayley, as did several other people in the room, at the harshness of Regina's words.

"Shame on you! Go on! Get out! Let us mourn our friend in peace!" Regina wailed.

Sheila, Celeste, and Jane exchanged horrified and humiliated looks, and, left with no choice, all stood up and fled the church.

Regina broke down, sobbing, drained. Her husband leaped out of his seat and scurried over to help her down the steps, past the coffin, and out the side door where the refreshments were being set up for after the service.

A discombobulated Reverend Staples stumbled back to the podium to try to get the service back under his control. "Is there anyone else here who would like to speak?"

There wasn't one taker.

Everyone was still too much in a state of shock.

And no one was about to follow that act.

Hayley jumped up and excused herself as she made her way out of the pew and down the aisle, hoping to catch her mother and make sure she was okay.

Chapter 20

"What kind of woman uses a funeral as a forum to make such wild, baseless accusations?" Sheila cried in the kitchen of Hayley's house later that evening.

"It was entirely inappropriate," Hayley said, trying to back her mother up.

"I should sue her for defamation!" Sheila said, nodding her head as if she was agreeing with herself before turning to Bruce. "What do you think, Bruce? Do I have a case? Can I sue Regina Knoxville for libel?"

Bruce wavered, not wanting to dash her hopes entirely but also not eager to give her false hope. "I'm not sure. You should probably consult with a lawyer."

Sheila wagged her finger at Bruce. "You're right. That's exactly what I'm going to do. Isn't Liddy engaged to a lawyer? Can I go talk to him?"

"They, um, are no longer together. It sort of ended rather badly. I'm surprised Celeste didn't tell you."

"I'm sure she did at some point," Sheila scoffed. "But you know Celeste, she spins everything into such major drama, I've learned to tune out most of what she says."

Hayley popped open a bottle of red wine, poured her mother a glass and held it out to her, which Sheila gratefully accepted. "Mom, I know you're upset about what happened at Caskie's memorial, and you have every right to be—"

"Regina excoriated the three of us! It was humiliating and totally uncalled for!" Sheila griped.

"You're absolutely right, it was unacceptable and I'm sure she's regretting it right now—"

Bruce piped in. "Oh, I wouldn't be too sure about that—"

Hayley threw him a fierce look and Bruce immediately backtracked. "I mean, now that she's had time to think about it, I'm sure she's feeling bad about what she said."

"She shouldn't have done it! Not in front of all those people! I know she and Caskie were close and she needed to lash out at somebody, but why us? Just because we weren't good friends with Caskie doesn't give her the right to publicly point the finger at us and insinuate that we are some kind of depraved killers!" Sheila cried.

Hayley didn't have the heart to remind her mother that the whole town was still talking about their confrontation with Caskie at Drinks Like a Fish, that there were undoubtedly at least a handful of people at the service who agreed with what Regina Knoxville had to say. But her mother was upset enough, and Hayley had no desire to make it any worse.

"I can't just stand by and do nothing . . ." Sheila said to no one in particular.

"Like we discussed, you need to stay out of it and let the police do their job," Hayley reminded her.

Sheila gave her daughter a disbelieving look. "Hello. Pot, kettle . . ."

"I know, I know, I need to follow my own advice, but I'm serious, Mom. The more you get involved, the more guilty you will look. I think it's best if you just lie low and wait until Sergio concludes his investigation and we finally know the truth about what really happened."

Sheila listened to what her daughter was saying, and then, as if completely discarding it, turned to Bruce. "What do you think?"

Bruce was caught off guard, surprised he was being drawn back into the conversation, and simply shrugged. "I think I'd rather be playing shuffleboard on the lido deck of a Caribbean cruise right about now."

Sheila deflated, a look of remorse on her face, and she walked over and placed a hand on Bruce's cheek. "Oh, Bruce, I'm so sorry I ruined your honeymoon."

Bruce suddenly felt bad for speaking so honestly. "No, it's okay. Really. It's important we be here while you're going through this."

"I feel just terrible. You were so looking forward to your cruise and here I show up and get into all kinds of trouble, and now you're stuck here at home dealing with me and my crisis!"

Sheila looked as if she was about to cry, and Hayley did not want to see that happen, so she rushed to her mother's side. "Mom, we can rebook the cruise. Please don't feel bad about it."

Sheila clapped her hands, startling both Hayley and Bruce. "I insist on paying for any cancellation or change fee. How much do you think it is?"

"I'm not sure, but I think I read there's a two-hundred-dollar-per-person change fee," Bruce mumbled.

Sheila gasped. "That much? What do they want you to do, buy the boat?"

"Mom, don't worry about it!" Hayley pleaded, desperate to change the conversation.

Sheila clapped her hands again, having made a snap decision. "If you can't be on your honeymoon, then at least I can get out of your hair so you can have some time alone tonight."

"Honestly, Sheila, you don't have to do that," Bruce argued.

Hayley threw him a stern look because she actually thought it was a good idea. Picking up on her signal, Bruce quickly backtracked again.

"I mean, that's awfully kind of you," he said, smiling.

"I read in the *Island Times* that there is a Meryl Streep movie playing at the Criterion tonight. She plays some historical figure, I can't remember which one, but who cares really, it's Meryl Streep. I'd pay to see her read the popcorn prices at the concession stand," Sheila said, glancing around for her purse. "I'll call Celeste and Jane and see if they will join me. We'll have a girls' night out."

Much to Hayley's relief, Celeste and Jane agreed to meet Sheila at the Criterion for the film. A little escapism would actually be a welcome release from the trauma of the day's events. Once Sheila was out the door and on her way in Hayley's car, Hayley and Bruce were finally left to themselves.

"Should we go out for a romantic dinner?" Bruce suggested.

Hayley shook her head. "No, why go on one of those excursions with the rest of the passengers when we can stay on board the ship and have it all to ourselves?"

"I like the way you think, Mrs. Linney," he said, kissing her softly on the lips.

"And I like the way you kiss, Mr. Linney."

"Does this mean you're going to take my name?"

"And have to get a new passport and change all my accounts and credit cards? Not on your life."

"Okay, I'm good with it as long as you let me keep doing this," he said, winking at her and stealing another kiss.

After lighting a few scented candles and polishing off the bottle of wine and a quick dinner of leftover rosemary chicken, Hayley and Bruce found themselves on the couch making out like two teenagers while playing their favorite bands from the 1990s, like Pearl Jam, Green Day, and Blink 182.

Hayley pulled away and looked into Bruce's eyes. "I feel like I'm back in high school, with a boy over at the house, hoping my mother doesn't come home too early and catch us fooling around."

"We can always take this upstairs to the bedroom and lock the door so she can't walk in on us," Bruce said, grinning. Actually it was more like leering.

They stood up, holding hands, and turned to head up the staircase when Hayley's cell phone buzzed.

Bruce sighed. "Please, whoever it is, let it go to voicemail."

Hayley glanced at the screen. "Bar Harbor Police Department . . ."

They were both too curious to ignore it.

Hayley answered the call and held the phone to her ear. "Hello?"

"Hayley, it's Mom!" Sheila said.

"Mom, what are you doing at—?"

"Listen carefully because they're only allowing me to make one call—"

"Who? The police?"

"Yes, I've been arrested," Sheila said, trying not to panic but failing miserably.

"*Arrested?* Did something happen at the Criterion?" Bruce's eyes widened. "Your mother's been arrested?"

Hayley held up a finger to silence him so that she could hear.

"No, we never made it to the Criterion . . ."

"Why not?"

There was a long pause on the other end of the phone.

"*Mom . . .*"

"I met up with Celeste and Jane and after talking, we knew we could not just stand by and let people think we were somehow involved with what happened to Caskie Lemon-Hogg, and so we made the decision to continue with our investigation . . ."

"*Your* investigation? Mom, please tell me this is some kind of joke!"

"I'm afraid not . . ." Sheila muttered before talking to someone nearby. "Don't rush me! I'm talking to my daughter! Is there a law limiting the time I have for my one phone call?" There was a brief muffled discussion and then Sheila was back on the line. "Apparently there is some time limit on how long I can talk! That Officer Earl is *just* like his grandfather. Impatient and pigheaded!"

"Mom, what did you three do?"

Another pause.

Sheila was clearly not eager to confess her apparent crime.

"*Mom . . .*"

"We were frustrated that Owen Meyers refused to speak with us about why he had been arguing with Caskie on the same day I found her body . . ."

Hayley's stomach started churning as she sensed what was coming. "Oh no . . ."

"So we decided to break into his restaurant and see if we could find any evidence that might link him to the murder . . ."

"You didn't . . ."

"Jane picked the lock. I had no idea how good she was at it. It's such a valuable skill set. Anyway, Celeste stood outside to keep watch in case anyone showed up. But unfortunately we tripped some kind of silent alarm because before we even had a chance to jimmy open the file cabinet in his office, the whole place was crawling with cops."

Hayley sighed. "So basically you've been charged with breaking and entering?"

"That's about the gist of it, dear, yes," Sheila said. "Any chance you can bail me out?"

Island Food & Spirits
BY HAYLEY POWELL

I never realized how having my mother back in town would stir up so many childhood memories with my posse, Liddy and Mona, especially seeing her pal around with her own two besties from her childhood, Celeste and Jane. They were the original three musketeers, a whole generation before their daughters bonded for life. My mother has always kept mum about all the trouble she and her friends got into when they were kids running around the streets of Bar Harbor in the 1960s, and whenever I pressed her about their wild antics when they were in high school, which Jane would allude to every now and then, my mother would always demur and say in the sweetest voice, "Oh, Hayley, we were absolute angels." I never bought that line for a minute, and I can tell you in no uncertain terms, that when it came to getting into trouble, their offspring took first prize a couple of decades later.

Recently the girls and I were enjoying a sunset cocktail hour on Liddy's porch with Blueberry Basil Vodka Martinis, which Liddy insisted we try after having had one at an up-scale restaurant in Boston last month. Well, the vodka seemed to lubricate our memories, and we found ourselves reliving all the wild stories from our youth. One particular adventure stood out above the rest. It happened one late summer afternoon, just a couple of weeks before we were slated to return for our senior year in high school. We were all at that sweet-sixteen point, armed with driver's licenses but with really nowhere to go.

We were hanging out at Liddy's house, scarfing down homemade blueberry bread that Liddy's grandmother, who lived next door, had made, and whining about how boring it was in Bar Harbor and how there was nothing to do. We were desperate for some excitement.

We were also very angry at our mothers. Earlier that morning, the three of them took off on what they described as "a girls' getaway weekend" to Salmon Cove, a small fishing village down east where Mona's family owned a rustic cabin. When we asked if we could go, we were given a quick and stern "No!" Our mothers wanted quality time together, and had no intention of spending their weekend chaperoning three rowdy, loud teenage girls.

Mona was especially miffed because she had been going to Salmon Cove with her parents every summer starting when she was seven years old. Mona looked forward to the trip every year, mostly because she had met a local boy named Corey Guildford and they had become fast friends. A little crush had now blossomed into a teenage romance. The young couple would keep in touch throughout the year with letters and phone calls, and Mona had been looking forward to seeing her beau again this summer, but it was not to be. This would be the first summer she didn't get to go to Salmon Cove and she was fuming about it.

Liddy was also furious because her mother always took her clothes shopping at the Portland Mall at the end of the summer so she could begin the new school year in true high fashion. Her mother broke the news that because of her Salmon Cove trip, they would have to delay their shopping trip to Portland until late September. Liddy did not appreciate this in the least because it meant she would have to buy her first few fall debut outfits at the Bangor Mall, which had a fraction of the inventory found in Portland. There was a huge risk that she could actually show up for the first day of school in the same outfit as another girl, or, gasp, even two girls! Everyone in their class went school shopping at the Bangor Mall! In Liddy's mind, this could potentially be worse than the Hindenburg disaster!

I was enjoying the blueberry bread, not really paying much attention, wondering what kind of pizza my brother Randy and I would order for dinner, when I heard Liddy say, "Well, Hayley, are you in?"

My mouth full of blueberry bread, I stared at them blankly and asked sheepishly, "In what?"

Apparently while my mind wandered to food (as it reliably does), Liddy and Mona had hatched a plan to "borrow" Mona's mother's Ford Taurus the next morning after her father left for work, drive the three hours to the Portland Mall to go school shopping, and be home that night before anyone was the wiser, with a trunk load of new school clothes!

I was wary at first, knowing full well our mothers would be apoplectic (if I knew what that word meant at the time), especially since we were forbidden to drive anywhere beyond Ellsworth, which was only thirty minutes from town. But with the promise of a few stylish looks for the new school year dancing around in my head, I quickly succumbed to peer pressure and was totally on board.

Bright and early the next morning we found ourselves heading down Interstate 95 South singing loudly along to Huey Lewis and the News on the radio on our way to the Portland Mall. And a little over three hours later, we were pulling into the huge expansive parking lot, cheering loudly and ready to shop till we dropped!

We had never felt so grown-up, pretending to be supermodels as we tried on a variety of different looks, breaking only to have pizza slices at the food court, before making our way to more stores in a whole other section of the mall. We finally ended up at Lacey's Lingerie, a racy boutique that only went out of business when a Victoria's Secret opened up in the mall a few years later. Liddy and I decided that Mona needed to woo Corey on her next trip to Salmon Cove, and what better way to do that than with some sexy lingerie! Mona stubbornly refused to try anything on at first, but Liddy and I helped her along by throwing on baby doll nighties and sequin teddies, finally shaming Mona into trying on a floral plunge bustier! We all stood in front of the giant wall mirror checking ourselves out, thinking we were hilarious, when suddenly we heard a booming voice yell, "Girls!"

We all froze in front of the mirror, our eyes wide. We knew that voice. It was Liddy's mother. But it couldn't be. She was in Salmon Cove. We all slowly turned around and our mouths dropped open at the sight of all our mothers—Sheila, Celeste and Jane—standing outside the other changing rooms on the other side of the store, decked out in their own sexy slips, bras, and corsets.

Liddy, without missing a beat, blurted out, "Mother, what are you doing here dressed like that?"

I remember Jane having to restrain Celeste from lunging at her daughter at that point. I was so scared to be caught that everything was a blur after that. There was a lot of yelling and screaming, the manager and salesclerks had to get involved, and there were a lot of gawking customers who were drawn to this circus of three angry mothers and three crying daughters, all dressed like—well, there really is no other word for it—hookers! We were ordered to get back into our street clothes, and after our mothers apologized profusely to the manager for causing such a scene, we were hustled out. I knew my mother was serious when she gripped my arm and hissed in my ear, "You're grounded . . . for life!"

Apparently our mothers had never intended to go to Salmon Cove. They had always secretly planned to have a relaxing weekend in the big city, in a nice hotel, with a little retail therapy, and NO kids! If we had known our mothers were going on a shopping spree in Portland without us, there would have been no living with us, and so in order for them to have a little break sans kids, they had come up with a little white lie. Only it had backfired on them big-time. Not to mention us too! We were all going to be spending a lot more time with our moms for the rest of the summer, confined to our houses, and no, we didn't get to come home with any new school clothes!

LIDDY'S FAVORITE BLUEBERRY BASIL COCKTAIL

INGREDIENTS
1 cup fresh blueberries
6 basil leaves
1 tablespoon fresh lime juice
1 ounce St-Germain liqueur
2 ounces vodka
Splash of sparkling water

In a cocktail shaker add your blueberries, bay leaves, and lime juice and muddle all those ingredients. Add the vodka, St-Germain liqueur and a little ice, cover, and shake well. Pour through a strainer into a martini glass with a splash of sparkling water. Garnish with a fresh basil leaf and a couple of blueberries if you desire, and enjoy!

BLUEBERRY CREAM CHEESE BREAD

INGREDIENTS
2 cups fresh blueberries
8 ounces softened cream cheese
1 cup butter, softened
1½ cups sugar
2 teaspoons vanilla
4 eggs
2 cups all-purpose flour
1½ teaspoons baking powder
1 teaspoon salt
2 tablespoons flour

Preheat your oven to 350 degrees F.

In a mixing bowl, toss the blueberries with two tablespoons flour, then set aside.

In a stand mixer cream together butter, cream cheese, sugar, and vanilla. Add one egg at a time, beating well after each egg.

In another bowl combine the flour, baking powder, and salt. Slowly mix it into the wet batter until combined. Fold in your blueberries with a spatula.

Pour the batter into two greased 9 x 5 bread pans and bake for 45 minutes or until a toothpick inserted in the middle comes out clean. Let rest for ten minutes, then flip the bread out onto a wire cooling rack and let cool completely.

This is always a wonderful treat in the morning with a good cup of piping-hot coffee.

Chapter 21

Hayley couldn't remember when she had last seen the Bar Harbor Police Station buzzing with so much activity. Officer Donnie had just hauled in a local punk who had tried stealing Betsy Dyer's purse when she had set it down at the pharmacy to pay for her monthly prescriptions and wandered off to look for a new heating pad while the pharmacist fulfilled her order. Luckily the kid wasn't looking where he was going while making his escape and walked right into a pantyhose display. He knocked it over and that got the attention of Officer Donnie, who was on his break and there to buy some cold medicine, which led to the juvenile delinquent's arrest. The kid looked dazed as Officer Donnie escorted him to the booking room, a red-faced and furious Betsy Dyer right behind him, eager to press charges.

According to Donnie, Betsy had whacked the kid over the head with her bag once she got it back. Crowded into the reception area was also a young couple from England who were there to file a police report about a stolen computer, along with Hayley, Liddy, and Mona, who were waiting to bail their mothers out of jail. Bruce had gone out to pick up some sub sandwiches in case it took a while and everybody got hungry.

After what seemed like hours, the door to the police chief's office banged open and Owen Meyers flew out, marching down the hallway into the reception area. He stopped short at the sight of Mona, who stepped in front of him and offered him a weak smile.

"Hey there, Owen, how's it going?"

Owen glared at her and then muttered, with his fists clenched, "Out of my way, Mona."

Mona quickly stepped to the side. As he passed, Owen cranked his head in her direction and seethed, "And for the record, I won't be placing any more orders for your lobsters. I'm taking my business elsewhere."

And then he scurried out of the police station.

"What's *his* problem?" Mona huffed.

"I told him it was you who saw him arguing with Caskie Lemon-Hogg on the day she was killed, so he probably blames you for all of this," Sergio said as he ambled out of his office and walked down the hall to the reception area to join them.

"Well, did Owen finally explain what he and Caskie were fighting about?" Hayley asked.

"He said Caskie was price gouging, doubling her price for her blueberries from three dollars to six dollars a basket. He felt he was being treated unfairly, especially as a longtime customer," Sergio said.

Mona thought about it and shook her head. "Nope, I'm not buying it. Owen just told me he was going to buy his lobsters from somebody else. He could easily have done the same thing with Caskie. A lot of people in town pick blueberries and I bet they are just as tasty as Caskie's. Nobody was forcing him to buy from her. The way he looked, how upset he got, I have the feeling it had to do with more than just getting ripped off."

"Unless you actually overheard what they were talking about, I'm going to have to take him at his word," Sergio said with a shrug. "Especially since Caskie is no longer around to refute his story."

"What about our mothers?" Liddy asked. "When can we bail them out?"

Sergio sighed. "You don't have to. I talked to Owen, and although it took a bit of convincing, he's decided not to press charges."

Hayley breathed a heavy sigh of relief. "Thank God!"

"But they *are* banned from ever setting foot in The Shack ever again," Sergio warned. "And they have to stop harassing Owen."

"I'm sure they will be happy to accept those terms," Hayley said.

Officer Earl, his big belly bouncing up and down, scurried down the hallway. "Chief, it's those women again! They won't leave poor Rupert Stiles alone. He's in the cell next to them and they won't let up questioning him about his involvement in the Lemon-Hogg murder, and now he's threatening to hang himself with his bedsheet!"

"You can release the ladies, Earl, they're free to go," Sergio said.

Earl glanced at Hayley, Liddy, and Mona, and scowled. "I don't know which mother belongs to which one of you, but one of them is *really* rude. She said if I didn't take better care of myself and cut out a few carbs, I'd never find a nice girl and end up spending the rest of my life alone!"

"That would be mine," Hayley said guiltily.

"You can have her!" Earl sniffed before spinning back around and marching down the hall to the back, where the jail cells were located.

Liddy turned to Hayley. "I don't know, it kind of sounds like my mother too."

"Well, it certainly wasn't mine!" Mona said confidently. "My mother raised us kids on carbs. The extra layer of fat kept us warmer in the winter when our parents couldn't pay the heating bill!"

"Try to keep your mothers out of trouble from here on in," Sergio said before crossing over to the young English couple and escorting them to his office to deal with their stolen laptop.

After a few more minutes, Earl, who was still in full-blown sourpuss mode, brought Sheila, Celeste, and Jane out from the jail cells to be reunited with their daughters. Jane was rummaging through her large shoulder bag, which had just been returned to her. "I swear there is some change missing! These cops, they're all on the take!"

Celeste collapsed into Liddy's arms. "It was awful, Liddy. All they served us was a ham sandwich and a lousy pickle for dinner. The bread was soggy and the pickle tasted funny. Can a pickle go bad if it's not refrigerated?"

"I don't know, Mother. Did you eat the whole thing?" Liddy exclaimed.

"Of course I did. I didn't know how long we were going to be stuck in there. I had to keep up my strength!"

Hayley went to hug Sheila, who gave her a brief squeeze and a light pat on the back. Hayley found it odd that her mother wasn't as talkative as her fellow jailbirds. "Is everything okay, Mom?"

"Yes," Sheila said. "I'm just tired."

Hayley's phone buzzed and she checked the screen. "Bruce just texted. He's on the way with sandwiches."

Celeste groaned. "Sandwiches? I can't eat another sandwich. I'm going to need something more substantial. Donate mine to a food shelter, would you, please? Come on, Liddy, Havana is open until nine. If we hurry, we can make it before the kitchen closes."

Havana was one of the pricier restaurants in town, but Celeste could afford it every night if she chose to dine there.

"Just don't mention to anyone I was in the hoosegow. I have a reputation to maintain," Celeste said as she glided out the door.

Liddy turned to Hayley. "I'll call you later."

Hayley nodded and Liddy chased after her mother.

Mona put an arm around Jane. "Come on, Mom. I'm taking you home."

Jane scoffed. "Wait, didn't you hear Hayley? Bruce is on his way with some food. I couldn't eat that slop they served in jail. I'm starving."

"I'll make you something at home. Now let's go. I have hungry kids waiting to be fed! I'm sure Dennis just threw a bag of chips at them and went back to watching the Red Sox on TV."

Mona dragged Jane out the door, leaving Hayley alone with Sheila.

Hayley glanced at her mother. "You're awfully quiet."

"Just thinking . . ."

"About what?"

Sheila opened her mouth to speak but decided against telling Hayley what was on her mind. "Nothing."

"You're acting weird."

"I was in jail, dear. It can change a person."

"You were in jail for less than an hour, Mom. Now Sergio wanted me to make sure your days of playing police detective are officially over. Can I promise him that you won't be doing that anymore?"

Sheila bristled, insulted that the roles were suddenly reversed and Hayley was treating her like a misbehaving child.

"Mom?"

"Yes, Hayley," Sheila said, sighing.

"Okay . . . is there something you're not telling me?"

"What do you mean?"

"I don't know. I get the feeling you know more than you're letting on and it's worrying me."

Sheila was obviously struggling inside, wrestling with something, perhaps not wanting to lie to her daughter, but then she closed her eyes and said emphatically, "Don't be worried. I told you everything I know."

"Good," Hayley said. "Bruce just pulled up. Let's go home."

She led her mother out the door, but she was not at all assuaged by her mother's claim that all was fine. Because if there was one person in the world she knew, it was her mother. And ever since she was a little girl, Hayley always noticed that if her mother closed her eyes when she spoke, that clearly meant she was lying. If she blinked a few times, it was just a fib. But if she kept her eyes squeezed shut for more than a few seconds, it was a big ole whopping lie. And as Sheila walked down the stone steps of the police station to Bruce's waiting car, Hayley had to catch her, because her eyes were still closed.

She was definitely, unequivocally lying.

Chapter 22

Sheila spent the rest of her night as a free woman somewhat subdued at the house. She watched some television with Bruce and then excused herself and went up to Gemma's room to go to bed.

Hayley knew there was something on her mother's mind and she found it frustrating that Sheila was purposely not sharing her thoughts. She also did not expect her mother to keep her promise and stop investigating in order to clear her name, and so the following afternoon, instead of doing laundry, which was Hayley's weekly tradition on a Saturday, she followed her mother, who had borrowed Bruce's car to take Celeste and Jane to the Jordan Pond House for tea and popovers.

The Jordan Pond House, the only full-service restaurant within Acadia National Park, has been around for over a hundred years, offering a unique experience of tea and popovers outside on the lawn with breathtaking views of its namesake pond and the North- and South Bubble Mountains. A fire destroyed the original restaurant in 1979, but private funds rebuilt the two-story structure that still stands today with an observation deck and gift shop. Tourists from around the world flock to the site every season and the restaurant has become more popular than ever. Sheila always made a point of going at least once during every visit, as she couldn't resist the fluffy, fresh-from-the-oven popovers slathered in butter and strawberry jam.

Hayley followed them in her Kia, remaining a safe distance behind them. She half expected them to turn off before they hit the Park Loop Road, which led to the restaurant, but they stayed on course, parking the car in the lot and heading inside. Hayley found a parking spot a few rows away, and then hurried across the lot, hovering just outside until she saw the hostess lead the three women out to a table on the lawn.

Hayley donned her sunglasses and then ducked into the gift shop and bought an Acadia National Park baseball cap. She stuffed her hair up inside the cap and then wandered back to the hostess station, where a young college-age girl greeted her with a bright smile. "Do you have a reservation?"

"No, sorry, do you have a table for one? I'd really like to sit outside."

Worry lines appeared on the girl's forehead. "Let me check."

She disappeared for two minutes and then returned, waving Hayley forward. "You're in luck. We do have a table on the lawn."

It was still early and a lot of the tables were empty. Hayley instantly spotted Sheila, Celeste, and Jane at a table nearest the pond. They had just sat down and were perusing their menus. The hostess escorted Hayley to a small table for two about fifty feet away, far out of earshot.

"Could I get a table closer to the water?" Hayley asked.

The worry lines returned and the hostess frowned. "A lot of our tables are already reserved . . ."

Hayley pointed to a small rickety table right behind her mother's. "What about that one?"

The hostess checked her watch. "I'm afraid that one's reserved for noon."

"I'll eat really fast."

"But it's already eleven thirty. You may not have time for your second popover . . ."

"I promise I'll be gone by the time they get here. If I'm not done by noon, I'll take it to go."

The hostess was not sure if she should relent, especially since she looked as if she thought Hayley might be some kind of a crazy person, but her training had prepared her for how to handle such situations. "As long as you agree to leave by—"

Hayley snatched the menu out of the startled hostess's hand. "Thanks! I can show myself there!"

Hayley bounded down the lawn toward the table. Her mother and Celeste were seated with their backs to her, but Jane was on the other side facing her. Still, Jane didn't even bother to look in her direction as she approached them and sat down at the smaller table behind them, making sure her back was to them.

Hayley picked up the menu and held it up in front of her face as she eavesdropped on their conversation.

"Why couldn't we talk about the case on the car ride over here?" Celeste asked.

"Because we were in Bruce's car and he's an investigative reporter, and with all the technology they have today, the whole thing could be wired, and I didn't want him listening to us through the radio or something!" Sheila exclaimed.

"He can do that?" Jane asked.

"People can do anything these days, Jane," Sheila warned. "The government could be taping our conversation through your phone right now! There could be a spy posted at a nearby table listening to our every word!"

Hayley sunk down in her seat as far as she could.

"Okay, so why didn't you tell Chief Alvarez what we found?" Celeste asked. "If he knew what we know, he might focus more on Owen as a suspect."

Hayley's ears perked up.

What did they know?

"Because it's not proof of anything. I can't just go to him and say, 'I found two dozen boxes of store-bought blueberry pies in Owen Meyers's freezer!' He needs more than that to make an arrest," Sheila cried.

"I'm still confused. What do a bunch of frozen pies in his freezer have to do with Owen strangling Caskie?" Jane asked.

Hayley leaned back in her chair because she was dying to know as well.

"We've been over this, Jane. Owen Meyers has boasted for years that he serves only fresh homemade blueberry pies at his restaurant, just like he buys live lobsters from Mona for his fresh lobster rolls. That's a big reason his business is so successful. Locals and tourists alike want to eat there because everything is made from scratch and from the freshest ingredients. But what if word got out that he was serving frozen store-bought blueberry pies? Well, you can imagine the negative Yelp reviews that would pile up! Suddenly The Shack wouldn't be so special and it could seriously hurt his business—who knows, maybe kill it altogether."

"What does any of that have to do with Caskie?"

Jane asked, frustrated that she was still not quite grasping the situation.

"I have a theory, it's just a theory mind you, but it makes sense," Sheila said confidently. "Owen has already admitted that Caskie was price-gouging him for her fresh blueberries, doubling the cost. So Owen decided it was too much and kicked her to the curb. But it's the height of the tourist season. He needed pies for his customers, so what if he went out and stocked up on store-bought blueberry pies and hid them in his freezer? He could save money, make an even bigger profit, and nobody would be the wiser. Unless someone found out, someone like Caskie . . ."

Celeste gasped. "So Caskie somehow discovered what he was up to, maybe she saw the pies in the freezer like we did, or tasted one and could tell the difference right away, and then she confronted him!"

Sheila jumped in. "Exactly! He could not risk her exposing him. It might cost him his business so he took matters into his own hands!"

"By wrapping them around Caskie's throat!" Jane yelled, finally getting it.

There was a brief pause as the women considered their next move.

Celeste spoke first. "I think we should at least let Chief Alvarez know our theory."

"Not until we gather more evidence," Sheila said.

"But didn't you promise Hayley we'd stay out of it?" Jane asked.

"I also promised Hayley that Santa Claus was real until she was seven years old. A mother does what she has to do."

"Hey, Mrs. Powell, remember me? I'm Kevin Vassey, I went to school with your daughter Gemma!"

Hayley's heart skipped a beat.

She looked up at a tall, lanky blond kid in his early twenties, in a blue polo shirt and khaki shorts, which all the servers were wearing, as he stood at her table with his hands clasped behind his back, a big welcoming grin on his face.

Hayley leaned over toward him and whispered, "Yes, hi, Kevin . . ."

"I hear through the grapevine that Gemma is studying in New York to be a master chef. Wow, that is so impressive. You must be so proud!" Kevin seemed to blare at the top of his lungs for everyone to hear.

Hayley nodded and whispered, "Yes, yes, I am . . ."

Another voice entered the conversation. "I am proud of her too."

Kevin looked at the next table, a puzzled look on his face. "And you are . . . ?"

"Gemma's grandmother! Hayley's *mother*!"

There was no hiding anymore. Hayley slowly turned to find Sheila, Celeste, and Jane all well aware of her presence. Kevin was still oblivious to the drama he had just stirred up. He looked back and forth, confused. "Would you like to sit with your mother and her friends? There is plenty of room at their table."

"No, I don't think I'll be staying . . ." Hayley moaned. "I'll just take the check, please."

"You didn't order anything . . ." Kevin reminded her.

Hayley stood up, hoping to make a hasty exit. "I'm suddenly not hungry. Thank you. I'll be sure to say hi to Gemma for you."

"That would be great," Kevin said before turning to Sheila, Celeste, and Jane. "Ladies, I'll be right back to take your order."

He scooted off.

Hayley slowly turned to face her mother, who said to Celeste and Jane pointedly, "See? Spies *everywhere*."

"I knew you were keeping something from me and so I figured I might find out what it was if I followed you—"

"Hayley, how *could* you?" Sheila cried.

"You would have done the same thing!" Hayley said, pointing a finger at her. "And I was right, wasn't I?"

"That's not the point!" Sheila snapped.

"Yes, it is. I'm just trying to keep the three of you from going to jail again! You should have told Sergio right away what you saw in Owen's freezer!"

"Would *you* have?" Sheila asked with a raised eyebrow.

Hayley folded her arms. "What do you mean?"

"I'm just curious. If you had seen those frozen pies in the freezer, would you have gone running to Sergio and risk him laughing you out of his office, or would you have dug a little deeper until you uncovered more concrete evidence?"

Hayley wavered, not sure how to answer. "I don't know . . ."

"Yes, you do. You would have done the *same* thing!"

"Okay, fine, but this needs to stop! You were arrested!"

"Yes, once. How many times have you been arrested?"

Checkmate.

Hayley's curiosity and zest for investigating crimes had led to her incarceration two times.

Maybe it was three.

She had been playing detective for a while now.

But she was not going to allow her mother to win this one.

"We're not talking about me!"

That was the best she could do in the moment.

Kevin returned with his big grin. "Ladies, may I—"

"We're not ready yet!" Jane snapped.

Kevin quickly retreated.

Hayley bowed her head and muttered, "I just really want you three to stay out of trouble."

"Fine," Sheila said. "If you are so hell-bent on us not defending ourselves and letting the whole town believe we're evil witches who teamed up to get rid of our sworn enemy Caskie, then maybe you should stop sneaking around and following us and put your energies into something more useful! Like finding out who really did kill Caskie!"

Her mother was right.

The only way she was ever going to get her mother to stop trying to solve Caskie's murder was for her to solve it herself.

And she had to do it fast, before the groundswell of suspicion around Sheila, Celeste, and Jane reached an unmanageable fever pitch.

Chapter 23

The Shop 'n Save was nearly empty when Hayley showed up the next morning, promptly at seven when the doors opened. Usually around this time she was slamming the palm of her hand down on her clock on top of the nightstand next to her bed to stop the annoying, piercing alarm trying to rouse her from underneath her plush white goose-down comforter and force her to drag her lazy butt into the shower. But not today. Today she was on a mission and had showered well before six in order to be at the grocery store at the same time as Owen Meyers. It was no secret in town that Owen was up early every morning to shop for the ingredients he needed when he opened The Shack promptly at eleven for the lunch crowd. Depending on what special he scribbled on the chalkboard he set up outside the front door to lure in the locals and tourists, Owen was laser-focused on every last detail, whether it was dried thyme for his lentil soup or fresh celery for his lobster rolls. Whatever it was he needed to pick up at the Shop 'n Save, like the fire department blowing the noon whistle, you could always count on seeing Owen rolling his cart up and down the aisles just after the break of dawn, like clockwork, at the start of each day.

Hayley had only managed to down her first cup of coffee as she shot out the door in order to get to the store by the time they unlocked the doors, so her brain was still a bit fuzzy. She grabbed a cart and paraded up and down the aisles in search of Owen. She knew she was acting suspicious, mostly due to the fact that none of the Shop 'n Save employees had ever laid eyes on her in the store before eleven. A couple of stock boys gave her surprised looks as she raced past them and mumbled, "Good morning."

Rounding the corner into aisle six, which housed baking needs like flour, sugar, and chocolate, Hayley came to a screeching halt at the sight of Owen at the spice section, perusing two different brands of Cajun seasoning, debating with himself on which one he should buy. Hayley stood frozen in the middle of the aisle, waiting to be noticed. Finally, when it became clear to Owen he wasn't alone, he glanced up and scowled at the sight of Hayley.

"Good morning, Owen," Hayley chirped, a big smile on her face.

Owen dropped one of the seasonings in his cart and threw the other back on the shelf, did an about-face, and hurriedly pushed his cart in the opposite direction. Hayley chased after him as he disappeared around the corner and down the cereal aisle.

"Owen! Owen!" Hayley shouted, to no avail. He had no intention of stopping to talk to her.

This was ridiculous. She couldn't just follow him up and down every aisle like their grocery carts were in the Indy 500, but it was becoming quite clear Owen was determined to remain elusive. And so she whirled her cart around and headed back up toward the front of the store. She cut across the wine section, her eyes briefly falling on a tasty pinot noir that had recently been marked down for a two-for-one sale. She made a mental note to come back later for it.

Hayley finally made it to the produce section and pushed her cart, with its rubber wheels swiveling, past the romaine lettuce and grape tomatoes until she was right in front of a giant basket of yellow onions. She stopped and waited, knowing Owen would soon be turning the corner from the dairy products. Sure enough, within seconds, she spotted his cart careening toward hers. Owen's head was twisted around, looking to see if Hayley was still in hot pursuit, having no clue she was right in front of him. And that's when their carts collided and Owen nearly did a flip over the metal bar his hands were gripping so tightly. He whipped his head around and his eyes popped open at the sight of Hayley.

"Good morning, Owen," Hayley said sweetly, as if it was the most unexpected development in the world that they were now face-to-face.

"What do you want?" Owen hollered, discombobulated as he rubbed his elbow, which he had banged upon impact when he crashed into Hayley's cart.

"Blueberries," Hayley said, searching the produce section. "Ever since poor Caskie Lemon-Hogg passed away, I haven't been able to find fresh blueberries, so I'm hoping they have some here."

He glared at her suspiciously. He knew she was up to something and so he remained guarded.

Hayley plowed ahead, still smiling sweetly. "Of course, Caskie's prices had gotten so ridiculously high, if you ask me. Wouldn't you agree?"

He didn't answer her, just stared at her glumly.

"I can't imagine buying from her in bulk like you did. I mean, how are you supposed to make a profit with Caskie jacking up the prices and you relying on her to supply you with your cakes and pies?"

"I know what you're doing, Hayley. Your mother saw what was in my freezer, didn't she? She told you and now you want to blackmail me too!"

Hayley arched an eyebrow. "*Too*? For the record, Owen, I have no intention or interest in blackmailing you for anything, but apparently *someone* did . . ."

Owen looked around the produce section to make sure there were no curious ears around, but as it was still early, they were pretty much alone except for a stock boy listening to music through his earbuds as he sprayed some spinach and kale with a small water hose.

Owen sighed, resigned to the fact that he was never going to physically escape Hayley's never-ending nosiness. "All right, all right, fine! You're right! Yes, Caskie *was* blackmailing me!"

Hayley leaned in, eyes widening, curious to hear more.

"She came into my restaurant a few weeks back and told me she was raising the price of her blueberries and I told her where she could go! Well, I couldn't find anybody else to sell me the amount of blueberries I needed, you know how fast they sell out here at the Shop 'n Save, so I was in a bind. I needed at least thirty boxes of blueberries a day, and I'm working at The Shack ten, twelve hours a day, so it's not like I can go pick them myself. She's the biggest supplier in town and so I got desperate! I was running low and every morning I was having an overflow of customers, so I bit the bullet and started buying frozen blueberry pies just to keep up with the demand. Nobody seemed to notice the difference except for that damn Caskie, who showed up for lunch one day, took one bite, and just looked at me with this knowing smile. She confronted me about it in the kitchen, and threatened to make a big fuss, and I didn't know what I was going to do . . ." His voice trailed off and he shook his head. "I pride myself on making sure every item on my menu is fresh and homemade and she was going to expose me as some kind of fraud . . . But I swear, it was just going to be a temporary fix, until I could figure out how to get a new supply . . ."

Before Hayley had the chance to ask, Owen grabbed her by the arm and got up close, staring straight into her eyes. "But I didn't kill her, Hayley! If I'm being completely honest, I would have to say I sure wanted to, but I didn't! I just don't have it in me to do anything like that!"

"She was at your restaurant on the day she was killed . . ."

"Yes, she came by to tell me she wanted me to pay for her silence . . . she was asking for way more than the hiked-up cost of her blueberries. In hindsight, I should have just shut up and kept buying those stupid berries from her. I never would have ended up in this ugly mess with people suspecting I had something to do with her death!"

Hayley pulled her arm out of his grip and nodded. "Okay, Owen, if you didn't kill Caskie, do you have any idea who might have?"

Owen shrugged. "Truthfully, I thought it was your mother."

This was not what Hayley wanted to hear.

She needed to find some answers soon before the whole population of Bar Harbor, including the summer tourists, was of the opinion that her mother, Sheila, was a cold-blooded killer.

Chapter 24

When Hayley received word via text from Mona that Sergio was releasing Rupert Stiles, she raced down to the police station right after work to find out exactly what was going on. When Hayley pulled into the parking lot, she spotted Mona standing by her white pickup truck helping Rupert Stiles into the passenger seat. He was struggling with the seat belt and she had to reach over to assist him.

Hayley jumped out of her Kia and scurried over to where Mona was buckling in Rupert. His eyes were droopy and his hands were shaking.

"Mona, what's happening? Where are you taking Rupert?"

"I'm taking him home to his apartment!" Mona howled. "The poor old codger has suffered through enough already! He deserves to have a good night's sleep in his own bed tonight instead of that lumpy cot in that god-forsaken jail cell!"

"I don't understand," Hayley said. "Why has he been released?"

"Because he didn't kill anybody, that's why!" Mona snapped. "And thanks to my deadbeat husband, Rupert was arrested for no good reason!"

"Wait, what does Dennis have to do with any of this?"

Mona patted the old man on the back of the head. "You comfortable, Rupert?"

"Yes, thank you, Mona," Rupert whispered hoarsely. "Would you mind dropping me off at Drinks Like a Fish? I wouldn't mind partaking in a nightcap before going home to bed."

"I most certainly will not!" Mona roared. "Your drinking is what got you caught up in this mess in the first place!" Mona slammed the car door shut. "Now stay put while I talk to Hayley."

Hayley threw her hands up, at a loss. "Mona . . ."

"My idiot husband fell out of the stupid tree and hit every branch on the way down! It took him all this time to stop staring at ESPN long enough to tell me that he picked up Rupert hitchhiking and gave him a ride to Ellsworth on the day your mother found Caskie's body at the B and B!"

"Dennis gave Rupert an alibi?"

"Can you believe that? I can never get him off the damn couch to fix a running toilet, let alone actually leave the house for a breath of fresh air! But apparently on that particular day he took my truck while I was working at the lobster shop and decided to drive up to Darling's Auto Mall in Ellsworth to test drive a new Dodge Grand Caravan! He saw Rupert by the roadside with his thumb out around three in the afternoon at the top of West Street on his way out of town and pulled over to pick him up."

"Where did he drop him off?"

"Some bar on High Street in Ellsworth, I forget the

name," Mona said. "I asked him why he'd go all the way to Ellsworth to a bar when he could've just gone to your brother's place, and he got all quiet and shy and wouldn't give me a straight answer until I finally guessed it had something to do with a pretty cocktail waitress up there he has his eye on and, well, let's just say he didn't deny it!"

Hayley leaned to the side so she could see past Mona to Rupert, sitting quietly in Mona's truck. "You got a girlfriend in Ellsworth, Rupert?"

His face reddened and he shrugged. "Maybe . . ."

"Rupert, if you were at a bar in Ellsworth and there was a girl who could back up your alibi, why didn't you tell the chief when he arrested you?" Hayley asked.

Rupert shrugged again. "Didn't want to drag her name into any of this mess. Besides, if she found out I was in jail, she might lose respect for me . . ."

"*Respect?*" Mona howled. "Rupert, you've been arrested for public intoxication more times than—"

Hayley cut her off. "Mona!" She turned back to Rupert. "Well, I'm happy you're finally free!"

Mona nodded. "The chief didn't have much choice after he called the bar and got both the waitress and the bartender to confirm that Rupert was there drinking from around four in the afternoon until after ten o'clock!"

"Mona! I'm awfully thirsty!" Rupert wailed from inside the truck.

"Hold your horses, old man! I'm talking to my friend here!" Mona bellowed.

"Is Sergio inside?" Hayley asked.

Mona nodded again. "Back to square one. He's not happy about it either."

"Thanks, Mona!" Hayley dashed up the stone steps

into the police station. She heard Mona shout at Rupert as she got into the driver's seat of her pickup truck, "I'll buy you a soda at the Big Apple, but you are not consuming alcohol on my watch!"

It was quiet in the station, and Officer Earl, who was reading some kind of *Walking Dead* type graphic novel behind the reception desk, barely bothered to look up at her as she breezed past him.

"I just need to speak to Sergio for a second, Earl. It won't take long!" Hayley chirped.

"Even if I said he was in a meeting, it wouldn't matter because you never listen anyway!" Earl growled before returning his attention back to his comic book.

Hayley marched down the hall to Sergio's office. The door was open and he was at his desk, scribbling notes on a pad of paper. She rapped on the door frame. "Knock, knock . . ."

He looked up and sighed. "I suppose you heard . . ."

"Yes. His alibi checked out . . ."

"Rupert's been hitching rides up to the Blue Parrot bar in Ellsworth for a few weeks now because he's got a crush on a cocktail waitress named Betty who he met on the town pier when she was down here one weekend last month. She's about thirty years his junior and has zero romantic interest, but I guess he's an eternal optimologist."

"Optimist," Hayley politely corrected.

"Isn't that what I said?"

"No, not really," Hayley said quietly.

English was Sergio's second language and occasionally he mixed up his words.

"The owner even provided a video from his surveillance camera of Rupert arriving at four and staggering out drunk around ten thirty. A cab driver picked him up outside the bar and dropped him off at his place around eleven. Apparently Rupert was passed out in the back seat when they got to his place, and the driver had to half carry, half drag Rupert inside and put him to bed."

"Eleven o'clock? That's well after my mother discovered Caskie Lemon-Hogg's body."

"Which puts him in the clear," Sergio said.

"Then somebody must have stolen or found Rupert's credit card and used it to pay for the room at the B and B. But who?"

"I talked to the cabbie and he said Rupert had him stop at an ATM once they got to town so he could get some cash to pay the fare because Rupert told him that he had lost his credit card a few days earlier."

Hayley folded her arms. "So did someone deliberately lift Rupert's credit card so they could set him up for the murder?"

"Your guess is as good as mine at this point." Sergio sighed, frustrated.

Chapter 25

The last thing Hayley ever thought she would be witnessing on this sunny, breezy Saturday afternoon in the Bear Brook Picnic Area, located on the Park Loop Road just east of Sieur de Monts Spring in Acadia National Park, was her mother lip-locked with her old high school beau Carl Flippen. But that's exactly what she was looking at while quietly picking at a fried clam roll that she had just taken from the picnic basket on top of the wooden table. Bruce kept averting his eyes, chugging down a canned soda, clearly wishing he was anywhere else.

The day had started out innocently enough. Sheila had been up at the crack of dawn, brewing a pot of coffee for Hayley and Bruce. She had repeatedly promised to finally leave the whole Caskie Lemon-Hogg murder to the police and not get involved any more. Hayley had told her mother that she was grateful that Sheila was finally being reasonable, while neglecting to mention she had been knee-deep in her own freelance investigation. The fact was, Sheila had been too preoccupied getting, in her own words, "reacquainted" with Carl, who had turned up on Hayley's doorstep the night before, shyly asking if Sheila was home like some lovestruck teenage boy with his hormones racing, eager to ask the prettiest girl in high school out on a date. Sheila, eager to start something new after her last relationship had gone bust, was only too happy to invite him in for a glass of wine. They had talked well into the night, and Carl, ever the gentleman, finally took his leave around twelve thirty, departing quite satisfied with a sweet albeit brief kiss on the check from Sheila. Before he left, however, a plan was set to meet the next day for a romantic picnic in the park.

After he left, Sheila had kept Hayley and Bruce up another hour and a half, until nearly two in the morning, obsessing over whether or not Carl might be some kind of rebound relationship. Perhaps her judgment was clouded after Lenny had so unceremoniously dumped her and this was a way for her not to feel so empty and alone. When Hayley calmly suggested that her mother might be overthinking it, Sheila snapped back that she had had to listen to Hayley prattle on about dating again after her own divorce from Danny, so she might want to indulge her own emotionally bruised and battered mother for at least a few minutes. That shut Hayley up, and she was a pillar of support from that moment forward.

Bruce was less inclined to offer advice or even stick around while the two of them hashed it all out ad nauseam, but he knew if he tried to bolt he would never hear the end of it from both his wife and mother-in-law, and so he worked hard to suppress his yawns and pretend he was interested in the topic of Sheila's love life.

Finally, when both Hayley and Bruce were fighting

to stay awake and Sheila had run out of reasons why she should not date Carl, she finally had decided to just see where the relationship went and mercifully stood up and announced it was probably time for them all to go to bed.

Hayley and Bruce had just about made a clean get-away when Sheila called up after them as they were halfway up the stairs, and told them that she would feel more comfortable if they came with her and Carl on their picnic, make it like a double date. Hayley had started to protest that serving as chaperones might cramp her mother's style, not to mention Carl's, but Sheila would hear none of her arguments and remained steadfastly insistent. As she wore Hayley down, who eventually had agreed she and Bruce would come along, Hayley couldn't help but notice the defeated look on Bruce's face as whatever plans he had been looking forward to doing on his day off slowly fell by the wayside.

When Carl had shown up to pick up Sheila around noon, he made an admirable attempt to hide his surprise and disappointment that he was not going to have Sheila all to himself. Bruce had just smiled at him apologetically, as if trying to signal to him that he had had nothing to do with this, that if it had been up to him, he would not be tagging along. Hayley had made an effort to be upbeat and chatty, as if double dating with her mother was the most natural thing in the world.

The foursome had made their way into Acadia National Park, with Carl behind the wheel of his Buick LaCrosse. Sheila had excitedly remarked about how impressed she was with all the car's technological details like the heated front seats and rear park-assist features. Carl had nodded in agreement as Sheila swiveled her head around to wink at Hayley and Bruce, who both sat quietly in the back seat. It was as if she was signaling her acknowledgment that Carl Flippen, like his choice of automobile, was a real winner.

Despite the awkwardness, Hayley actually had found herself enjoying the picnic. Bruce had loosened up a bit once he was eating and was now cracking a few of his lame jokes, which both Carl and Sheila astonishingly found hilarious. Bruce had savored the attention and so he was no longer wishing he was anywhere else. But of course that had lasted only through the first couple of beers. Once Carl himself had felt more relaxed, the easier it was for him to flirt with Sheila, subtly at first, once squeezing her bare shoulder with his beefy hand, another time stroking the back of her hair and complimenting her on how pretty she looked today. Pretty soon he had gotten bolder and more obvious and Sheila, for her part, eagerly lapped it up until finally neither of them could control themselves any longer. As the undeniable chemistry between them was exploding, the two retirees could hardly keep their hands off each other. And without any further thought as to just how agonizing it had to be for their two picnic companions to watch, Sheila and Carl were now quite literally sucking face.

Bruce was now looking straight up at the sky, anywhere except what was right in front of him at the moment. "It sure is a beautiful day."

Hayley shoved the last fried clam from her roll into her mouth and chewed quickly. "I know, there was a twenty percent chance of rain, but there isn't a cloud in the sky."

"Nope, not one," Bruce said, eyes up.

Hayley could not help herself. She glanced over at just the moment when Carl slipped his tongue into

Sheila's mouth. She quickly averted her eyes over toward Bruce. "Do you want to go for a walk?"

"Yes, please!" Bruce begged.

They both popped up to their feet.

Hayley's eyes were fixed on the grass underneath them. "We'll be back in a little while."

She didn't expect her mother to answer, but she still waited a few seconds anyway. Upon hearing a slurp, she decided that was as good an answer as she was going to get, and so she and Bruce hurried off, crossing the road to Bear Brook Pond with a sweeping view of Champlain Mountain steeply above.

Once they were a safe distance away, Bruce took Hayley's hand and they strolled along in silence, enjoying the restful sights and sounds of nature.

Finally, Bruce squeezed Hayley's hand and spoke. "I'd really like to kiss you right now but I'm afraid I might have a flashback to what I saw back there at the picnic table."

Hayley giggled. "I guess we should be grateful that my mother is happy."

"There is happy and then there is *happy*! And that is *way* too much happy for me!"

"Are you traumatized by public displays of affection?"

"No, I'm traumatized by having to watch your mother swap spit with the man who used to coach my Little League baseball team. You just can't unsee something like that, Hayley."

"I don't know, I think it was kind of cute. And if having a new man in her life distracts her from getting into any more trouble, I'm all for it."

"Just promise me if they get married, we won't have to go on a joint honeymoon cruise to the Bahamas."

"Well, we're not going anytime soon. I went on the

website and found out the two-hundred-dollar change fee is only valid until the start of the cruise. We missed the deadlines, so now the tickets are totally nonrefundable, which means we have to start our honeymoon fund all over again."

"Maybe we can go on our tenth anniversary." Bruce sighed.

Hayley and Bruce walked a bit farther, and the trail opened up into a clearing near Dorr Mountain. Hayley glanced down to see blueberry bushes lined up along the way. She bent down, plucked one berry and tossed it in her mouth. After chewing and swallowing, she opened her mouth to show Bruce her purplish-gray tongue.

"The blueberries are really ripening now. They're so sweet and juicy," Hayley said, picking another one and handing it to Bruce, who threw it in the air and tried catching it with his mouth as it came down, but he missed.

Hayley picked one up and tried the same thing. She managed to catch hers and swallow it.

"You trying to show me up?" Bruce asked.

"No, I'm just better at it than you."

Bruce feigned offense. He picked another blueberry off the bush and tried again.

And he missed again.

Hayley laughed. "No wonder you got cut from the football team in high school. You can't even catch a blueberry."

"I got cut because I was failing half my classes. I was an awesome running back. Here, I'll prove it to you. Give me a head start and then you throw the blueberry and I'll show you just how good I can be."

"This is such an exercise in humiliation," Hayley said, shaking her head.

Bruce began jogging backward into the open clearing that was full of blueberry bushes, his mouth wide open.

Hayley knew he wouldn't stop until he caught one, so she picked one more blueberry and threw it as hard as she could at him.

It flew right at him, and it looked as if he was poised to finally catch it when suddenly he went down, flat on his back.

Hayley gasped. "Bruce, are you okay?"

"Yeah, I just tripped."

"Anything broken?"

"Just my spirit."

Hayley ran toward him, but didn't see him at first. "Where are you?"

He raised an arm in the air.

As she got closer to him, she suddenly heard him yell, "Oh my God!"

"Bruce, what is it? What's wrong?"

"I just saw what I tripped over . . . I thought it was a log or something . . ."

As Hayley finally reached Bruce, she followed his stunned gaze to the ground, where a body was facedown in a blueberry patch.

Bruce gingerly reached down and turned the body over enough to see that it was a woman, her white summer blouse stained purple by squashed blueberries.

Hayley threw a hand to her mouth. "It's Regina Knoxville!"

Island Food & Spirits
BY HAYLEY POWELL

Growing up on Mount Desert Island on the Down East coast of Maine, that old phrase, "there are plenty of fish in the sea" usually meant a good haul for the local fishermen who went out every day to catch the lobsters and crabs that the local restaurants served to the millions of tourists who descended upon our small island during the busy tourist season.

However, for Liddy Crawford's mother, Celeste, the saying "plenty of fish in the sea" had nothing to do with shellfish. In her mind, it squarely meant something else entirely—the men who were available to marry her one-and-only, precious daughter. And as far as Celeste was concerned, once Liddy had graduated from college and moved back home to follow in her mother's footsteps, hoping to become a successful Realtor, the island's dating pool had sadly dried up!

In Celeste's eyes, no boy had ever been good enough for her darling Liddy. She attributed this to the fact that Liddy's choices had been impulsive and wrong-headed, and none of the boys she had brought home during high school and college even came close to deserving her stamp of approval. As for Liddy, she considered her mother's ideas about having "a man to take care of you" antiquated and outdated, and she was having none of it. She could take care of herself, and set out to prove it by making the goal to sell more houses in one year than her mother! That would keep her so busy she wouldn't have time to worry about any kind of love life!

Unfortunately, Celeste had other plans, and she was determined to find someone for her daughter, who she felt "wasn't getting any younger." When Liddy reminded her that she was only twenty-two, her mother quipped, "There's another phrase besides 'plenty of fish in the sea,' and that's 'the early bird gets the worm.'"

There was plenty of eye-rolling over that one.

So as Liddy worked tirelessly to build her career, Celeste was hard at work playing matchmaker to find Mr. Right. First there was a young, eager salesman at Darling's Auto Mall in Ellsworth who could only talk about himself, and when he wasn't talking about himself, he talked about his work. The few minutes he did focus on Liddy were spent trying to convince her to buy a new Ford Mustang convertible just off the assembly line, which he could get for her for a good price. Since Liddy also preferred talking about herself most of the time, it was not a good match at all. Then there was the young scientist from the Jackson Laboratory biomedical research facility, and no pun intended, there was literally zero chemistry. An up-and-coming nature photographer seemed promising, but Celeste had been misinformed about the kind of pictures he took. She thought nature meant trees and frogs and ponds, but his portfolio was actually "au naturel" and his models posed nude. Liddy politely declined his request for a photo session after dessert.

Finally, Liddy put her foot down and after a lot of yelling, begging, and pleading, her mother grudgingly agreed to finally stay out of Liddy's dating life. Well, as it happened, a couple of weeks later, when Liddy popped into the new florist shop in town to pick up fresh bouquets of flowers for an open house that she was helping her mother stage, she met the new owner, who introduced himself as Barry. Barry was in his late twenties, movie-star handsome in a Brad Pitt sort of way, and he was also funny and he had Liddy laughing while he gathered up her order. By the time she left his shop, Liddy was in love.

Liddy and Barry became inseparable, and Celeste could not have been happier that her only daughter had finally, after much searching, found the love of her life. The icing on the cake was that he owned his own business, which was definitely a major plus in her book!

Liddy was so happy that she actually invited her mother out to dinner one evening with her and Barry at the Chart Room in

Hulls Cove. However, Barry seemed unchar-
acteristically distant at the table. Liddy attributed it to nerves. Her mother seemed totally
oblivious and was enjoying herself immensely
as they ordered their second round of blueberry cosmos. Barry answered all of Celeste's
probing questions about his family. At some
point, Liddy excused herself to go to the
ladies' room when Celeste pointed out that
her nose was shiny. Upon her return, Liddy
saw her mother and Barry huddling close, in
deep conversation, and for a brief moment,
she let herself imagine that Barry might be
asking her mother's permission to propose
marriage. But as she got closer, she heard
Barry say insistently to her mother, "I can't
keep your money!" To which her mother
replied, "A deal is a deal!"

When they finally noticed Liddy had returned and overheard them, Barry's face had
guilt written all over it. Then he jumped up
from the table, mumbling "I'm sorry," and
ran right out of the restaurant. Liddy stared
after him, and then turned to her mother
and yelled, "Mother, what did you do?"

It took some coaxing, but Celeste finally
admitted that she had met Barry before and
thought he and Liddy would be a good
match, and so she offered him money to take
Liddy out on a date. Barry had accepted, jus-
tifying it as a business deal in his mind, since
he could use the extra cash for more inventory at his fledgling flower shop. He never
dreamed he would even like Liddy, nor did
he ever imagine that he might even fall in

love with her. Barry had been trying to return Celeste's money. He wanted to confess everything to Liddy, hoping she would take it with a sense of humor. Unfortunately, Liddy did not see it that way at all.

Liddy was furious with her mother and she moved out of Celeste's house and didn't speak to her for a few months. But eventually she realized that her mother only had her best interests at heart, and forgave her, but not before making her promise to never meddle in Liddy's love life ever again. Celeste readily agreed, but broke the promise a week later when she sold a summer cottage to a wealthy single banker from New York.

As for poor Barry, he had called Liddy for a month straight after that ill-fated dinner, but she refused to answer. She just couldn't get past the fact that her mother had paid a man to date her. She was utterly humiliated.

Small towns are funny though, and eventually Liddy and Barry kept running into each other at the grocery store, at after-hour work events, and occasionally at mutual friends' parties. They did try dating again, but in the long run they were not meant to be. However, on a happy note, they are the best of friends still to this day.

Of course, my favorite part of that story is the mention of a blueberry cosmo, one of my all-time favorite cocktails, and believe me, after you try one you too will be hooked.

Blueberry Cosmo

Ingredients
4 ounces blueberry juice
1 ounce lime juice
2 ounces Cointreau
6 ounces vodka

Combine all your ingredients with ice in a shaker and shake until chilled.

Rim a martini glass with the lime juice.

Strain the chilled mixture into the glass and garnish with a lime slice and enjoy.

BLUEBERRY COBBLER

INGREDIENTS
3 cups fresh blueberries
3 tablespoons sugar
⅓ cup orange juice
⅔ cup all-purpose flour
½ teaspoon baking powder
1 teaspoon salt
½ cup room temperature butter
½ cup sugar
1 egg
1 teaspoon vanilla extract

Preheat your oven to 375 degrees F.

In an 8-inch baking dish mix your blueberries,
three tablespoons sugar, and orange juice
together and set aside. In a bowl mix your flour,
baking powder, and salt and set aside.

In a stand mixer or bowl with hand mixer, cream
the butter and ½ cup sugar until light and fluffy.
Beat in the egg and vanilla extract. Gradually add
the flour mixture until just combined. Drop the
batter by tablespoonfuls over the blueberry mixture.

Try to cover as much of the blueberries as you
can.

Bake in preheated oven for 35 to 40 minutes,
until the topping is golden brown and the filling
is bubbly.

Chapter 26

After Bruce checked Regina's pulse and found none, Hayley scooped out her cell phone and called 911, reporting what they had found. Bruce jogged up to the main road to wait for the police to arrive while Hayley stayed with the body.

Chief Alvarez raced to the scene as fast as he could after receiving the call, but since they were deep inside Acadia National Park in a remote area, Bruce did not spot the flashing blue lights of the chief's squad car approaching for a tense and uncomfortable twenty-five minutes. Within that time, Hayley had enough time to examine the body without touching it.

She had first noticed that there were red splotchy marks all over Regina's face, bare arms, and legs. Her throat appeared to be swollen along with her tongue, which stuck out of her mouth. After swatting away a few bees that kept buzzing around and irritating her, Hayley noticed a hive nearby. It was lodged in one of the blueberry bushes close to Regina's body. There was a wicker basket upended and blueberries were spread around all over the dirt and grass. Hayley quickly determined that Regina had been out picking blueberries when she died. The hive was also an important clue because the red marks and swollen neck and tongue possibly indicated symptoms of an allergic reaction to bee stings.

What Hayley found odd was how the hive was positioned. She didn't get too close, fearing she might surprise the bees still inside and get attacked herself, but it seemed so out of place. The hive was tilted to the right, and just resting in the bush, not hanging anywhere, as if someone had deliberately placed it there.

The pounding footsteps of her husband, Sergio, and a couple of his officers snapped her out of her thoughts and she turned to see the cavalry finally arriving on the scene. Hayley didn't have to give her brother-in-law the rundown of what she had noticed because he was a smart enough investigator to deduce all of what she had discovered on his own. Instead, she stepped back with Bruce as the cops took over. She did, however, turn to Bruce, who was sweating from the hot sun and clearly upset over having stumbled over Regina Knoxville's dead body.

"You okay?" she asked.

Bruce nodded. "Just kind of a shock to find her out here like that. I told you dead bodies freak me out!"

Hayley rubbed his back with her hand to comfort him. "I know. Poor Regina . . ."

"Sergio wants us to stick around for a few minutes so he can ask us some questions once he's done looking around," Bruce said.

"Of course," Hayley said, having no intention of leaving just yet anyway. She wanted to make sure that she and the police were both on the same page.

A bee buzzed past them and over to the hive lodged

in the blueberry patch. Then another. Hayley turned to see Bruce waving his hand in front of his face as a third one danced around his head before flying away and over to the hive. Hayley touched Bruce's arm. "I'll be right back."

"Where are you going?"

"Just over there," Hayley said, not pointing in any particular direction. She watched as one bee after another whizzed through the air toward the hive. She set off due west, in the direction from which the bees seemed to be coming. She hadn't gotten very far, maybe fifty yards, when she noticed a balsam fir tree with hundreds of bees hovering around one of the branches as groups of them, flying in ever increasing figure eights, buzzed off toward the honeycomb hive lodged in the blueberry patch. Hayley suddenly knew exactly what had happened.

When she dashed back to Bruce, he was already engaged in a deep discussion with Sergio, recounting how he and Hayley had first encountered the body.

"She was murdered!" Hayley shouted.

Bruce and Sergio stopped talking and turned toward her, both staring at her blankly.

"What?" Sergio asked.

"Regina! Somebody *wanted* her dead!"

Sergio tried not to come off as patronizing and so he pretended to be taking Hayley seriously. "We may come to that conclusion when we're done investigating, but I have to be honest, Hayley, right now it looks like Regina bumped into a beehive and got a hell of a lot of stings all over her body—"

"Yes, I know, and from the flushing and swelling, it's quite possible Regina was allergic to bees, but I think somebody already *knew* that!"

"How so?"

"Because that beehive is manmade. Most wild bees in nature colonize in hollowed-out trees or in rock cavities to protect themselves from predators. That hive was hung on a tree branch about fifty yards down the trail. But somebody moved it and placed it in that blueberry patch."

"How do you know that?" Sergio asked, curious.

"Because I did a high school science project on beehives and I know for a fact that when a hive is moved, the returning bees will hover near its original location. Then they will start looking for their lost hive by flying in figure eights. They use their sense of smell to find where the hive is. Look, you can see the bees coming toward their nest."

Sergio watched the bees arriving and knew there was no arguing with her.

She was right.

Bruce arched an eyebrow, impressed with his wife's knowledge of the bee kingdom.

Sergio scratched his chin, still trying to put it all together. "But, Hayley, Regina's body was a good distance from the blueberry patch with the hive. If we are dealing with a killer, how did he or she know the bees would go after Regina? It's not as if she was doused in honey."

"Maybe she knocked into the blueberry patch and she panicked and ran away when the bees swarmed around her, but she didn't drop dead from her allergic reaction until she got to the point where we found her."

Sergio considered the theory and nodded slightly. "You could be right. But I'm still not sure."

Hayley had just come up with this wild murder theory off the top of her head, and so she couldn't blame Sergio for hesitating to immediately classify Regina Knoxville's death as a homicide. Because frankly, Hayley wasn't entirely sure she had it right either. Would somebody actually come all the way out here wearing protective gear, move an active beehive to a blueberry patch, and just hope and pray that Regina would decide to go blueberry picking out in the park on this particular day and just coincidentally walk right into it?

No, there were pieces of the puzzle still missing.

And Hayley was more determined than ever to find them and put them all together.

Chapter 27

Sergio rubbed his eyes with his thumb and forefinger as Sheila, Celeste, and Jane, sitting together on the couch in Hayley's living room, all chattered at once, their decibel levels rising the more frantic and panicked they got.

Sergio, frustrated, finally shouted at the top of his lungs, "Ladies, please! Calm down! I never meant to imply that you are official suspects when I asked where you were today! I'm not even sure this is a murder case."

"It is, trust me," Hayley said.

"Hayley, you're not helping," Sergio moaned. "I just want to know in case the autopsy report suggests some kind of foul play."

Celeste huffed, "I know how you cops operate! You like to lull your suspects into a false sense of security and then you pounce when we least expect it!"

Sheila gasped. "Are you going to arrest me, Sergio, your own mother-in-law?"

"No, Sheila," Sergio insisted.

"Well I should certainly hope not," Celeste said. "We all have to live in this town, and it would be hard to maintain a decent reputation if suddenly you booked us for Regina's murder, not to mention Caskie's."

Bruce strolled in from the kitchen with a can of beer, having heard Celeste's last comment. "Yeah, Sergio, getting arrested for breaking and entering is one thing, but *murder*? That's a whole other ball game."

Sheila stared daggers at Bruce, which he totally missed. He sat down in his recliner and wanted to turn on the TV, but knew it was hardly an appropriate time so he just settled in for the drama unfolding in front of him in the living room.

"Sergio's just trying to rule you out so he can move on to *actual* suspects who might have wanted to do away with Regina Knoxville," Hayley added helpfully.

"Did none of you hear me? This is not a murder case!" Sergio cried.

"Not yet, but it will be. I can feel it in my bones," Hayley said confidently.

"Well, one thing is for certain. I am in the clear," Celeste said. "I had an appointment at Julio's Salon today. He was over in Northeast Harbor doing hair for a bridal party, so I took a chance and let his cousin Juan take care of me. I was rather impressed, don't you agree?"

"Oh, yes, I love how it's so beautifully layered," Sheila said. "He did a wonderful job. It's hard to believe he is still in training."

Celeste nodded. "I was going to go for a blunt cut, like what's-her-name, the one they based that Meryl Streep movie on, about the fashion magazine editor . . ."

"*The Devil Wears Prada*," Jane piped in.

"Yes, her. What's her name?" Celeste said.

"Anna Winter," Jane said.

"Anna Win*tour*," Sheila corrected her.

"Yes, I was in the mood for something different, almost a bob, but then I thought, what the heck, let Juan work with what I've got."

"That's the perfect style for a woman with thinning hair," Jane said.

Celeste deflated right in front of their eyes. "*What?*"

Sheila was quick to rush in and patch up the wound. "She just means it's nice your hair isn't so puffy, right, Jane?"

"She's got thinning hair. What's the big deal? It's not a crime," Jane said, her giant faux pas still completely lost on her.

Sergio had heard enough. "Ladies, can we please get back to the crime at hand?"

"See? You said crime! You think Regina was murdered too!" Hayley cried, pointing a finger at Sergio.

Sergio dropped his head. "There's no harm in gathering a few facts in case I might need them later."

"When you classify Regina's death as a homicide," Hayley said.

"If." Sergio sighed.

"Girls, please, Sergio would like us to focus," Sheila said with a tight smile, nervously glancing over at Celeste, who now appeared to be having a silent meltdown. "We know Celeste was at the hairdresser's this afternoon. What about you, Jane?"

"I was babysitting my grandchildren, and let me tell you, after four hours with those hellions, I have to say I wish I was out in the park killing Regina Knoxville!"

"Jane! You're not helping your case!" Sheila admonished.

Sergio sighed. "Sheila?"

"Well, obviously I could not have done it. I was with Hayley and Bruce and Carl Flippen in the park. We were on a double date," Sheila said.

"You like Carl, don't you?" Jane said, grinning.

Sheila playfully swatted Jane on the knee. "We'll talk later."

Sergio sighed. "What about in the morning before you left for the park?"

Sheila shrugged. "I was at Hayley's house."

Bruce cleared his throat. "Except for when you went out to pick up lunch. You were gone almost two hours. I thought we were going to have to send out a search party."

Sheila glared at him, and he realized he was not exactly helping her case, so he just chugged some more of his beer.

"I couldn't decide on what sandwiches we should have for our picnic. I didn't want to serve something Carl didn't like so I decided to have plenty of everything and went to the grocery store, some takeout restaurants, the bakery. I'm sure the workers there will remember me."

"I'm sure they will too." Bruce laughed before catching himself and getting serious. "Which means you'll be in the clear!"

"Hayley, do you think my hair is thinning?" Celeste asked, bereft and cheerless as she checked herself out in a compact mirror she had grabbed from her purse.

"You have beautiful hair, Celeste. I wish I had hair like yours," Hayley said reassuringly.

Sheila was done being interrogated and wanted the attention off herself and her friends. "Listen, Sergio, I appreciate the fact that you have to speak to everyone who disliked Caskie and Regina, and I imagine it's a very long list. But have you considered the fact that we might have a serial killer on the loose who is targeting older women?"

"In Bar Harbor?" Bruce asked incredulously.

"Just because we live on such a beautiful, picturesque island doesn't mean there aren't ugly things around us," Sheila argued.

Celeste gasped. "You mean we could be potential *victims*?"

Jane sat up. "If it gets me out of babysitting my awful grandchildren ever again, I say take me, take me!"

Sergio raised his hands to try to get control of the room one more time. "Ladies, I honestly don't think we're dealing with a serial killer, but I will not rule anything out at this point, okay?"

"If anyone had thinning hair, it was Caskie Lemon-Hogg," Celeste suddenly announced. "To be perfectly frank, I think they put a wig on her for the funeral. It did not look at all natural."

"Do you really think so?" Sheila asked.

"It took every ounce of self-control for me not to reach down into the casket and give it a tug."

"You're probably right. Everything else about her was fake, so why not her hair?" Jane offered.

"She was such a despicable woman," Celeste said.

"God, I couldn't stand the sight of her," Sheila said, nodding vigorously.

"Regina too," Jane said, staring off into space.

"You know, in some ways, Regina was worse," Sheila said.

"Mom, you three are not exactly proving your innocence by constantly bad-mouthing the two murder victims!"

Sergio interrupted her. "Hayley, I never said Regina was—"

"I know, I know. But you will," Hayley said, brimming with confidence.

"She's usually right, Sergio," Bruce added.

Sergio tried plowing ahead. "I spoke to Regina's husband, Albert, and he confirmed that she was allergic to bees."

"What was she doing all that way out in the park picking blueberries?" Hayley asked.

"According to Albert, once a week, usually every Saturday, Regina would go out and pick blueberries. She found it calming and she liked helping Caskie out with her blueberry business. She'd always keep a few baskets to make pancakes and muffins for Albert. After Caskie died, she didn't want to stop and so she decided to keep the tradition going in honor of Caskie's memory."

"That's sweet," Hayley said.

"I don't buy it," Jane huffed. "I bet Regina just wanted to take over the business."

"Why would she need it? Isn't Albert loaded?" Celeste asked.

"Maybe the killer already knew Regina's schedule and the exact spot where she would usually go to pick blueberries, and that's how he or she knew where to place the beehive," Hayley surmised.

"But how did the killer know Regina was allergic to bees?" Bruce asked.

"Everyone knew, at least I did," Sheila said. "I remember back when we were in high school we went on a field trip with our science class taught by Mr. Long . . ."

"Oh, Mr. Long! What a dreamboat! He was so handsome," Celeste gushed. "I had a mad crush on him! I know at the time I was just a teenage girl, but I am confident he had a little thing for me too . . ."

"He must have liked girls with thin hair," Jane couldn't resist commenting.

Celeste wilted again.

"I had a big crush on him too!" Sheila continued. "Anyway, I remember we were in the park studying nature, like plants or wildlife or some such thing, who can really remember stuff like that, and Regina got stung by a bee and her face just blew up!"

Jane scrunched her nose. "I don't remember that."

"You probably skipped school again that day, which is why you barely graduated, dear," Celeste said, a vengeful look on her face.

"It was horrible," Sheila said. "She couldn't breathe and her face looked like a big red beach ball! Mr. Long picked her up in his arms and ran her to the school bus and we all piled on and raced to the hospital. I remember thinking *God, I wish that was me being carried in Mr. Long's arms! Why Regina? I hate her so much!*" Sheila was lost in thought for a few seconds.

"I thought you liked Mr. Cadwell, our history teacher?" Jane asked.

"What, I can't have a crush on more than one teacher?" Sheila snapped. "Anyway, we got her there in the nick of time and she got a shot and everything turned out fine. She had to stay home sick for a few days, and Mr. Long made us write 'get well soon' cards. I worked really hard on mine, not because I liked Regina, I just wanted to impress Mr. Long, and it worked because he said mine was the best! I wonder if he's still alive . . ."

"We could look him up on Facebook!" Jane suggested.

Before Sheila had a chance to jump up and run to the nearest computer, Sergio stepped in front of her. "So you're telling me you *knew* Regina was allergic to bees?"

"Yes, as do all the living students of our graduating class," Sheila said sourly.

"Except Jane, because she was a truant." Celeste sniffed.

Hayley caught Bruce smirking. He was enjoying watching his mother-in-law continue to incriminate herself without even knowing it.

Chapter 28

Hayley sat up in bed, her arms folded, her mind racing. The lamp on her night table was still shining brightly as Bruce burrowed underneath the covers next to her, a pillow tossed over his head, held down by the crook of his arm in a desperate bid to block out the light.

"Regina's death was obviously no accident, don't you agree, Bruce?"

Bruce didn't answer her, and Hayley knew he was just pretending to be asleep so she nudged him a little. "Bruce?"

"Yes, yes, I agree," he mumbled. "Can we talk about this in the morning?"

"I mean it's too much of a coincidence that Regina just happened to be allergic to bees and then someone placed a man-made beehive in the bushes where she picks blueberries every Saturday, am I right?"

Nothing.

Hayley cleared her throat, followed by another little nudge.

"You're right, you're right . . ." Bruce groaned.

"Maybe Mom is on to something. Maybe there is some mad killer on the loose who is targeting women of a certain age. At least I have nothing to worry about. I mean, I am *way* too young to fit the profile . . ."

Hayley waited for her husband to second that motion.

He didn't.

"Bruce?"

"Way too young . . ." he grumbled into his pillow.

"Decades too young . . ."

Bruce tossed the pillow aside, threw off the covers and sat up until he was eye level with Hayley. "I know you can't sleep, and your brain is working overtime, but, honey, mine isn't. I'm tired and I have a lot of work to do at the office tomorrow, and I really, really need to get some shut-eye so can we please table this discussion until morning?"

Hayley reached over and kissed him sweetly on the cheek. "Yes, I'm sorry. Go to sleep. I'll stop talking."

Bruce sighed. "Thank you."

"You're welcome," Hayley said, reaching over to shut off the lamp on her nightstand.

They snuggled together underneath the covers, Hayley turning over to one side, and Bruce spooning her with an arm slung around her waist, and they closed their eyes.

Not even thirty seconds passed before they heard screaming.

Bruce tightened his grip in surprise. "What the—?"

Hayley freed herself, quickly shot back up in bed and turned on the light. "It's my mother!"

Before either of them had time to jump out of bed, the door swung open and Sheila came barreling into the room, panting and crying.

"Mom, what is it? What happened?"

She stood there, breathless for a moment, her eyes bulging out of her head, her hand to her mouth. She took some time to calm herself down before finally speaking. "I had a nightmare . . ."

"What kind of nightmare?" Bruce asked, not really wanting to hear what she had to say, but feeling obligated since the poor woman was standing at the foot of his bed in a puddle of tears.

"I was being strangled by a man. I couldn't see his face because it was dark, but I felt his hot breath on my neck . . ."

"Are you sure it wasn't Leroy, sneaking up on your bed trying to cuddle?" Bruce asked seriously.

"I think I would know if it was a dog, Bruce," Sheila snapped. "I couldn't breathe and I thought I was going to die . . ."

"How could your mind not go there after what's happened to Caskie and Regina?" Hayley said, trying to comfort her mother. "I was just saying to Bruce that you have every right to be scared, right, Bruce?"

Bruce nodded as he yawned.

Sheila sat down on the edge of the bed. "I just hope Sergio starts focusing on who is responsible instead of constantly grilling me, Celeste, and Jane about where we were every time this happens! I mean, it's ridiculous to think my own son-in-law suspects me of doing such a vile, contemptible act . . . twice! You're my son-in-law too, Bruce. You don't believe I'm capable of anything like that, do you?"

"No, ma'am," Bruce blurted out.

"Sergio is just doing his job, Mom. Of course he doesn't actually think you did anything," Hayley said.

"I'm beginning to wonder," Sheila said before she

started staring at Bruce. "I didn't know you slept like that, Bruce."

"Like what?" Bruce asked.

"Without a shirt."

Bruce looked down at his bare chest and suddenly began to feel self-conscious. "Um, yes, I guess I do."

"What's wrong with that, Mom?" Hayley asked.

"Nothing, it just surprises me, that's all. Your father loved sleeping naked."

Bruce raised his hand. "For the record, I'm wearing boxer shorts."

"I just always had the impression, you know, before the two of you got married, when you just worked together, that you were a little uptight, so I always envisioned you as the pajama type."

"Mom!"

"What? I'm just being honest," Sheila protested.

"Let's go back for a second," Bruce said, shifting in bed uncomfortably. "You envisioned me in bed?"

"Oh my God!" Hayley wailed.

"Oh, don't make such a big deal out of it, Hayley, I picture lots of men in bed. That doesn't mean I want to be in there with them!"

There was an awkward silence.

"I really want to put on a T-shirt right now," Bruce said, reaching down and searching the floor for one he discarded earlier.

Suddenly they heard a high-pitched screeching sound coming from underneath the bed and Bruce yelped in pain.

Blueberry scooted out from under the bed and bolted for the door, slipping on the hardwood floor as he rounded the corner. Bruce held up his hand. It was bloody from a deep scratch.

"Look what that damn cat just did to me!" Bruce howled.

"I'll get some peroxide and a washcloth!" Sheila said, leaping up and racing out the door.

Bruce didn't wait for her to come back. He picked his gray T-shirt up off the floor and wrapped it around his hand to use as a tourniquet to stop the bleeding.

Hayley rubbed his back with her hand. "I'm so sorry, Bruce . . ."

Bruce opened his mouth to say something, but he just erupted into a violent, loud sneeze.

"Oh no . . ." Hayley whispered.

He sneezed again.

And then again.

He reached over to his own nightstand, grabbed a handful of tissues out of a box of Kleenex, and started blowing his nose.

And then he sneezed again.

"That's it, Hayley. I've had enough . . ."

"Enough of what? My mother?"

"No, that cat! My nose is stuffed up all the time, I'm in constant misery, I live in fear of waking up to find it sitting on my face. I can't take it anymore!"

"Oh, Bruce—"

"I thought when we got married and I moved in here, some Benadryl would do the trick, or those allergy shots I tried for a month. At one point I was hoping my immune system would just naturally adjust to living with a cat, but it hasn't! I can't live like this anymore! It's too much!"

"I'm sorry, Bruce, I'm not sure what we can do about it," Hayley said, feeling bad for her husband but at a complete loss.

"Well, you're going to have to do something, because either Blueberry goes or I do!"

Hayley almost laughed. She thought it was a joke at first. But as she looked into her husband's eyes, she suddenly realized his ultimatum this time was for real. He was being dead serious.

One of them was going to have to go.

Chapter 29

"Miss Hendricks, our English teacher, absolutely hated both Caskie and Regina because they used to make fun of her weight," Sheila said over pancakes at Side Street Cafe with Hayley. "One time Miss Hendricks wore this bright yellow dress and was walking down the hall, and when she passed by Caskie and Regina, who were standing by their lockers, Caskie yelled, 'Taxi!'"

"That's horrible!" Hayley said, staring at a black-and-white photo of Miss Hendricks—who had short white hair and wore small rectangular glasses that didn't quite fit her chubby face—in the last yearbook ever put out by Bar Harbor High School in the spring of 1968.

"Miss Hendricks pretended she didn't hear them, but she got her revenge when she caught them plagiarizing their book reports on *Silas Marner* by George Eliot and flunked them both!" Sheila declared with more than a hint of satisfaction. "Regina's parents were so upset they forced her to quit cheerleading and focus on her studies."

"Is Miss Hendricks still around?"

"No, she died in the late nineties, as did Mr. Peterman, who also had it out for them," Sheila said with a sigh.

"The janitor?"

Hayley stared at a picture of Ralph Peterman, smiling but with one front tooth missing, his complexion pockmarked, just a few wisps of gray hair sprouting on top of his weirdly curved head.

Sheila nodded. "He used to stutter and they would constantly make fun of him. One day Caskie purposely dropped her food tray in the cafeteria so he'd have to come and clean it up. She was just awful."

"Was there *anyone* in high school who didn't hate Caskie and Regina?"

"They had their followers, the girls who thought they should be just like them because they were pretty and had nice bodies and were cheerleaders, and of course a lot of the *boys* in school paid attention to them because they had hormones, but most decent people knew exactly how stuck-up they were," Sheila said.

"Do you remember anyone who was at the reunion recently who might have had a particular hatred of them?"

"You mean besides me, Celeste, and Jane? Well, yes, Cammie Metcalf once threatened to run them down in the school parking lot with her father's Dodge Charger after they drew a nasty caricature of her and posted it in the gym, but she's in a wheelchair now with MS and physically incapable of harming anyone."

"There must be someone we're missing," Hayley wondered as she poured syrup on top of her stack of blueberry pancakes at her kitchen table. After cutting some with her fork and knife and shoveling them in her mouth, Hayley resumed flipping through the pages of her mother's yearbook. She stopped on a page and looked at the picture of a striking young man in a football uniform. "My, he's handsome."

"You don't recognize him? That's Carl Flippen," Sheila said with a smile.

"Wow, he was a real stud back in the day," Hayley marveled.

"He still is, if you ask me," Sheila said. "I'm so happy we reconnected."

"What was his relationship with Caskie and Regina back in high school?"

"I honestly don't remember. I mean he certainly knew them, it was before the schools merged to form Mount Desert Island High School, so we had a very small class, but I don't think he dated either of them, at least as far as I can recall. But let's face it. Carl Flippen had discerning taste. His wife, Bev, was such a treasure. He would never have lowered his standards to go out with Caskie or Regina."

Hayley turned a few more pages, settling on a collage of photos from the prom, which was held in the gym. She zeroed in on one photo of Caskie and Regina, in beady, puffy dresses, posing together.

Sheila turned up her nose. "I actually remember those awful dresses. The only saving grace is that the photo is in black and white, because those dresses were even worse in color. Definitely not pretty in pink. Caskie looked like a bottle of Pepto-Bismol."

Hayley noticed a kid in an ill-fitting suit, one much too big for him, hovering in the background, gawking at them. "Who's that?"

"Who?"

Hayley pointed at the boy. "Him."

"I think that's Rupert Stiles."

"Rupert? Are you sure?"

"Yes, he was the smallest kid in our class. There were a few bullies who picked on him and called him the runt of the litter. Look how small he is. Yes, I'm positive that's Rupert."

"Did he have a crush on Caskie? He seems to be staring longingly at her."

"Not Caskie. He's looking at Regina. See? If you follow his line of sight, he is focused on her," Sheila said, tracing her finger from Rupert to Regina.

"Do you remember anything about that?" Hayley asked.

Sheila thought about it, and after taking a sip of her coffee, said, "I heard something about it. There was some incident where Regina caught some Peeping Tom gawking at her while she was showering in the girls' locker room, and there was a rumor going around that it had been Rupert. But she didn't get a good enough look to be certain it was him. And there was another story where I heard Rupert paid Kenny Epstein, who had the desk directly behind Regina in Chemistry because we were seated alphabetically and Regina's maiden name was Eisenhower, to switch seats with him so he could sit behind her and smell her hair. Miss D'Agostino made him switch back because he made Regina feel uncomfortable. But all of that was over fifty years ago, Hayley, so I could be wrong about some of the details."

"So his crush was unrequited?"

"As far as I know. After graduation, Regina played the field and dated lots of men until she met Albert, who arrived in town while on summer break from Colby College. It was love at first sight and they got married a few months later and have been together ever since."

Hayley couldn't take her eyes off the picture of the awkward-looking Rupert Stiles in the old yearbook photo. Mostly because upon closer inspection, the look on Rupert's face was not one of adoration. It looked more like unbridled rage.

"Hayley, you can't possibly think Rupert, after all these years, still harbors resentment toward Regina for rejecting him, do you?"

"I don't know . . ."

"But you heard Sergio. He has an alibi. He couldn't have done it."

"Rupert has an alibi for Caskie's murder. But what about Regina's?"

Sheila bolted upright, suddenly intrigued.

Had the reunion at Drinks Like a Fish possibly reignited long forgotten feelings and painful old wounds?

Had Regina's past finally come back to haunt her?

Just because Rupert Stiles had been officially cleared of one murder didn't necessarily mean he was innocent of another.

Chapter 30

Later that afternoon, Hayley took a sip of her Jack and Coke as she sat atop a bar stool in her brother Randy's bar. She listened as Rupert Stiles, nursing a bottle of beer, and nervously scratching his beard, kept his eyes glued to the floor as he spoke in a tired, scratchy voice. "Yes, truth be told, Hayley, I did have a big crush on Regina back in high school, but as you know that was a long time ago . . ." He looked up at her and his bloodshot eyes were watering. "I can't believe she's gone. She was a good woman who didn't deserve to die the way she did . . ."

Hayley reached into her bag and pulled out her mother's yearbook. She flipped through it to the page where she had seen the photograph of Rupert looking angry as he stared at Regina. She gently set it down in front of him. "Do you recall that picture being taken?"

Rupert shook his head. "Like I said, it was a long time ago and a lot has happened in the world since then . . ."

"It's just that I know the picture is a little blurry, but

if you look really close, you can see the expression on your face, and to be blunt, you seem very angry," Hayley said calmly.

Rupert bent over to get a better look at the picture. He grunted and then took a sip of his beer. "Guess I was."

"Do you remember why?"

Rupert pointed at a poster on a wall behind them promoting senior prom, which was coming up soon. "Must have been around May of 1968 when that photo was taken. I remember . . ." His voice trailed off as the memories came flooding back. "I remember I was head over heels in love with Regina around that time . . . there's no denying it . . . ask anybody who still has a clear memory of high school and they'll tell you the same thing . . ."

"Do you remember what she did to upset you?"

Rupert hemmed and hawed a bit, but then put his beer down on the bar and turned to face Hayley, his eyes full of sadness. "I sure do . . . Deep down I knew I was out of her league. She was real popular with the boys at that time, but I figured I'd always regret it if I didn't at least try, so I asked her to be my date for prom. And she laughed. Right in my face. She turned and told her friends what had just happened, that I actually asked her to go to the prom with me, and they all laughed too. I knew right then and there she would never be interested in someone like me, and so I just walked away and never really spoke to her again. I gotta say though, even though I was mad as hell, and you can see it right there in that picture, I still couldn't shake my feelings for her, not for a few years. Finally, about the time she met Albert, I was able to move on." Rupert paused. "Mostly."

"So where were you last Saturday when Regina was killed?"

"At my apartment, like I am most Saturdays, watching a Red Sox game."

"Alone?"

"Pretty much."

"Did anybody call or drop by?"

"Nope. I don't have many visitors, and the only calls I usually get are those annoying telemarketers trying to sell me something. I was home, Hayley, all day. And I'll tell you where I wasn't. Anywhere near the park or any blueberry patch."

He studied Hayley's face to determine whether she believed him or not. He seemed unable to come to any kind of conclusion and so he added, "Besides, it couldn't have been me who killed Regina."

Hayley arched an eyebrow. "Why not?"

"You said the police suspect that maybe someone moved a beehive over to where Regina was known to pick blueberries, right?"

"Yes, that's the theory, at least for now . . ."

"Well, Regina and I may have been totally opposite of one another but we did share one thing . . ."

"And what's what?"

"We're both allergic to bees."

Hayley sat upright, surprised. "You too?"

"Don't take my word for it, ask anyone who knows me. Got stung once in my early twenties and blew up like a Macy's Thanksgiving Day float."

"I can see why you would want to avoid bees."

"You could put me in one of them hazmat suits and I still wouldn't get near anything that has those damn things buzzing around it! I may have a few problems, but I sure ain't suicidal."

Hayley put a hand on Rupert's arm. "Thank you, Rupert."

She finished her Jack and Coke and flashed him an appreciative smile, and then got up to leave, waving goodbye to Randy, who was at the other end of the bar chatting with a few of his customers. She wasn't sure what to make of anything at this point. If Rupert was at a bar in Ellsworth during Caskie's murder and at home watching sports all day when Regina was killed, then who was it who looked just like him and used Rupert's credit card to pay for the room Caskie was found in? If he was truly innocent, then someone had to definitely be setting him up.

Hayley was halfway out the door when she ran into Liddy, who clutched her Gucci handbag, harried and in a rush. She practically pushed Hayley back inside the bar. "Where are you going?"

"Home," Hayley said.

"Not yet. I need to talk to you."

"About what?"

"I need a cosmo first. It's been one of those days." Liddy moaned.

"Tell me about it."

Liddy grabbed Hayley's hand and led her back over to the bar. They sat a few stools away from Rupert so he was out of earshot. Liddy raised her hand to signal Randy that she was in desperate need of a refreshment, and Randy got to work making her usual cocktail. Liddy glanced around to make sure no one was eavesdropping before leaning in close to Hayley. "I sold the Hinkley place down on Derby Lane."

"Congratulations."

"I was hoping for a bidding war, the house is a dream, but the Hinkleys wanted a fast sale, so I had to settle for the first offer that came in, a couple from

New Jersey, the wife's a scientist who's moving here to work at the Jackson Lab."

Hayley waited to hear the rest of her story, but Liddy was already more interested in how long Randy was taking to make her cosmo. He had stopped to chat with a young fisherman who had just strolled into the bar.

Hayley cleared her throat. "Is *that* your big news?"

"No, Hayley, I sell houses practically every day, that's not the headline, I'm just setting the table."

"Sorry, go on."

"I had to mail some signing documents to the couple in Jersey and so I stopped by the post office to send them off, and while I was waiting in line, I could hear Ginny O'Conner, the loudmouth who works there, gossiping with another mail carrier as they were sorting through this big basket of letters and packages, and that's when I heard her mention Regina Knoxville."

"Everyone in town is talking about Regina Knoxville."

Liddy glared at Hayley, not happy that she was questioning the scope and dramatic impact of her news. "Is everyone talking about the extramarital affair Regina was supposedly having?"

"She was cheating on Albert?"

Liddy nodded excitedly. "Apparently Ginny was out delivering mail on her route last week, and when she walked up to the mail slot of a house down on Ash Street, she happened to see through the living room window Regina kissing the man who lives there. And it wasn't the kind of kiss you give your brother or an old friend."

"Ash Street? Who lives on Ash Street?" Hayley's mind was racing. "Mr. Foley?"

"He's literally a hundred years old, Hayley!"

"But he's still in great shape. I heard all the old women

fall all over themselves to sit next to him on bingo night at the senior center."

"It wasn't Mr. Foley! It was next door to Mr. Foley!"

"Let me think. Who lives next door to Mr. Foley?" Hayley thought a few seconds and then suddenly gasped. "Julio? The hairdresser?"

"That's the one."

"But Julio's married!"

"Duh," Liddy cried, slapping her forehead. "So is Regina! That's why they call affairs *extramarital*!"

"Where was Julio's wife?"

"Jeanette . . ."

"Right, Jeanette . . . Why wasn't she around?"

"Because she volunteers three days a week up in Bangor at a children's hospital."

Hayley's head was spinning.

This was potentially big news.

Especially when it came to the circumstances surrounding Regina Knoxville's untimely death.

Randy finally delivered Liddy's cosmo. She grabbed the glass by the stem and downed it. "I so deserve this!"

"What are you two talking about?" Randy asked, curious because they both looked like cats who swallowed a couple of canaries.

"Nothing!" they both exclaimed.

Randy eyed them suspiciously for a moment but then gave up and walked back to his customers seated at the other end of the bar.

Hayley noticed Liddy grimacing. "What's the matter?"

"I just can't believe it . . ."

"I know. Regina and Albert seemed so happy. And so did Julio and Jeanette . . ."

"It's not that! Of course we've heard all the rumors over the years about Julio's secret dalliances, but come on! He's so handsome and manly and muscular! He could have any woman he wants. Why Regina Knoxville? I mean, she looks good, but she's ancient! If he was going to step out on his wife, why wouldn't he pick somebody younger and more alluring like . . ."

"Like *you*?"

"Well, yes!"

"I'm going to pretend you did not just say that!"

"I'm just saying, Hayley, if someone is going to be 'the other woman,' I'm a much more logical choice!"

As much as Hayley wanted to scold Liddy for even considering having an affair with a married man, she knew Liddy wasn't alone. There were a number of single women, not to mention a few married ones, who would have gleefully welcomed the opportunity to embark on an illicit affair with a sexy stud such as Julio.

But apparently, despite that fact, Julio preferred the company of women much older than himself.

Chapter 31

A woman's blood-curdling scream stopped Hayley and Bruce in their tracks as they approached Julio's Salon on Rodick Street. Hayley grabbed Bruce's arm and they both gaped at each other in shock before Bruce bolted forward and charged his way toward the shop to rescue whatever damsel was in distress. Hayley followed on his heels.

An elderly woman in her mid to late seventies, her wet hair still in curlers and a black nylon cape tied around her neck, flew out of the shop, nearly colliding with Bruce and Hayley as she scrambled down the wooden steps that led into the salon. It was Gretchen Maxwell, who worked at a local insurance company and handled Hayley's home and auto policies. "Hayley, you better call the cops before somebody gets killed in there!"

Hayley stared blankly at Gretchen as she pushed her way past them and ran for her car, which was parked in the lot across the street.

Hayley and Bruce exchanged another wary look,

not sure they should enter the salon without police backup, but then another scream and something crashing on the floor propelled them forward and they raced inside, stopping near the reception desk. The entire salon had emptied out of customers, leaving Julio, who was ducking behind one of his hydraulic black leather salon chairs. Across the room, brandishing a curling iron in her fist, was his wife, Jeanette, her face flushed with anger and her eyes blazing.

It didn't take Hayley more than a few seconds to size up the situation. Apparently Liddy wasn't the only one who had heard the latest hot gossip. Word had already spread around town about Julio's possible affair with the late Regina Knoxville. And the news had obviously landed on Jeanette's doorstep.

"Would you please just calm down, Jeanette?" Julio pleaded, peeking out from behind the salon chair.

"Don't tell me what to do, you two-timing fink lothario!" Jeanette cried, hurling the curling iron at him. It flew over him and smacked into the wall mirror, cracking it slightly.

Julio peered up at the crack, aghast. "Look what you did! Do you know how much that's going to cost me to replace?"

"I don't care!" Jeanette wailed. "I just know it won't be coming out of my alimony check!"

Hayley was not completely surprised by the bitter scene unfolding in front of them between Julio and Jeanette. In fact, she had never really expected the marriage to last as long as it had. Jeanette was from a wealthy family who owned a lot of local real estate, and was very spoiled and used to getting what she wanted. She had dated a lot of local boys during her younger years. However, it turned out most of them were more interested in her daddy's money than Jeanette herself. Being rich was her curse. It didn't help that she had a grating personality that put off most people. Still, when the handsome Argentinean hairdresser Julio first arrived in town, Jeanette had set her sights on him immediately. It took a while for her to wear him down, but finally he agreed to go out on a date with her. A lot of locals were skeptical because Julio was such a handsome man, and Jeanette was, well, rather plain to put it politely. It also didn't help that they started dating around the time Julio was looking for a business loan to start his own salon, and Jeanette was happy to gift the twenty grand he needed to get started as an engagement present. The flirty, impossibly sexy Julio was loyal and faithful to his wife for about a year, but then, according to word on the street, he couldn't resist some of the temptations that came waltzing into his shop looking for a cut and dry. Although Julio had successfully kept his suspected dalliances on the down low, his purported exploits kept the gossips in town buzzing on a regular basis, mostly because a lot of his customers relished picturing themselves as "the other woman." Everyone just assumed Jeanette knew what was going on and had accepted it, that perhaps they had some kind of arrangement, but now it was crystal clear the poor little rich girl, now an embittered, betrayed older woman, had been kept in the dark, totally ignorant.

Until now.

Bruce, trying to tamp down the escalating tensions, stepped forward cautiously just as Jeanette scooped up a purple hairbrush off the counter. "Jeanette, why don't you put down the hairbrush, and we will all take a deep breath and talk about whatever is going on here rationally, like adults . . ."

Jeanette flared up like a sudden brush fire. "Nobody

asked you to butt into this, Bruce Linney! Get the hell out of here!" She pitched the hairbrush directly at him, and Bruce practically had to dive out of the way to avoid getting beaned in the forehead.

"Bruce, maybe we should go . . ." Hayley quietly suggested.

"No! Don't leave me alone with her! She's a raging lunatic!" Julio yelled.

Jeanette whipped her head back around toward her husband and stood silently for a moment, processing what he had just said to her. Then she burst into tears, ran to the bathroom in the back of the salon, and locked herself inside.

"You can stay in there all night for all I care!" Julio bellowed before jumping up from his crouching position behind the chair and marching over to Bruce and Hayley, who stood tentatively near the reception desk.

"I am so sorry you had to see that," he said, trying to regain some sense of professionalism. "Sometimes she gets these crazy ideas into her head and I have to talk her down from the ledge."

"I guess somebody told her about you and Regina Knoxville," Hayley said pointedly, anticipating a reaction.

She got one.

Julio bristled and his face darkened. "I do not know what you are talking about. I have never cheated on my wife, if that was what you were implying."

The denial was almost laughable.

"Especially with someone as old . . . I mean as mature as Regina. She was my client here at the salon, that's all."

He was so obviously lying.

Hayley considered presenting him with what Liddy

had told her about Ginny O'Conner delivering mail to the Knoxville house and what she had witnessed, but decided against it. Why rile him up even more?

"You okay, buddy? Your head's bleeding," Bruce noticed.

A trickle of blood was slowly rolling down the left side of Julio's face. He picked up a towel and wiped it off. "Yeah, I'll be fine. She got me in the temple with some thinning shears."

"Ouch," Hayley said, grimacing.

Julio suddenly snapped back to his jovial self, slapping a friendly smile on his face "All this unpleasantness will pass, believe me. Once Jeanette realizes she overreacted and has nothing to worry about, she'll be fine."

"I'm happy to hear that," Hayley said, not buying it.

"Hayley, why don't you call here tomorrow and I'll give you a free shampoo and style, on the house for your inconvenience. You too, Bruce. You could use a trim."

Bruce ran his fingers through his hair. "Really?"

"You just need a little cleanup," Julio said, leading them to the door. It was clear he wanted them to get out of his shop.

Hayley took Bruce's hand. "Let's go, Bruce. Julio, please tell Jeanette I hope she feels better."

"Will do," Julio said with a thin smile.

And then they left. As they headed down the wooden steps, Hayley heard Julio locking the door behind them to prevent anyone else from entering the salon until he had fully regained control of his emotional mess of a wife.

Hayley and Bruce were still talking about what had happened at the salon as they arrived at home and were in the kitchen. Bruce grabbed a beer from the fridge as Hayley opened the oven to see a chicken potpie bubbling on the rack.

"Mom made dinner," she said gratefully.

Bruce popped the top off his Bud Light with a bottle opener. "That was nice of her."

"I'm going to make us a salad," Hayley said, opening the fridge and perusing the vegetable bin. She settled on a head of romaine lettuce, a couple of Persian cucumbers, and some grape tomatoes. As she began chopping the lettuce, Bruce leaned against the counter and said, "So what do you think?"

"You mean do I think Jeanette was the one who planted the hive full of bees that stung Regina Knoxville to death?"

"Makes sense. The vengeful wife going after the woman out to destroy her marriage."

"Well, if the gossips in town are right, there would be about twenty other women in town that Jeanette would have to go after for sleeping with her husband too. What makes Regina so special?"

"Maybe with the others she was totally clueless. You saw how angry she was. This could be the first one she actually found out about."

"It's possible, but improbable. Julio is such a flirt it's hard to imagine she didn't suspect something at some point," Hayley said.

They both heard a creaking sound.

Bruce opened his mouth to say something but Hayley raised her hand, stopping him. She knew that creak. She heard it every time she went up the stairs and her foot hit a certain point on the second to top step.

Bruce mouthed, "What?"

Hayley leaned in and whispered in Bruce's ear. "Somebody is eavesdropping on our conversation."

They waited a few seconds.

"Mom, is that you?"

No answer.

Hayley tiptoed from the kitchen to the hallway and peered up through the railing to see a foot in a slipper perched on the second step. It was definitely Sheila. Leroy was sniffing the slipper and then began licking her bare ankle.

"Mom?"

Sheila knew she was caught and chirped, feigning surprise, "Hayley, I had no idea you were home. I didn't hear you come in. Is Bruce with you?"

"Yes, he is."

Sheila then bounded down the stairs, pretending she had been in her room reading a book or watching the news, but definitely not listening in on their conversation from the top of the staircase. "I cooked dinner. I hope Bruce likes chicken potpie."

"I love it," Bruce said from the kitchen with a knowing smile.

"Oh, good, now tell me all about your day," Sheila said, grabbing the pot holders and opening the oven to check on her casserole.

Julio Garcia was not the only unconvincing liar they had encountered today.

Island Food & Spirits
BY HAYLEY POWELL

It is hardly a typical week in my life if my bestie Mona Barnes doesn't call me with some sort of complaint about her mother, Jane, and last night was certainly no exception.

Mona and her mother are so close that at times they sound just like each other. They tend to finish each other's sentences and mimic the other's mannerisms while in the midst of a conversation. However, when they happen to disagree with each other, boy howdy, watch out! Mona's father once compared their fights to an atomic bomb going off! He would take shelter in the basement until all the screaming and stomping finally came to an end and a truce was called.

No one would ever dispute the fact that Mona and Jane love each other, but that doesn't stop most people from pussyfooting around those two, fearing a brand-new argument could erupt between them at a moment's notice.

Last night Mona called me and the first words out of her mouth after I answered with a cheery "Hello," were "Holy crap! You will never guess what that woman did now!" I immediately made myself a Blueberry Jam Cocktail and settled in my chair out on the deck, getting comfortable for the latest mother-daughter drama.

Mona recounted her harrowing story that had unfolded just hours ago when she was heading to the Shop 'n Save to do her weekly grocery shopping. She saw her mother walking to the store on the street, carrying an armful of her reusable bags. Mona thought it might be fun if she and Jane shopped together and shared a little bonding time. Well, that idea proved to be her fatal mistake. Because from the moment they entered the store and were rolling their carts side by side, laughing about something silly one of Mona's kids had done that day in school, that's when the trouble started.

Every time Mona reached for a grocery item, in this case a bunch of Lunchables for her kids—a couple of Pizza Kabobbles, Mini Hotdogs, and Chicken Dunks, tossing them into her cart—Jane couldn't help but snort her disapproval. Mona chose to ignore it at first. But then there was this annoying constant clicking of her mother's tongue when Mona stockpiled her kids' favorite breakfast cereals in her cart, including Cap'n Crunch, Lucky Charms, and Froot Loops. Jane was sending a clear signal that this was not acceptable breakfast food. But still, she refused to just come out and say it.

After an eye roll from her mother in the bread aisle, when Mona was loading up on four loaves of Wonder Bread, Mona couldn't stand it anymore and grabbed her cart and raced away from her mother, refusing to endure any more of her judgmental looks. In her haste to escape her mother, Mona nearly knocked over the nice lady handing out free cake samples near the snack aisle.

Finally, it all came to a head. Jane caught up with her daughter just as Mona was grabbing box after box of Hostess processed desserts such as Ding Dongs, Suzy Q's, and vanilla Zingers. Jane apparently had finally seen enough. "Oh, dear Lord, Mona, are you *trying* to give my grandchildren type two diabetes?"

Mona was dumbfounded. This was so out of character for her mother, who never cared one whit about what Mona chowed down on as a kid. As long as she didn't get sick, or have too many cavities at the dentist's office, all was good. But *now* she had decided she was some kind of professional nutritionist?

Still, Mona did not want to cause a scene.

"Do we have to do this now?" Mona hissed.

"No wonder those kids of yours just run around not listening to a word you say! They're on a constant sugar high!"

That was the proverbial last straw. It was one thing for Mona to complain about her children, but it was quite another for her own mother, the queen of spoiling her grandkids with candy, cakes, and ice cream, to dare suggest to Mona how she should parent her children.

Mona suddenly snapped and tore open a

box of Sno Balls and started firing them at her mother. Jane, who was as tough and ornery as her daughter, wasn't about to retreat or surrender. Instead, she snatched a box of orange-flavored cupcakes off the shelf, ripped them open and began hurling them back at her daughter. It was an all-out war of flying snack cakes!

The poor woman handing out cake samples had to duck underneath her cardboard table to protect herself from the sweet-tasting artillery flying over her. A few shoppers on both ends of the aisle began cheering them on, some rooting for Mona, others yelling and clapping for Jane.

Luckily, before the shelves were empty, Officer Donnie appeared on the scene to restore order. The startled young policeman had just swung in to pick up a few ingredients for his girlfriend, who fancied herself a budding Martha Stewart. Officer Donnie shouted at Mona and her mother to cease fire as he pushed his way through the crowd.

Unfortunately, due to the cheers and their own shouting, Mona and Jane didn't hear him warning them to stop and he got pelted in the face with a few stray Ho Hos. By the time Officer Donnie had drawn his baton and was flashing his badge, mother and daughter finally decided it might be a good time to stop their public spat, although under their breath they continued blaming the other for starting the cake war.

True to form, Mona and Jane did offer to stick around and clean up the mess after paying for everything, but the store manager politely declined their offer and begged Officer Donnie to just escort them out of the store as quickly as he could. Mona not only paid for all the destroyed snack cakes, but also sent over a case of fresh lobsters to the manager's home as a peace offering (thus also insuring she would not be permanently banned from the Shop 'n Save).

Mother and daughter were back on speaking terms, at least until about three days later, when Jane commented that Mona's new haircut made her look like her cousin Ricky, who still sported a mullet.

Speaking of Jane, I have a great Easy Blueberry Jam recipe today that goes beautifully on her blueberry scones recipe. I also have a fantastic cocktail recipe, so I hope you try them both!

When it is summertime and we are in the heart of blueberry season, you will love this blueberry jam slathered all over your morning toast, or even better, enjoy a blueberry jam cocktail. You can thank me later!

BLUEBERRY JAM PROSECCO COCKTAIL

INGREDIENTS
1½ tablespoons blueberry jam
1 ounce lemon juice
2 ounces vodka
3 ounces Prosecco
Ice

In a cocktail shaker, add the ice and all the ingredients except the Prosecco, shake until well chilled, then strain into an ice-filled cocktail glass, top with the Prosecco, and enjoy.

Easy Breezy Blueberry Jam

Ingredients
2 cups fresh blueberries
¼ cup honey
½ teaspoon cinnamon
1 tablespoon lemon juice

Put all your ingredients into a saucepan and mix together. Bring to a boil, then simmer for 30 to 35 minutes. When the mixture has a jam-like consistency, turn off the heat and store in a jar in the refrigerator until you are ready to enjoy!

Chapter 32

Bonnie Henkel was faced with unbridled skepticism when she first introduced a Zumba class to the YMCA gym. Many of the locals had trouble pronouncing the word, let alone drumming up the interest to actually attend the one-hour workout mixing high and low intensity moves with Latin and world rhythms. After recruiting a few brave souls to partake in her brand-new calorie-burning dance party, word slowly started to spread, and after a few months people were being turned away at the door because the studio could only hold so many people.

Bonnie then expanded her classes, offering different versions including the immensely popular U-Jam Fitness, designed for all ages and fitness levels, a slight twist on Zumba that Bonnie promised would leave you dripping in sweat and glowing with smiles. And she managed to deliver every time. Bonnie herself was upbeat, energetic, and stunningly gorgeous, which would explain the number of men who decided to check her out, or rather check the class out. She had learned Zumba from her college roommate Kamala, who was born in Mumbai and incorporated a lot of songs from Bollywood movies, including her favorite, *Desi Boyz*, from 2011, featuring two men suffering from the recession who decide to make some money as male strippers. It was a giant hit in India, and one of the dance numbers, a rollicking, high energy song called "Make Some Noise for the Desi Boyz" was now a staple in her U-Jam Fitness class and it was blasting through the speakers when Hayley, Liddy, and Mona showed up fifteen minutes late for the class.

The room was packed with about twenty people trying their best to follow Bonnie's lead. Mona took one look at the complicated choreography, and yelled, "I'm out!"

As she turned around to leave, Hayley grabbed her arm. "Where are you going?"

"Your brother's bar for a beer." Mona grunted. "I'm not breaking a hip just so you can talk to Jeanette Garcia."

Liddy eyed Mona's midsection. "Mona, don't you want to drop a few pounds?"

"I'd like to drop about a hundred and fifteen pounds, like right now, but I'm afraid you'd just show up again," Mona growled.

And then she stormed out.

Liddy shook her head. "I don't know why she always insists on being so difficult."

Bonnie had already managed to whip the crowd up into a frenzy, and they were now singing along with the song as they danced. "'Make some noise for the Desi Boyz!'"

Not one of them had probably seen the movie where the song had come from.

Hayley was already scanning the crowd for Jeanette

Garcia. She knew from Liddy, who attended Bonnie's class at least twice a week, that Jeanette was a regular, and so even though Hayley loathed the idea of engaging in any kind of protracted physical activity, let alone something this high energy, she felt it might be the best way to casually approach Jeanette about what had happened with her husband, Julio, at the salon.

"There she is, right up front, near Bonnie," Hayley said.

"Should we move up closer to her?" Liddy asked.

"It would be kind of hard. Those three older ladies are kind of crowding around her . . ." Hayley said, observing the three women in colorful leotards and headbands, as if they had just jumped out of Olivia Newton John's 1980s video "Physical." Suddenly Hayley gasped.

"What is it?" Liddy asked.

"You don't recognize them?"

"How could I? Their backs are to us . . ." Liddy's voice trailed off and then she grimaced. "Oh God, that's my mother."

"And mine. And Mona's," Hayley groaned.

"What are they doing here?"

"I knew my mother was eavesdropping on my conversation with Bruce when we got home last night. She heard me talking about Jeanette's fight with Julio at the salon, and how it probably involved Regina, so she's recruited her fellow Golden Girls to hunt her down here and question her."

Liddy scoffed. "Of all the nerve! Look at them stalking poor Jeanette and surrounding her like that! They're like tigers trying to separate an unsuspecting spotted deer from the herd!"

"You watch too many nature shows, Liddy. And to be fair, that's exactly what we're trying to do too," Hayley said.

"That's not true! I really am here for the workout. I had a double scoop of the blueberry sour cream crumble at Mount Desert Island Ice Cream between open houses today."

"Okay, fine, *I'm* the stalker, but we're already here, so we might as well find out as much as we can. Come on!"

They weaved their way through the crowd of people jumping around the room. Liddy got slapped in the head by an overzealous grandmother who was swinging her arms around, trying to keep up with Bonnie. Hayley ducked and managed to avoid colliding with a couple of elderly men who were busy leering at Bonnie and were not paying attention to where they were swinging their loose limbs.

When Hayley and Liddy finally reached the front, Hayley couldn't help but notice Bonnie staring at her with wide eyes, full of wonderment. She didn't need a psychic to tell her what Bonnie was thinking. What on earth was Hayley Powell doing in her class? Truth be told, Hayley would expect that reaction from anyone who was a personal trainer, taught a yoga class, or was just a regular gym goer. Hayley was certainly not known around town for being a jock.

Hayley and Liddy fell in behind Sheila, Celeste, and Jane, who were desperately trying to follow the choreography with decidedly mixed results. Jane was moving about three steps slower than the rest of the class, trudging along, her face puffy and red. Celeste was going in all kinds of directions, pretending to be as skilled as a Fosse dancer, but coming off more like someone suffering from an epileptic seizure. And then there was Sheila, who remarkably was the most adept of the three at U-Jam Fitness, surprising even herself as she moved in concert with Bonnie, swiveling her hips, sweating profusely, and genuinely enjoying herself.

At one point, Bonnie signaled everyone to turn around and face the wall as they walked and clapped to the music, and that's when Sheila suddenly noticed Hayley, who was late in turning and was still facing her mother when she spun around.

"Hayley!" Sheila gasped.

"Hi, Mom," Hayley said, waving sheepishly.

The shock of Hayley in an exercise class threw Sheila off, and she fell behind in the choreography and got frustrated. Finally, she gave up and walked over to where she had draped a towel over a chair. She wiped the sweat off her face, and marched back over to Hayley, who was apparently hopeless when it came to picking up the steps.

"This is the *last* place I ever thought I'd see *you*," Sheila said, studying Bonnie's moves so she could join in with the rest of the crowd again.

"I thought it was time I got back into shape," Hayley said, never expecting her mother to believe that.

And she didn't.

"Hayley, please. Don't insult my intelligence. I've always been able to tell when you're lying. Ever since you were a little girl. That's why you never got away with anything."

"You have no idea what I got away with," Hayley said.

"I knew you threw a big party the police had to break up that time when your father and I went to visit his uncle in Dixmont and you tried to tell me you just had Liddy and Mona over for a slumber party."

"Yes, and you believed me until Dad found the beer line from the keg behind the couch!"

Sheila couldn't rebut this claim because she knew it

was true. A stern look from Bonnie, who was annoyed they were disrupting her class by standing still and having a conversation, forced Hayley and Sheila to resume dancing once again.

After an excruciating forty more minutes, Bonnie shifted gears into a cooldown with some slower moves and light stretching to Prince's "Kiss" and then the class was finally, mercifully over.

Celeste wasted no time in racing over and buttering up Jeanette. "I was so happy I was behind you, Jeanette! I just watched you and followed along! You are so good at this!"

Jeanette beamed. "Thank you, Celeste. The more you do it, the easier it gets."

"I'm really looking forward to your Tupperware party tomorrow evening!" Jane cooed.

"I'm glad you talked me into it," Jeanette said.

"What Tupperware party?" Hayley asked.

Jeanette suddenly noticed Hayley, and her mood changed. She became a little awkward and embarrassed. She was still smarting from the loud scene with her husband at the salon the previous day that Hayley had witnessed. She grabbed her towel and bottle of water and muttered, "You're welcome to come if you want, Hayley."

And then she raced out of the studio.

Sheila watched her go, a triumphant look on her face.

"I'm guessing the Tupperware party was *your* idea?" Hayley asked her mother pointedly.

"Actually, it was Celeste's. She can be so brilliant," Sheila gushed.

"You convinced Jeanette to throw a Tupperware party so you three can get inside her house and search for evidence that will prove she killed Regina Knoxville," Hayley said, folding her arms.

"That's right," Celeste said, dabbing at her face with a plush pink towel. "Besides, she's always coming to the parties at my house and not once has she ever hosted one. That's how we got her. Pure guilt."

"I don't believe it," Hayley said, shaking her head.

"You're just sorry *you* didn't think of it," Sheila said as she passed her daughter and headed toward the exit.

Hayley couldn't argue with Sheila because in this particular case her mother was absolutely right.

Chapter 33

It was standing room only at Jeanette Garcia's hastily planned Tupperware party and orders were being placed fast and furious. The brightly colored retro chic Impressions Classic Bowl Set was the top seller, but Hayley found herself getting caught up in the festive, almost frenzied atmosphere and bought herself four microwave-reheatable cereal bowls, a Classic Sheer Pitcher in sky blue, large hourglass salt and pepper shakers, and three snack cups. At one point, Mona, who was too cheap to buy anything, and Liddy, whose cupboards were already overflowing with life-time-guarantee products from previous Tupperware parties she had attended, had to remind her why they were here in the first place.

Hayley noticed Sheila, Celeste, and Jane huddled near the fireplace, quietly conversing out of earshot of the other guests, who were spread about the room handling the items for sale, indulging their sweet tooths with the trays of cookies, cakes, and brownies Jeanette had set out on the dining room table, and engaging in the town's latest gossip, much of it, of course, involving the recent untimely deaths of two of their own, Caskie Lemon-Hogg and Regina Knoxville.

When it appeared that Jeanette was about to wrap up her orders, Celeste and Jane made a beeline for her, armed with some round storage containers and a flurry of questions. Hayley knew exactly what the ladies were up to. The plan was for Celeste and Jane to keep Jeanette occupied while Sheila searched for any evidence that might link her to Regina's death. Sure enough, Hayley spotted her mother creeping up the stairs, her eyes darting back and forth, making sure that no one saw her slipping away from the party.

Hayley groaned. "She just won't stop . . ."

"Who?" Liddy asked.

"My mother. I just saw her sneaking upstairs to search the bedrooms. Honestly, what makes her think she can just go around playing detective?"

"Beats me," Mona said. "What makes you think *you* can do it?"

Hayley glared at Mona.

Mona threw her hands up. "I'm just saying you got it from somewhere. Makes perfect sense."

"Well, I'm not going to just stand here and let her ransack the place on her own," Hayley said. "I'm going up there. You two stay down here and make sure Jeanette doesn't come up while we're poking around, okay?"

"Finally, something to do. This is the worst party ever. You'd think she'd serve booze or something to loosen people up so they'd buy more," Mona said.

"Mona, it's eleven thirty in the morning," Liddy said.

"What's your point?" Mona growled.

"It's a little too early for cocktails," Liddy snapped.

Mona turned to Hayley. "She's such a hypocrite. Remember the time we were having brunch on the patio of Eggs-istential, that new breakfast spot in town, one Sunday morning and Liddy saw some people going into your brother's bar across the street, and she went on and on about how sad it was that people had to drink so early in the day as she gulped down her third mimosa?"

Hayley chuckled. "Yes, I remember. Now keep watch and I'll be back down soon."

Hayley turned to make sure Jeanette was preoccupied with her party guests, and then she hurried up the staircase. Upstairs in the hallway, she heard some rummaging coming from the master bedroom and walked in to find Sheila searching the drawers of Julio and Jeanette's dresser.

"Find anything interesting?" Hayley asked.

Sheila screamed and jumped back.

"Mom, keep your voice down or Jeanette will hear you!"

"Well, don't sneak up on me like that! What are you doing here?"

"Same as you. Looking for clues. I cannot believe I am actually competing with my own mother to solve this case."

"I have no choice, Hayley. Celeste, Jane, and I have to clear our names; otherwise we'll never escape this heavy cloud of suspicion."

"You were specifically ordered by Sergio to stay out of it, and yet you continually refuse to listen. You're just asking for trouble! If you don't wise up, you're all going to wind up in jail again, this time for obstruction of justice!"

"Would you please relax, Hayley? I was invited here. There is no breaking and entering this time."

She had a point.

And Hayley didn't want to waste any more time because the party was threatening to break up soon.

"Okay, fine, we'll cover more ground if we both look around. Did you already check the closet?"

"No, just the nightstand and this dresser."

Hayley sighed and marched over to the large walk-in closet. One side was devoted to Jeanette's entire wardrobe, the other side was filled with Julio's shirts, pants, suits, and shoes. She got down on her hands and knees and looked behind some boxes and found some cashmere sweaters from Macy's that Jeanette had not even taken out of the bag yet. She then crawled over to Julio's side and looked behind some luggage but found nothing. She stood back up and started whipping through a row of suits on hangers when something caught her eye just above her. It looked like a cat at first or some kind of animal perched on the top shelf. She gasped, surprised, but it didn't move. When she reached up to touch it, she suddenly realized it wasn't alive, it was a folded-up fake gray beard. Hayley smoothed it out and then carried it out of the closet to where her mother was just closing the last drawer in the dresser.

Sheila turned around and crinkled her nose. "What's that?"

"A fake beard."

Sheila studied it. "It looks just like the one . . ."

"Rupert Stiles has."

"The desk clerk at the bed-and-breakfast said the man who checked in using Rupert's credit card had a long gray beard."

"I don't understand. Julio was supposedly having an affair with Regina, not Caskie."

Hayley looked at the beard. "What if Julio was having an affair with more than one woman?"

"Regina *and* Caskie?"

Hayley nodded. "Jeanette could have found out about both affairs and gone into a jealous rage."

Sheila pointed to the beard. "You mean Jeanette somehow lifted Rupert's credit card and then disguised herself as a man who looked like Rupert . . . ?"

"They're both about the same height . . . She could have sent Caskie a message, pretending to be Julio asking her to meet him. Caskie may have already been on her way over there looking for you when she got it and—"

"Jeanette strangled her to death and then moved on to Regina . . ."

Hayley snapped her fingers. "I bet if we keep searching we'll find a pair of gloves and maybe some netting she used to protect herself from the bees!"

Sheila's phone buzzed and she checked it. "We have to go back downstairs now!"

"Why?"

"Jane just texted me. She and Celeste got into an argument downstairs with Mona and Liddy and they lost track of Jeanette!"

"What?"

Hayley's phone suddenly buzzed.

It was a text from Liddy.

Get out!

Hayley and Sheila both spun around to flee from the bedroom when they both gasped at the sight of Jeanette standing in the doorway, a stern look on her face.

"What are you doing up here?"

"I'm sorry?" Sheila asked, her voice cracking, in a desperate bid to buy them more time so they could come up with some kind of reasonable answer.

"You forgot to properly fill out your order form,

Sheila. You didn't include your address or credit card information, so I've been looking all over for you."

Sheila's lips quivered slightly, panic rising, before a lightbulb seemed to pop on in her head. "You know, I've always admired your style, Jeanette. I wish I had half the fashion sense you do, and I was downstairs telling Hayley how I want to refresh my wardrobe, and the next thing you know we were up here looking for a few ideas. I hope that's all right."

Hayley had to hand it to her mother. Her quick-thinking excuse wasn't half as lame as she had expected it to be.

Jeanette, however, wasn't quite buying it.

Especially since Hayley was still holding the gray beard.

"What are you doing with that?" Jeanette asked, eyes narrowing.

Hayley held up the scraggly fake beard. "This?"

"Yes," Jeanette muttered impatiently.

"It fell off the shelf and nearly scared me half to death. I thought it was an animal and I was just going to put it back—"

Jeanette knew she was lying and she cut her off. "It's part of a Halloween costume Julio wore last year. He went as Gandolf the Grey from the *Lord of the Rings* movies. I went as Galadriel, the Lady of the Wood. Cate Blanchett played her in the movie."

Hayley nodded and managed to squeak out a soft, "Oh . . ."

"We looked fabulous and we took lots of selfies that night and posted them on Facebook. You should definitely take a look sometime," Jeanette said, challenging her to do just that.

Sheila walked over to Jeanette and snatched the order form out of her hand. "Well, I better go find a pen and take care of this right away. I don't want any delay in getting my new Tupperware."

She scurried out the door.

Hayley sheepishly stepped forward and handed the fake beard to Jeanette. "I'm sure you made a spectacular Galadriel."

And then she quickly followed her mother back down the stairs. It was a believable explanation. But just like Jeanette, who failed to buy the flimsy excuse that Hayley and her mother were snooping around in her bedroom for fashion tips, Hayley wasn't about to buy the Halloween costume story.

At least not yet.

Chapter 34

Hayley leaned against the bar at Drinks Like a Fish later that afternoon and quietly absorbed what Rupert Stiles had just told her. She was not entirely surprised, but it still raised her suspicions, enough so that she thought she better hear it again just to be sure.

"You told him what?"

Rupert, who was hunched over on his bar stool, clutching his glass as if he was holding on to it for dear life, took a generous swig of the whiskey, and then turned to Hayley with his vacant, watery eyes. He had probably been drinking for quite some time. "I told him I've pretty much been in love with Regina Knoxville my whole life."

"Julio Garcia."

Rupert nodded. "Yup."

"When did this happen?"

"In his shop. I got my beard trimmed a few weeks ago. I go in once a year in the summer and he cleans it up a bit before I let it grow long during the fall and inter months. Keeps me warm. But by spring, the dang thing is practically down to my kneecaps."

"How did the topic of Regina Knoxville even come up?"

"Because she was there."

"In the salon?"

"Yup. Two chairs down from me. She couldn't hear us talking though, on account of her being underneath one of Julio's old-fashioned hair dryers. Julio noticed me staring at her through the mirror, and he asked if I had a little crush on Regina. Well, I told him I'd been carrying a torch for her ever since we met on the playground in the fifth grade. She didn't pay me much mind though, back then. Fact is, like I told you before, she's never paid me much mind, ever. Except to laugh at me. Still, all these years, right up until the day she died, whenever I'd see her my heart would get this little flutter."

Hayley hadn't expected to learn such a revelation when she first arrived at her brother's bar to meet Bruce for a drink after work and saw Rupert at the far end of the bar singing along to an old Reba McEntire ditty playing on the jukebox. She had decided to just stop by and say hello, but then the topic of Regina Knoxville came up and not long after that Rupert had made this stunning admission. It wasn't proof of anything, but it sure was odd that Rupert had at one point been arrested for Caskie Lemon-Hogg's murder and that Hayley may have uncovered some circumstantial evidence that Julio or his wife may have been involved. But the gray beard Hayley had found in the closet connected one or both of them to Caskie Lemon-Hogg's murder, not Regina Knoxville's killing. Still, someone was trying very hard to pin Caskie Lemon-Hogg's murder on Rupert. And maybe that same person was going to try to do the same with Regina Knoxville's murder, knowing Rupert had long-simmering, unrequited feelings for her that could have somehow given way to bitter resentment.

A thought popped into Hayley's head and she leaned in closer to Rupert. "When exactly did you notice your credit card was missing?"

"Let me think," Rupert said, scratching his beard and then taking another swig of his whiskey. "Might have been later that day, after I got my beard trimmed, I'm not sure. I kept meaning to call and cancel the card, but I got to drinking and forgot all about it."

Perhaps Caskie's killer had counted on that.

The desk clerk's description of the gray-bearded man and Rupert's actual credit card being used to reserve the room was enough to get him arrested. The killer just didn't expect him to have such an airtight alibi, since Rupert spent much of his time alone and inebriated at home.

Hayley strongly suspected that both murders were connected, but how? There was nothing yet that suggested Rupert was responsible for strategically placing that beehive near where Regina Knoxville was picking blueberries. Besides, according to him, he was allergic to bees too.

At that moment, Bruce breezed through the door of the bar, late as usual. He signaled Randy to get him a bottle of Stella Artois since Bruce hated the flat taste of beer from the tap. Hayley squeezed Rupert's arm and thanked him for talking to her, and then she made a beeline over to Bruce. He noticed she didn't have a cocktail in her hand.

"This is a first. No drink. Since when are you on the wagon?"

"I got distracted. I think Julio Garcia is trying to frame Rupert Stiles for both murders!"

"Whoa, hold on. What? Why?"

"Well, we know Julio was having an affair with Regina. Maybe the whole thing went south and there was some reason he wanted to get rid of her—"

"And so he just trotted out to the park with a bee-hive, hoping the bees would target Regina? That's insane! And how does that frame Rupert?"

"It doesn't. Not yet. But Rupert admitted he still carried a torch for Regina, and maybe Julio was going to plan to use that against him . . ."

"Yes, but, Hayley, Rupert was arrested for Caskie's murder, not Regina's. It doesn't make a lick of sense."

"I know. But the gray beard I found in Julio's closet, the credit card Julio could have easily swiped when Rupert was in the salon getting his beard trimmed . . . all the signs keep pointing back to him . . ."

"But why frame Rupert for Caskie's murder? I understand why he would use Rupert to cover his tracks for Regina. But as far as we know, Rupert didn't care about Caskie at all, so why set him up for that one?"

"I don't know. We're still missing some pieces of the puzzle." Hayley ran the facts over in her mind again. "But what if Julio was having affairs with both Caskie and Regina, and they found out about each other and things got out of hand and Julio was afraid they would tell Jeanette?"

"It's not possible," Bruce said.

"Why not?"

"Because Julio wasn't attracted to Caskie Lemon-Hogg. He told me so himself when he was cutting my hair a couple of months ago, and Caskie was at the cash register causing a scene, claiming she had been overcharged for some skin creams she had bought on her last visit, which she had seen for half the price on Amazon. I remember Julio specifically telling me he didn't like women taller than himself, especially tall women who talked too loud, like Caskie."

"He could have made an exception."

"Trust me, he was pretty emphatic about it. I'm sorry, babe, but there is no way Julio would ever have an affair with Caskie, which blows a big wide hole through your theory."

"Then what did he have against her? Other than her complaints about him charging too much for a bottle of facial cream?"

"That's hardly a reason to kill her."

"It still could be Jeanette," Hayley suggested.

"But if Julio was sleeping with Regina, why would the scorned wife kill Caskie?"

Hayley sighed, frustrated. "I don't know . . ."

The questions just kept piling up.

With no concrete answers in sight.

Chapter 35

The next day at the *Island Times* office, Hayley sat at her desk, working her way through her in-box, answering a few emails, and fielding a handful of calls from business owners interested in placing ads in upcoming issues. All in all, it was a pretty typical if not exciting day at the local daily paper. That lasted until about ten thirty, when her phone rang and she had the regrettable misfortune of picking it up.

"*Island Times*, this is Hayley."

"Hayley, this is Julio Garcia."

She was caught a little off guard and couldn't help but feel slightly nervous. She assumed Jeanette had told him how she had caught Hayley snooping around in their walk-in closet and perhaps he was calling to chew her out and tell her to mind her own business. But as it turned out, that wasn't why he was calling at all.

"Yes, Julio, how can I help you today?" Hayley said tentatively.

"You need to come over to the salon right now and pick up your mother!"

"My mother? I'm sorry, I'm a little confused. Is she there for a hair appointment?"

"No! I don't want her business! I don't want her in my shop! I want her gone!"

"Can you please put her on the phone?"

"Come and get her right now, Hayley!"

"But I really don't understand—"

"Come now or I am going to call the police!"

Julio hung up.

Hayley knew that whatever her mother had done was probably bad, and the last thing she or her mother needed was Sergio or any of his officers involved again, so she shot up from her desk, grabbed her bag, and raced out the door, hoping she would manage to get back to the office before anyone noticed she had been gone.

Once she was behind the wheel of her car, it was roughly a four-minute drive to Julio's Salon, and when she pulled up in front, through the window she could see a commotion happening inside. Julio was waving his arms around, screaming, while her mother stood defiantly by a shelf of his beauty products, her arms folded.

Hayley jumped out of her car and raced up the steps and into the shop. A few women, in various stages of having their hair done, all stared at Julio yelling and presumably cursing in Spanish as Sheila stared him down, not budging an inch.

Finally, when Julio stopped for a moment to catch his breath and noticed Hayley standing in the doorway, staring numbly at him berating her mother, he sighed.

"Hayley, thank you for coming." He gestured toward Sheila. "Here, take her."

"Mom, what's going on?"

"I just asked him a simple question and suddenly he just went crazy."

Hayley took a step forward, not anxious to get involved, but she knew she didn't have much of a choice. She already was involved. "What did you ask him?"

Sheila hesitated and then mumbled, "I don't want to set him off again. He gets so dramatic and the veins on his forehead pop out."

Hayley looked to Julio and noticed her mother was right about his protruding veins.

Julio said under his breath, "She asked me if I was having a secret affair with Caskie Lemon-Hogg . . ."

Hayley whipped around to her mother. "What?"

Sheila shrugged. "I was curious. It's not my fault he has such a short fuse. I guess that's why everyone says Spanish men are so hot-blooded."

"I'm not Spanish! I'm from Argentina!"

"Isn't that basically the same thing?" Sheila asked innocently.

"No, it is not!" Julio cried, raising his hands as if he was about to wrap them around Sheila's throat.

"See, it looks like he wants to strangle me. I find it rather strange that the police say Caskie died of strangulation, don't you?" Sheila remarked casually to the other ladies in the salon, not the least bit concerned that Julio might actually physically attack her at any moment.

Julio immediately dropped his hands to his sides. He didn't need his other customers getting it into their heads he had a violent temper.

This was not good. Sheila had no business riling up

Julio, who, in her mind, was a strong suspect for at least the Regina Knoxville murder. It is always smarter to lull the suspect into a false sense of security, let him feel as if he is getting away with his crimes, and eventually he will let his guard down and make a mistake. But with Sheila constantly insisting on confronting everyone, from Owen Meyers, to Caskie herself, to now Julio, she had everyone on edge.

"Come on, Mom, I think we should just go," Hayley said.

"I'm not going anywhere until he gives me an answer. I'm tired of everyone thinking I'm the one who killed Caskie," Sheila barked, still not budging.

"How did you even get the idea in your head that Julio and Caskie were romantically involved?" Hayley asked, thoroughly confused.

"As you know, I have been investigating on my own, with Celeste and Jane's help, of course, and we uncovered evidence—"

Julio's veins started popping again. "What *evidence*? There is no evidence because I have never touched a hair on Caskie Lemon-Hogg's head!"

"Well, we know that's a lie right there, because you're her *hairdresser*!" Sheila said calmly.

The other ladies in the salon nodded in agreement.

"It's a figure of speech!" Julio cried. "Of course I touched her hair . . . but *just* her hair!"

It suddenly dawned on Hayley where this had to be coming from. When Hayley and Bruce returned home from Randy's bar the night before, they were still discussing the theory of Julio's involvement with both women, even though Bruce had heard from Julio himself that he was not the least bit attracted to Caskie. In the kitchen, as they made themselves a late-night snack, Hayley threw out the possibility that Julio could have been lying to Bruce to cover his tracks. Maybe he was just pretending not to be interested in Caskie in order to keep their affair a secret. Bruce dismissed that theory because he felt in his gut Julio had told him the truth. And since Hayley was now acutely aware that her mother had been making a habit of eavesdropping on their conversations, she could only assume that Sheila was planted at the top of the stairs again, straining her ears to hear every word. And she had probably decided in that moment to get to the bottom of it herself. And now here Hayley was, standing in the middle of Julio's Salon, trying to defuse a rather combustible situation.

Julio, frustrated, spun around and shouted something in Spanish. After a moment, his cousin Juan poked his head out from behind a black curtain that led to the supply room, where he had obviously escaped to, hoping to avoid getting enmeshed in all the swirling drama.

Julio stomped his foot, and directed Juan to come over to where he was standing with Hayley and Sheila. Juan shyly trudged across the salon, all eyes in the shop watching him.

Julio yelled something in Spanish, but then caught himself, and repeated it in English. "Juan, tell these ladies where I was on the night Caskie Lemon-Hogg was killed at the bed-and-breakfast over on Mount Desert Street!"

Juan shuffled his feet, his eyes downcast, and mumbled, "Here at the shop."

"And how do you know that?" Julio asked.

"Because I was here with you . . ." Juan said shyly.

Sheila shook her head and scoffed. "Oh, please. He's your cousin. Of course he would try and cover for you—"

Hayley shot a scolding look at her mother. "Mom!"

Julio nudged Juan. "Go on."

Juan finally raised his eyes to meet Hayley's but didn't dare look anywhere near Sheila's direction. He was clearly frightened by her. He focused on Hayley because she appeared to be the more reasonable one. "He was training me. He had me work on one of those . . . man . . . man . . ." He turned to his cousin. "What are they called?"

"Mannequin training heads," Julio answered. "Go on. Show them."

Juan trotted back behind the black curtain and emerged a few seconds later carrying a mannequin head with a sleek long bob with curves and side-swept bang.

Julio smiled proudly. "See? What a nice job! He did it all by himself! I just supervised and gave him a few pointers."

Sheila still wasn't buying the story. "That doesn't prove a thing. Where's the security tape showing you were *really* here? Where are the witnesses who happened to pass by the shop and saw you both in here working late?"

Julio's popping veins returned with a vengeance every time he heard the sound of Sheila's voice, but he kept his temper in check and said evenly, "No one actually saw us, but a few customers called the landline to make appointments while we were here. I will give you their names. I am sure they would be happy to swear they talked to me personally."

Hayley gently took her mother by the arm. It was time to go. She smiled at Julio and Juan. "Thank you for your time."

Julio didn't answer her. He turned his back on them and hurried over to the three clients who had been trapped in the shop watching the whole ugly scene unfold, offering them free jars of his personalized cleansing purifying scrub with sea salt for their inconvenience.

As Hayley and her mother turned to leave, the door flew open and Liddy rushed in, her phone clamped to her ear. "I'm on the verge of a bidding war, so you tell your client that offering the asking price is a surefire way of *not* getting the house of his dreams!" She ended the call and shoved the phone back in her purse, then approached Juan, whom she saw first as he stood awkwardly by the register, still holding the mannequin head. "Julio, you have to help me! I have an open house in an hour and my hair looks like a rat's nest!"

"I'm Juan . . ." he said.

"Oh, you look *just* like Julio . . ." Liddy noted before finally noticing Hayley and Sheila. "I was going to call you. It's been a bear of a day. Let's meet for lunch so I can calm down with a glass of chardonnay. Is one o'clock good for you?"

Hayley nodded, but her mind was elsewhere. There was something about Liddy mistaking Juan for Julio that suddenly got her attention. They did look alike. And they also sounded alike. If she closed her eyes, she would have difficulty identifying who was speaking, which in her mind left open the possibility that Juan could have easily answered those phone calls and pretended to be his cousin.

Julio's alibi suddenly wasn't so airtight.

Island Food & Spirits
BY HAYLEY POWELL

When my son, Dustin, was born, I not only found myself juggling a newborn baby, but also a rambunctious toddler and a high-maintenance husband who was constantly bouncing from job to job looking for the next best thing. It was a particularly trying time, and after a few weeks, I finally hit my breaking point. My husband, Danny, had called me one morning on his break from his job at a local convenience store, and summarily announced he was quitting his job so he could, as he put it, "direct my creative side in a more positive direction." It was lucky for him that before I could open my mouth to respond, Dustin, who I was holding at the time, began spewing formula everywhere within a four-foot radius. It was like a scene right out of *The Exorcist.*

I quickly put Dustin down in the pack and play and ran to the kitchen for some towels, and that's where I found Gemma on the floor making snow angels in five pounds of flour, which she had somehow gotten down from the cupboard, the same cupboard that I had been begging her father to put a safety latch on for the past two years. I stood there for a moment, feeling horribly overwhelmed, and then I did what any new mother would do—I started to cry.

Then I called my mother.

My mother arrived within twenty minutes and immediately brought my house back to order. My two babies were clean, fed, and put down for a nap, and my mother insisted that I go lie down and get some rest too, while she prepared supper for that evening.

I was finally able to relax, knowing everyone was clean, quiet, and happy. Just as I was drifting off to sleep, my thoughts turned to Danny and I quickly jolted up in bed. Danny! He would be home soon. And he was not a big fan of my mother's! They had had a huge falling-out right after I came home from the hospital after giving birth to Dustin. Mom had offered to come and stay with us for a few days to help us settle in with the new baby and look after Gemma, but Danny put a stop to it before she even got one foot in the door. The problem was Mom and Danny never really liked each other. But now that he was refusing to allow her in the house for an extended period of time, well, that just added fuel to the fire.

I decided that Danny was a grown adult and was tough enough to make it through one evening meal with his mother-in-law. He would just have to grin and bear it for the sake of the kids, since she was going to always be their grandmother.

Dinner that evening was surprisingly un-eventful, and Mom and Danny were actually acting civil toward one another, so I was start-ing to feel a little more relaxed. Mom had made her special warm blueberry snack cake and Danny was clearly enjoying it.

And that's when the trouble started. Danny was happily scarfing down his second piece of cake when my mother unexpectedly an-nounced that she was definitely going to be staying for a while to help out, because I obvi-ously needed her help adjusting to having two children, and with everything I had to do alone around the house, since Danny was ob-viously no help, she was not going to take no for an answer. She stared pointedly at Danny as she spoke, and he did open his mouth to protest, but in the end he thought better of it, and just choked down the rest of his blue-berry snack cake in silence.

I pretended to be asleep when Danny fi-nally came to bed later that night because I didn't want to hear him complain or start a fight between us about my mother. I just prayed that it would all work out.

It didn't.

I woke up late the next morning because my mother let me sleep in while she attended to the kids. I had a weird feeling in the pit of my stomach, like something bad was about to happen. I got out of bed and made my way downstairs. I could practically hear the famil-iar drumbeat of war.

Danny was stretched out on the couch in the living room, casually reading the newspaper while my mother was vacuuming all around his feet. It was clear from their stiff body language that neither one of them was willing to budge for the other. I could see the battle lines being drawn. I knew at that point the situation was only going to get worse. Danny was not a happy camper.

I, on the other hand, loved having my mother around, helping out during the day. It was fun and we were enjoying each other, taking walks with the kids, sitting around catching up; and having her there doing all the cooking and cleaning was literally a dream come true. But as soon as Danny walked through the door at the end of his shift, the two of them were like attack dogs ready to pounce on each other. But giving credit where credit is due, they both did try their best to hold their tongues, at least until the kids were tucked safely into their beds. Then the barbs and jabs began to fly!

My mother relished saying things like "You're lazy," "You're such a slob," "Why don't you want to work like most able-bodied men?" Danny came back with "You meddle too much," "You're overbearing," "You are a real pain in the . . ." Well, you get the picture.

It all came to a boil about a week later, when I came down the stairs after putting the kids to bed and found the two of them shouting at each other about how to do the dishes properly.

Enough was enough. I stormed into the kitchen just as my mother was pestering Danny about how he was washing the pan wrong and

Danny's face was so red I thought his head was about to explode. I was just about ready to hurl my body in between them before they went for each other's throats when suddenly, in what felt like slow motion, Danny grabbed the sink sprayer, turned around, and nailed my mother with a torrent of water squarely in the face. And he didn't stop. He kept dousing her until she was sputtering and coughing and throwing her hands up in front of her face to protect herself.

"Danny!" I cried.

That snapped him out of it and he stopped. It's as if he had been in some kind of trance, like his whole body had been momentarily taken over by a devilish spirit. He looked surprised at what he had done and dropped the sprayer into the sink.

My mother stood there with her hair and face dripping wet, a shocked look on her face. For a full minute it was deadly silent in the kitchen as the two of them simply stared at one another. I considered calling the police, fearing they might kill each other.

But then my mother started to laugh. Danny looked more than a little relieved and started to chuckle too. Well, the next thing I knew, they were collapsing in each other's arms, barely able to breathe because they were laughing so hard.

I just wanted to throttle the both of them as I stared at my practically flooded kitchen floor.

I wish I could say Mom and Danny became best friends after that, but they didn't. There were more slights and insults and sharp comments over the next few years, but I will say as far as the kids were concerned, the two of them were always on their best behavior around them and I am grateful for that. I am also thankful for the two recipes my mother shared with me during that brief time that she stayed with us—her delicious blueberry snack cake and her refreshing blueberry smoothie, both featuring her favorite fruit—you guessed it—blueberries!

Easy Breezy Blueberry Smoothie

INGREDIENTS
1½ cups milk (or almond milk)
Half of a banana
1½ cups blueberries
¾ cup Greek vanilla yogurt

Place all your ingredients into a blender and blend until smooth. Pour into a glass and enjoy a refreshing smoothie for breakfast or snack.

Blueberry Coffee Cake

Cake
Ingredients
2 cups blueberries
2 teaspoons baking powder
2 cups flour
½ teaspoon salt
¼ cup oil
¾ cup milk
1 egg
1 cup sugar
1 teaspoon vanilla extract

Crumble Topping
Ingredients
⅓ cup sugar
½ cup flour
1 teaspoon cinnamon
4 tablespoons butter cut into small cubes

Preheat your oven to 375 degrees F. Spray a
9-inch baking dish with nonstick spray. In a bowl
mix your flour, baking powder, and salt together.

In the bowl of a stand mixer beat together the
egg, oil, sugar, and vanilla until well mixed, then
alternate adding the flour and milk until
combined. Batter will be thick. Gently fold in
your two cups of blueberries with a spatula just
until combined.

Spread your batter into the prepared baking dish.
Make your crumble topping by adding the sugar,

flour, cinnamon, and cubed butter to a small bowl and mix together with a fork or your fingers to crumble the mixture together, then pour all over your batter, trying to cover as much as you can.

Bake cake for 40 minutes until topping is golden brown and when you insert a toothpick in the center it comes out clean.

Cool for at least 20 minutes, then slice, serve, and enjoy.

Chapter 36

Hayley could feel her face burning as she sat upright in the chair across from Bruce, who was behind his desk, tapping keys on his computer. "Who is this woman again?"

Bruce smiled dumbly as he stared at her picture on the screen. "Sofia Ortiz."

"And how did you meet her?"

"One summer during college I went backpacking through South America with some buddies of mine, and I met Sofia when she was working as a local tour guide in Mendoza, Argentina, and we became friends."

"I see," Hayley said tightly. "How close of a friend?"

Bruce laughed. "I was a college kid on a world adventure and she was a beautiful girl who liked my eyes and said I made her laugh. You do the math."

Hayley stood up and crossed around the desk to get a look at her picture on Bruce's computer screen. It appeared to be a recent photo since she was roughly Bruce's age, but she was still a stunning beauty, with long raven hair and flawless skin. "She's gorgeous."

"Yeah, she hasn't aged a bit," Bruce said absently.

Hayley shot Bruce a look and then said, "I just find it odd you never mentioned her before."

"Well, she and I met so long ago and we certainly don't communicate that often . . ."

"Still . . ."

Bruce looked up from his computer and gave her a broad grin. "I love it when you get jealous."

"I'm not jealous," Hayley lied.

"You're jealous."

"I'm not."

"I know you, Hayley."

"Well, obviously you don't know me as well as you think you do or you would know that I am definitely not the jealous type. Now Liddy, there's the jealous type."

"Okay, let's agree to disagree," Bruce said with a wink.

"I'm not jealous."

"You already said that. People who aren't jealous don't have to say it so much."

Hayley decided to push forward, fearing they would remain in this conversation, running in circles. "Okay, fine. So you met her in Argentina, during college, and she just reached out to you after all these years out of the blue?"

"No, I was the one who reached out to her," Bruce said matter-of-factly.

"Oh . . ." Hayley said, trying to keep up a poker face and give him the impression that this revelation had absolutely no effect on her whatsoever.

Bruce studied her, trying to gauge her level of jealousy, and although it was a struggle, she did manage to remain calm and nonplussed.

"We're friends on Facebook," Bruce said.

Hayley nodded, biting her lip to keep from commenting.

"This is her profile picture," Bruce said, gesturing toward the near perfect supermodel photo on his computer screen.

"And why after all these years did you feel the burning desire to get back in touch with this old flame from South America?" Hayley said, not realizing she was tapping her foot loudly on the floor as she waited for him to answer.

"I thought you'd never ask. Sofia still lives in Mendoza. With her husband of twenty years. And their six kids."

The tension slowly began draining out of Hayley's body and she circled back around the desk and sat down in her chair again.

"She's now a big muckety-muck in the government, Minister of the Interior, or something like that. Anyway she has lots of contacts, so I reached out to her to see if she could help me get some information on Julio Garcia's cousin Juan."

Finally there was something in this unexpected and uncomfortable conversation that Hayley could grasp onto, and it instantly sparked her curiosity. "And?"

"I was right. She has a cousin who works in the Gendarmería Nacional Argentina . . ."

"The what?"

"In short, her cousin's a cop. And he has access to all kinds of information, and as a favor to her he did a search on Juan, and came up with some very interesting statistics—"

"Such as?"

"Lots of arrests over a long period, dating back to when he was just twelve years old and got caught picking the pockets of tourists in General San Martín Park. From there, he graduated to petty theft, breaking and entering, and then went on to more violent crimes like armed robbery and assault and a number of other gang-related offenses."

"Juan? Really? He seems so gentle and shy when I see him at Julio's salon," Hayley remarked.

"That's usually how someone acts when they are totally trying to reinvent themselves. Anyway, according to Sofia's cousin, Juan and Julio's family paid off a few officials to squash his rap sheet and cover up his past so it wouldn't follow him here. Otherwise, he never would have been allowed in the country."

"Julio told me Juan was just visiting when he first showed up in town a few months ago, but he never left," Hayley said.

"That's because according to documents filed with U.S. Citizenship and Immigration Services, Julio is applying to sponsor Juan as an invaluable employee of the salon in order to help him get his green card so he can stay here permanently."

Hayley began running through her mind these new facts about Julio and Juan Garcia, and how they might relate to the Caskie Lemon-Hogg and Regina Knoxville deaths. Her concentration, however, was disrupted by a short boyish giggle.

It was her husband, who was staring at his computer screen.

"What now?" Hayley asked.

"Oh, nothing . . ." Bruce said, averting his eyes from her.

"Bruce . . ."

"I just sent Sofia a message to thank her for all her help, and she wrote back, *When will I see your handsome face again back here in Argentina?* That's sweet, she's very nice, always was, just a lovely person all around . . ."

"Stop gushing, Bruce."

"I'm not gushing. We really should go sometime though, Hayley, you'd love it. The scenery is stunning and you do love wine . . . Sofia would be happy to show us around . . . and her husband too, of course . . . I think he's a professor at the university or something like that . . . I'm sure he's nice too, though I've never met him, just her, but like I said, she looks exactly the same, you'd never believe it's been something like twenty-five—"

"Bruce . . ."

"Yes, dear?"

"You're still gushing."

"Right. I'll stop now."

"I think that would be best."

Bruce reached over and clicked out of Facebook, so the photo of the stunning Sofia Ortiz disappeared and was replaced by his usual screen saver of scenic Cadillac Mountain in Acadia National Park.

As Hayley got up to leave, Bruce mumbled, "You're nothing like Liddy, you're not jealous at all."

She turned back and stared at him. "You really can't help yourself. You always need to have the last word."

"No, I don't."

"See?"

"I really don't. Go ahead and say something and I promise to keep my mouth shut, and then you leave and you'll see that I don't always need the last word."

"Fine. Goodbye, Bruce."

Hayley whipped around to make her escape, but had barely made it halfway out the door to his office when she heard him say cheerily, "I love you."

She slammed the door behind her.

Chapter 37

Hayley stood on the threshold of Albert and Regina Knoxville's bedroom, shifting uncomfortably, feeling strange at being in such close proximity to a deeply personal private space. But Albert didn't seem to mind at all. In fact, there was a look of relief as he opened the closet door and showed Hayley the rack of dresses and pantsuits that were crammed onto the small rack along with dozens of shoe and hat boxes stuffed on the top shelf. On the floor were more shoes and sandals.

"She was quite the clothes horse," Albert said softly as he stared at all of his late wife's belongings. "I've been meaning to clean all this out and donate it to Goodwill, but every time I come up here to do it, I get lost in the memories and I just can't seem to get anywhere."

"It's totally understandable, Albert. Maybe with some more time . . ." Hayley's voice trailed off.

"I guess I kind of keep hoping this is all a bad dream and I'll wake up and she'll still be here . . ."

His eyes welled up with tears.

Hayley didn't know what to say. When she had shown up at Albert's door to ask him if he knew about Regina's affair with Julio, it had seemed like a good idea at the time. But when confronted with Albert's sad, distraught eyes, she just couldn't bring herself to actually ask the question. Albert had invited her in, offered some tea, which she declined, and just stared at the walls as Hayley went on about every topic that popped into her head except the one that had brought her here. She just didn't want to hurt the poor man any more than he already had been by his beloved wife's untimely demise.

When Hayley finally ran out of things to say, Albert had asked if she might be interested in some of Regina's dresses, particularly since they were roughly around the same size. Regina had recently gone on a shopping spree in Boston and there were dresses she had not even worn. Hayley had politely declined the kind offer, but Albert had insisted she come upstairs and take a look anyway. Hayley had dragged her heels as hard as she could, but Albert wouldn't take no for an answer, and so finally, realizing it would be easier just to pretend she might accept one, she had followed Albert up the creaky steps of their weathered albeit sprawling five-bedroom house to the master bedroom.

Albert struggled to sift through the rack of garments, finally yanking out a glittery number that looked like it belonged in a flapper sketch from the 1970s in an old *Carol Burnett Show*, but she refrained from critiquing it and just said to Albert, "It's lovely, but I'm afraid it's just not my style."

Albert stuffed it back into the closet and kept searching for the right outfit for Hayley.

"Really, Albert, this is totally unnecessary. At home I already have a closet full of clothes I've hardly worn.

I was thinking of doing some wardrobe purging myself one of these days."

Albert finally got the hint and stepped out of the closet and nodded solemnly. Hayley couldn't help but notice his whole body was slumped over, like a hopelessly defeated, broken man. She felt so sorry for him.

"Are you sure you don't want some tea?" he asked.

"No, thank you, Albert," Hayley said. "Again, I am so sorry about everything. You and Regina seemed very happy."

He didn't want her to leave. She knew Albert had loved Regina deeply and was now lonely and lost without her. And she decided in that moment that despite her burning curiosity, she was not going to ask him about Julio Garcia. She was about to say her goodbye and quietly slip out when Albert, almost as if reading her mind, broached the subject himself.

"I'll miss her every day . . . But it's not like our marriage was perfect."

"Few marriages are," Hayley remarked with a wry smile.

Albert grinned. "No, I suppose not."

"I'm sure you remember my first husband, Danny. Now that marriage was about as far from perfect as you could get."

Albert chuckled and then caught himself. "Excuse me, Hayley, I didn't mean to make light of your relationship . . ."

"No, when I think back to all I put up with, it makes me laugh, but he gave me two great kids, so there was definitely an upside."

"Was he faithful?"

Hayley was surprised by the question. It was almost as if Albert wanted to open up and discuss his own marriage troubles. She thought about it for a moment and then shrugged. "You know, I'm not really sure. I thought he was, but by the end we were barely speaking, so who knows what he might have been up to? He was what you'd call a ladies' man . . ."

"Well, I never was, but that wouldn't surprise anybody. I'm more Mr. Magoo than Captain America."

Hayley cracked a smile. "I think you're a wonderful man, Albert, and I'm sure Regina did too."

"Oh, yes, I know Regina loved me, but it was more like how a little girl adores her cocker spaniel, which makes sense because she always had me fetching things."

Hayley laughed. Albert, if nothing else, had a charming sense of humor.

"But I often thought my loyalty and devotion to her just wasn't enough . . . I believe she had certain needs I just could not satisfy . . ." He seemed to be talking more to himself than to Hayley, and suddenly he snapped out of his own thoughts and raised his eyes to meet Hayley's. "I'm sorry, this is probably the last thing you came here to listen to . . ."

He couldn't have been more wrong.

Hayley knew her opportunity was right in front of her so she seized it. "Do you think Regina was having an affair?"

Albert scratched his chin and thought about it before nodding slightly. "I certainly had my suspicions. I caught her giggling and whispering to someone on the phone late at night once, and when she hung up and saw that I was awake, she told me it was her sister Betty in Philadelphia. But then the next day, Betty called and I answered and she mentioned that she hadn't talked to Regina in over a week. That was a big red flag. And I also had this nagging feeling in the pit of my stomach that wouldn't go away, but of course I didn't say anything."

"Why not?"

"In a way, I didn't want to know the truth. I was willing to turn a blind eye because if it did all come out into the open, I was afraid I might lose her."

Hayley walked over and gave Albert a hug.

He seemed grateful because he wrapped his short arms around her and squeezed so tightly, she could barely breathe.

He sniffed a few times before finally pulling away and wiping his nose with his hand.

She knew she had to know one more thing before she left. "Albert, do you have any idea who Regina might have been seeing? Was it someone local?"

Albert shook his head. "No, and I don't care. What does it matter at this point anyway? She's gone."

Hayley was not about to mention the name Julio Garcia at this point. If Albert didn't want to know, then she was not going to be the one to tell him. She turned to leave, but Albert stopped her.

"I will tell you this, I think it was over by the time of the accident."

"Accident?"

"The bees."

"Oh, yes."

Albert was firmly in the camp that believed Regina's death was *not* a homicide. Hayley was most definitely not. She turned back around to face Albert.

"What makes you think that?"

"Because the day before, she kept talking about how she wanted us to go on a trip, take a second honeymoon, maybe a cruise or something . . . it sounded like she wanted to try and rekindle our romance, which gave me high hopes that whatever she was doing behind my back was finished."

"I see," Hayley said, curious to hear more.

"I don't know if you know this, but over the last few years I've made a few bad business investments, and I've lost a lot of money . . . A *lot* of money . . ."

"No, Albert, I didn't know. I'm so sorry to hear that."

"Regina never wanted for anything . . . until recently. It's been a struggle for both of us. It nearly killed me, but I had to tell her money was too tight for us to take a trip, but she told me not to worry about it. She said she'd pay for everything, although I have no clue how—she was as broke as me. At first I figured she was just going to charge the whole thing to her one credit card that hadn't been canceled yet and we'd worry about it later. But then she mentioned she was about to come into some money but remained vague about the details and didn't want to talk about it. I was just happy she wanted to spend time with me so I didn't press her. Sadly she never got around to booking anything . . ." He sniffed again, and then before he got too emotional, cleared his throat and changed the subject. "Are you sure you don't want to take at least one dress with you, Hayley?"

"Thank you, Albert, I'm sure."

"Well, if you don't want any of Regina's clothes, how about some perfume?"

She knew what he was doing. He was making up excuses for her to stay because he didn't want to sit in this quiet house all by himself without the wife he had loved so much.

"Honestly, Albert, I don't need anything . . ."

But he was already dashing to the bathroom, perusing a few perfume bottles, picking one up and holding it out to Hayley. "She loved this one. Lavender Extreme by Tom Ford. She ordered it from Bergdorf Goodman and it just came the other day. It's never been used."

"I'm not a perfume kind of gal," Hayley said.

Albert was already on to the next beauty product on the bathroom countertop. He held up a bottle. "She wore this lotion every day. Slathered it all over herself. She bought it in bulk from Julio. No wonder she maxed out all her credit cards, buying so many dresses and beauty products."

This suddenly got Hayley's attention. "Julio Garcia?"

"Yeah, he sells all kinds of face creams, hand creams, body lotions, whatever a woman needs, but this stuff here, Regina was obsessed with it." He popped the top open and took a big whiff. "It smells real nice. Here, see for yourself, maybe you'd like a bottle or two to take with you, I've got about a half dozen she never got around to using . . ."

Albert bounded over to Hayley and shoved the open bottle right up underneath her nose. She couldn't help but inhale the fragrance, which was admittedly quite nice, but had an overpowering scent of . . .

"Honey . . ."

"Yes, it's pretty strong," Albert replied, nodding. "But you know what, it reminds me of her, and sometimes I'll open a bottle and take in the aroma and it's as if she's still here in the house."

Hayley studied the bottle and then arched an eyebrow. "That's odd."

"What?" Albert asked.

"Well, I was just reading the list of ingredients and I don't see honey extract."

"It has to be a misprint. All I smell is honey."

"Me too," Hayley said, reading through the list again. And then she gasped as if she had just been smacked in the head.

"What's wrong?"

"Nothing . . . It's just that . . ."

It had finally come to her.

How Julio Garcia had managed to kill Regina Knoxville without physically being in her presence at the time.

He had sold her his personal body lotion, which she loved so much and wore every day. What if he added one extra special ingredient to the bottle? Honey extract. And a ton of it. He knew Regina went blueberry picking in the park every Saturday. She probably told him the exact location where she liked to go. He was also probably aware that she was allergic to bees! What if he donned some gloves and a face net and moved the beehive close to the blueberry patch where he knew Regina would be? The bees would naturally be drawn to the honey slathered all over Regina's body. She would have panicked, the bees would have stung her, and after a severe reaction, she would have collapsed and died with no one around to save her!

It was the perfect murder.

Almost.

Chapter 38

"Albert, do you recall what you were doing on the day Caskie Lemon-Hogg was killed at the bed-and-breakfast?" Hayley asked as they descended the creaky steps back down to the foyer of the Knoxville home, clutching the bottle of honey-scented body lotion Albert had agreed to let her take with her.

"Was that a Tuesday?"

"I believe so, yes."

"Let me think . . ." Albert said, struggling to remember. "The days seem to blend together now that I'm retired, but I'm pretty certain I was right here, because I remember I had just watched the evening news and was getting ready to make myself some dinner when one of Regina's friends, Carol Wincott, called here asking if we had heard a body had been discovered downtown, although none of us knew who it was yet."

"Was Regina home with you at the time?"

"No, she wasn't. She had a book club meeting that night. I remember because usually the group gathers to discuss whatever they're reading on Thursdays, but for some reason, they decided to move it to Tuesday."

They reached the bottom of the stairs and Hayley stopped before opening the door to leave. "Who else is in Regina's book group?"

"I know Caskie Lemon-Hogg was in it because she was the one who got the whole thing started. She's an avid reader, always recommending books for Regina and me to read . . . Poor thing never made it to the meeting that night . . ."

"Anybody else you can think of?"

"Let's see, who else?" Albert suddenly gasped. "Come to think of it, Carol Wincott was a member of the book club too. Now why would she call here asking if Regina had heard about a murder in town if she was already with Regina? I guess I never thought about that at the time."

"Thank you for all your help, Albert," Hayley said as she reached for the door handle.

"Are you sure you don't want to stay for some tea, Hayley?"

Hayley hugged him again. "I'm sorry, I really have to go, but I promise to stop by later this week."

He nodded, not sure if she meant it or not, but appeared grateful that she was at least being nice to him. Hayley suspected Regina had found few occasions to be kind to her adoring and devoted husband other than toward the end when she mentioned planning that out-of-the-blue trip together.

Hayley dashed down the sidewalk to her car, and once she was in the driver's seat with the motor running, and had tossed the bottle of body lotion into her bag, she scrolled down the list of contacts on her phone and called Carol Wincott.

Carol answered on the second ring. "Hello?"

"Hi, Carol, it's Hayley Powell."

"Hayley, I must say this is a pleasant surprise. I hardly ever hear from you."

She was right.

Hayley usually didn't reach out to Carol, as they had very little in common. Although Carol was friendly and sweet, they just ran in different social circles. Hayley didn't want to come off as rude or self-serving, so she said in a sing-songy voice, "That's why I'm calling! I've been thinking about you, and I've been meaning to call and catch up, and I'm finally doing it! So let's do it! Let's catch up! How are you? How's the book club?"

Okay, so it wasn't the height of subtlety, but she didn't have a lot of time.

"The book club?" Carol asked, confused.

"You know, the one you're in that meets every Thursday . . ."

"Well, we've recently lost two members, so we've been on kind of a break . . ."

"Oh, that's right, I heard Regina Knoxville and Caskie Lemon-Hogg were members. I'm so sorry . . ."

"No, it's all right. If you're looking to join, I'm sure the other ladies would be happy to have you. When we do reconvene I've recommended the new Sally Thorne novel, even though Kate Addison is pushing for that new E. L. James piece of trash. I swear every time it's her pick, we have to slog through another one of those filthy *Fifty Shades*–type books that are dripping with sex and bad behavior."

Hayley refrained from mentioning that she had read them all. "I'm definitely interested, although I know sometimes you meet on Tuesdays, and Tuesdays don't work for me because that's my date night with Bruce."

"I don't know what you're talking about, Hayley, we *always* meet on Thursdays."

"I heard you met a few Tuesdays ago, the night Caskie Lemon-Hogg was killed, in fact."

"We certainly did *not* meet on that day."

"Are you sure?"

"I'm positive. We've never in the history of the book club ever had a meeting on any day but Thursday," Carol said flatly.

Hayley's suspicions had been confirmed.

Regina had lied to Albert about where she was on the day of Caskie's murder.

"It's been great catching up with you, Carol! Let's do this again real soon!"

"Wait, what about the book—?"

Hayley ended the call, tossed her phone on the passenger's seat, and peeled away from the curb. She felt bad about hanging up so abruptly on Carol and made a mental note to call her again in a few days to sincerely catch up, but she had to concentrate on pulling together all the information she had just learned.

Why would Regina lie to Albert? More than likely it was to cover up a secret rendezvous with Julio. But according to Julio, he was at his salon training his cousin Juan and had even answered a few calls on the landline from customers who wanted to make appointments. He supposedly didn't go anywhere all night. It wouldn't be hard for her to find the women who had called and spoken to him personally, to corroborate his story. So did Regina come to him? That was a possibility, but if Juan was truly there, then that would make a romantic rendezvous rather awkward. Julio could be lying about Juan being there. But what kept nagging at Hayley was what Albert had just told her. He had gotten the impression that Regina's affair with Julio was over. And what about this mysterious money that Regina had mentioned to Albert that she was going to use to pay for their vacation cruise?

Hayley tried hard to piece together a plausible theory. It might be reasonable to believe that Julio had broken it off with Regina, and she was angry and vindictive, and perhaps she threatened to spill everything to Jeanette if he didn't pay her off? That would explain why Regina was expecting an influx of cash, and it would also give Julio a clear motive to want to somehow silence her. And maybe he succeeded in getting rid of her permanently with the lotion and beehive and Regina's bee allergy. But then there was the beard she had found in the closet at the Garcia home. If Julio's alibi the night of Caskie's murder was airtight, then the bearded man who showed up at the bed-and-breakfast and killed Caskie could have been his cousin Juan! But why? Why kill Caskie?

And then she had a eureka moment.

Of course!

The answer had been in front of her all along!

Chapter 39

Hayley had to do one more thing before she went to Sergio to explain who killed Caskie Lemon-Hogg and Regina Knoxville. She needed one last piece of evidence, and she knew where she would find it. She drove from the Knoxville house straight over to Julio's Salon.

Her phone buzzed. It was Sheila. Hayley sighed and answered the call. "Mom, I can't talk right now—"

"I just want to know when you're coming home for dinner. I'm making short ribs and mashed potatoes and a beautiful blueberry tart for dessert. Oh, and I invited Sergio and Randy . . ."

That was perfect.

She didn't have to stop by the police station.

She could present her theory and evidence right at her own dinner table.

"I just have to make a quick stop first," Hayley said.

"Good, could you pick up some Cool Whip? Just in case people want a dollop on their tart?"

"Mom, I'm not going to the Shop 'n Save."

"The drug store? Because if you are, I'm out of orange-flavored baby aspirin. My doctor has me take one every day as a preventive measure against a heart attack. You know, your Aunt Margery died of heart failure, and she was younger than me!"

"I'm going to Julio's Salon!"

"Whatever for? The short ribs are almost done. I'm not going to make everyone wait to eat while you get your hair straightened and colored!"

Colored? Really? Of course she would just assume Hayley was going gray. And frankly, her hair *had* been turning gray at a much faster rate than normal ever since her mother had blown into town. But instead of engaging, Hayley simply said, "I'm not getting my hair done. I'll be home in ten minutes."

"But why do you have to—?"

Hayley ended the call as she pulled up Rodick Street toward Julio's Salon. When she stopped her car in front of the building, she saw the closed sign in the window. It was already a few minutes past six o'clock. Through the window she could see Julio with a broom sweeping up, and so she jumped out of the car, ran up to the front door and rapped her knuckles on the window a few times to get his attention. The sound of her knocking startled him. He turned to see Hayley waving frantically at him. He leaned the broom against the counter and sauntered over to talk to Hayley through the door. He glared at her grimly, not at all excited to see her again after she had shown up to drag her mother out of the shop for causing such a scene.

"I'm sorry, Hayley, I just finished up my last appointment for the day. Jeanette and I have a dinner reservation at Havana in a half hour."

"I'm not here to get my hair done, Julio, I just want to buy a bottle of your body lotion."

"I already cashed out the register. Can you come back when we open in the morning?"

"Please, I'll pay extra."

He stared at her quizzically, not quite understanding why it was so important, but then he shrugged—a sale was a sale, after all—and he unlocked the door and ushered her inside.

"I really appreciate this, Julio."

He circled around the counter to grab a bottle off the shelf behind him. "Did you talk to Sergio? After you left, I called and gave him all the phone numbers of the women I talked to on the phone here at the shop on the night Caskie Lemon-Hogg was killed."

"I haven't had a chance, but I have no reason to doubt you. Again, I am so sorry for my mother."

He eyed her suspiciously and then began tapping keys on the register until it rang and the empty cash drawer opened.

"That will be thirty-five sixty-seven," Julio said coldly.

Hayley opened her bag and fished around for some cash and withdrew two twenties and handed them to him.

He accepted the bills. "Like I said, I already cashed out and made the bank deposit for the day, so I don't have any change right now."

"Perfectly understandable. I don't need change. I just wanted a bottle of this lotion. Liddy swears by it so I'm desperate to try it out."

She unscrewed the cap and inhaled the scent. There was a strong scent of rosemary and mint but nothing remotely like honey. This was exactly what she needed to prove her theory: the original bottle with the listed ingredients, so the police could compare the bottle with the one Julio had personally prepared for Regina

Knoxville with the extra added ingredient of honey extract.

"Thank you so much for letting me come in here after closing, Julio. I'm going to call you tomorrow and make an appointment so you can help me tame this frizzy mess I'm dealing with," Hayley said quickly as she spun around to beat a hasty retreat. Unfortunately she slammed right into a wall, or at least that's what it felt like upon impact. She stumbled back in time to see that she had just collided with the broad, buffed, sculpted chest of Julio's cousin Juan, who had just walked through the door. She dropped her bag to the floor and the contents scattered everywhere, most notably the bottle of Julio's body lotion that she had borrowed from Albert Knoxville.

Julio's eyes fixed on the bottle instantly and he looked squarely at Hayley, frowning. "I thought you said you've never tried the lotion."

"I . . . I haven't . . . that's Liddy's bottle. She lent it to me so I could see if I liked it . . ."

Julio wasn't buying her story. He bent down, scooped up the bottle, unscrewed the top and took a whiff, overcome by the strong smell of honey. "You didn't get this from Liddy . . ."

Hayley knew there was no way she could talk her way out of a potentially dangerous situation this time. So she turned and made a run for it, but Juan was blocking the door and his arms were outstretched to intercept her like a football flying at him in the final few seconds of the game. He wrapped his giant, muscled arms around her in a bear hug and half dragged, half carried her over to a dryer chair, where he forced her down and then strapped her in using the wide leather belt he ripped out of the loops of his tight khaki pants. Meanwhile, Julio lowered the bamboo curtains down over the windows to block the view of anybody who might be passing by the salon.

Hayley struggled mightily in the dryer chair, but the leather belt holding her down was too thick and strong and Juan hovered over her menacingly, ready to intervene if she somehow managed to get herself free. But Hayley knew in her gut there would be no miraculous escape.

Julio marched over to Hayley, shaking his head. "It's such a shame. You've always been one of my favorite customers, Hayley. So friendly and charming. Most of the time I have to pretend to be interested in what my customers chat endlessly about while I do their hair, but you were different. You didn't bore me. You were interesting and funny. And now you've gone and ruined it."

"No, I didn't ruin anything, Julio! You did! You and Juan! By committing *two* murders!"

Juan shot Julio a panicked look, but with one wave of his hand, Julio calmed him down and he stood there like a docile animal.

"I told you I was here in the shop when—"

"I know you were. You had the perfect alibi with all of your adoring customers who called here that night, ready to back you up. But none of those women talked to Juan, did they? You just said he was here, that you were training him, but we only have your word. He wasn't here at all. He was over at the bed-and-breakfast strangling Caskie Lemon-Hogg!"

Julio flinched slightly, but kept up his steady, unruffled demeanor. "That's ridiculous. What would Juan have against Caskie? He's just arrived in town."

"With a long criminal record," Hayley said.

Juan gasped. "How did you know about—"

Another look from Julio instantly shut him up.

Hayley stared at Juan. "You're right. Juan had nothing against Caskie and neither did you."

"Finally, some progress. So tell me, Hayley, what is it you're talking about?" Julio said, appearing to feel a bit more confident and emboldened.

"Juan didn't go over there to kill Caskie. He went over there to kill Regina."

Julio's placid exterior finally began to slowly melt away at hearing the words come out of Hayley's mouth, and he became a bit more noticeably agitated.

"Your affair with her had ended, badly I presume, and Regina was threatening to go to your wife, Jeanette, and spill everything. You desperately didn't want that to happen so you offered to buy Regina's silence since you probably knew that she and Albert were having money problems after some bad investments. Albert said that Regina had told him right before she died that she was about to come into some money."

She could tell from Julio's pained expression that she had just nailed that bit, so she kept going. "But you never had any intention of paying her, did you? You arranged to meet her at the B and B, ostensibly to hand over a bag of cash, but instead you stayed behind at the salon to establish your alibi and sent your cousin to do your dirty work. Juan used Rupert Stiles's stolen credit card, the one you swiped from him when he came in here to get his beard trimmed. It was Juan who wore the long beard I found in the back of your bedroom closet, and probably some old smelly baggy clothes. Just in case anyone saw him, he resembled Rupert. The desk clerk probably didn't pay that much attention to him, but from his loose description and the credit card on file, the police would be able to confirm it was him. A lot of people knew Rupert had a mad crush on Regina his whole life. The cops would just assume it was a crime of passion. That Rupert somehow got Regina to agree to meet him over at the B and B, she rejected him again, and he just lost it, unable to accept that she didn't love him and would never love him and so he killed her, maybe by accident or in a moment of insanity. It would be so easy to mount a case against him."

Hayley let the theory hang there for a few quiet moments.

Julio bit his bottom lip, but was unwavering in his resolve to not react hysterically as Hayley plainly laid out the facts. Juan, on the other hand, was sweating as if he had just emerged fully clothed from a sweltering sauna.

"The only problem was, instead of Regina, Caskie showed up first. She went to the B and B to talk to my mother, who was staying in room nine. But instead, Caskie knocked on the door of room six. That's because Caskie had dyslexia, or some version of it, an affliction that had been diagnosed way back when she was in high school. She mixes up numbers. She looks at something and sees something else. And instead of a six, she saw a nine. Her fatal mistake was going to the wrong room. She walked right into a trap."

Juan started to shake. "Julio . . ."

"Shut up, Juan!" Julio barked.

Hayley kept going. "Juan, who was new to town and didn't really know either woman, was just waiting for his mark to arrive. He simply assumed Caskie was Regina when she entered the room and strangled her from behind, never getting a good look at her face. When Regina showed up for her money, she probably purposely avoided being seen by the desk clerk, not wanting anyone to witness her there with you. She knocked on the door to room six and when no one answered, she left, having no idea that Caskie's body was on the other side of that door, and Juan was probably still there too, ready to take care of her as well if she barged in and saw what he had just done. After that, Juan must have run off, leaving the door ajar, which was how my mother found the body. Poor Caskie was never the intended target. It was Regina all along."

Hayley looked at Juan and then at Julio. She had them dead to rights and they all knew it.

Hayley leaned forward, still restrained by the leather belt, and asked, "Once Regina found out what happened, why didn't she go directly to the police? Caskie was her close friend . . ."

Julio sneered. "Regina wasn't anyone's close friend. It was all an act. Once she realized our big mistake, she just tripled her price to keep quiet."

"Wasn't she afraid you might try to kill her again instead of paying her off?"

"No, because she didn't think we'd be stupid enough to risk committing two murders, and she was right. That's why it was so important that her death look like an accident."

"But why did Regina point the finger at my mother, Celeste, and Jane if she already knew that you and Juan had killed Caskie?"

"She was greedy. She wanted to keep the attention off us until she got her money. I told her I needed time to get the cash together, but I was just buying time until I could figure out how to solve the problem."

"And that's when you came up with the body lotion solution."

"There was a bee in the shop once when I was doing her hair and she freaked out and hid in the bathroom until we could squash it with a magazine. I knew from that point on she was allergic, and I knew where she went every Saturday, so I put the honey in her body lotion. Juan went out to move the beehive close to the blueberry patches. I honestly wasn't sure if it would work, but it did, like a charm. Chief Alvarez was certain Regina's death was just a tragic accident. And now, besides your mother, who doesn't have the brainpower to put all of the pieces together, you're the only one who knows the truth about what really happened."

Julio took a step toward Hayley, whose whole body tensed. She locked eyes with him. "How are you going to explain another dead body?"

"I won't have to," Julio said calmly.

"You're not going to kill me?" Hayley asked, a skeptical look on her face.

"No, not at all. I don't have the stomach for physical violence, never have," Julio said, before turning to his cousin, who scowled at Hayley. "Luckily, my cousin does. And nobody has to explain a dead body if it's never found."

Juan grabbed a black hair-stylist apron off the back of a chair and rolled it up into a taut noose, and then slowly advanced toward Hayley, sliding in behind her before dropping it down in front of her and tightening it around her neck.

Chapter 40

As Juan yanked back hard on the makeshift noose, Hayley opened her mouth and let out a quick gasp, but that was the only sound she managed to make as the pressure violently cut off her breathing. As hard as she fought to escape, she knew it was hopeless as the belt kept her firmly pinned to the chair and there was nowhere to go. Julio stood in front of her, his arms folded, calmly watching the scene with cold black eyes. His lips curled into a sickening sneer. Hayley reached up to claw at the apron wrapped around her throat, but Juan was too strong. She felt a sense of dread and hopelessness.

Suddenly there was a loud banging at the front door. Startled, Julio whipped his head around toward the salon entrance but couldn't see who was outside because he had drawn all the curtains. He turned back to Juan.

"Hurry up and get this done," Julio hissed, gesturing toward Hayley, whose eyes were about to roll up in the back of her head as she fought hard not to pass out. She managed to stay conscious long enough to see Julio tiptoe over and press his ear to the door to see if he could hear anyone talking on the other side. Another loud knock caused him to jump back, and then Hayley heard the sweet, welcoming sound of her mother's voice.

"Julio, I know you're in there with my daughter! Open up!"

Hayley, reignited with a faint bit of hope, tried calling to her mother, but anticipating the move, Juan squeezed the noose tighter, almost crushing her windpipe.

More banging, this time more aggressive, more insistent.

"Julio, open this door right now!" Sheila cried.

Julio walked back over to where Juan was in the final throes of asphyxiating Hayley. He kept one eye on the door but whispered, "She'll give up and go away soon enough . . ."

Suddenly, without warning, Hayley heard a hissing sound and a man screaming. The noose around her neck loosened and she was able to pull it away from her neck. She twisted her head around to see Jane, armed with a can of DevaCurl Flexible Hold Hairspray, her finger pressed firmly down on the nozzle, shooting it directly into Juan's eyes. She had come out of nowhere and surprised the two men. Juan fell back against the mirror, covering his eyes with his hands.

Julio was so stunned he didn't move at first.

Hayley seized the opportunity and grabbed the sides of the dryer chair with her free hands and drove her knee up into his groin. It knocked the air out of him and he doubled over in pain.

Then Celeste appeared with a curling iron and began violently whacking Julio on the head with it. Hayley couldn't believe her eyes. Liddy's prissy, socialite mother was screaming like a wild animal, thrusting the curling iron to and fro like she was a *Game of Thrones* warrior.

With Juan blinded and moaning from the chemicals in his eyes and Julio on his knees covering his head to protect himself from Celeste's relentless, vicious attack, Hayley felt someone behind her unbuckling the belt that was keeping her tied to the dryer chair, and she was finally freed. It was Jane. "Go let your mother in, I'll handle this one!"

She was referring to Juan, who had just lowered his hands to reveal the burning red skin around his eyes. He had just enough time to look around and see that the cavalry here to rescue Hayley were two elderly women, when Jane grabbed some cutting shears off the counter and wedged the sharp tips up underneath his Adam's apple, ready to draw blood. "One move, and I'll cut you a new smile!"

Hayley jumped to her feet, ran to the door, and unlocked it to let her mother inside. Sheila grabbed her in a hug and began to cry. "Oh, honey, I was so worried about you!"

A police car came roaring up the street, sirens blaring, and seconds later Sergio and Officer Donnie barged into the salon, but stopped short at the sight of Julio writhing on the floor as Celeste stood over him, ready to strike again with the curling iron. Juan stood up against the mirror, hands in the air, as Jane kept the shears pointed at his neck.

Sergio and Donnie exchanged astonished looks before taking the two men into custody.

Hayley turned to her mother. "I don't understand. How did you know?"

"A mother *always* knows," Sheila said matter-of-factly. "I already suspected Julio was behind all this, which is why he kicked me out of his shop. When you called and told me you were on your way to the salon, well, I had a bad feeling, call it a mother's intuition, and so I called the girls and told them to meet me over here, and then I texted Sergio and said we might need backup."

"But how did Jane and Celeste—?"

"We took a chance that Juan hadn't fixed the broken lock on the back window that Julio mentioned when we were last here getting our hair done. The plan was for me to keep them distracted by pounding on the door while Jane and Celeste snuck around back and climbed through the window."

Hayley stared at her mother, impressed. "You're like a post-menopausal Navy SEAL team."

"You could have just left it at Navy SEAL team, dear."

"Sorry."

Chapter 41

As hard as she tried, Hayley couldn't stop herself from crying. The tears rolled down her cheeks and she tried wiping them away with the palms of her hands, but they just kept coming.

Sheila, who stood in the kitchen with her and a large suitcase, pressed a hand to her heart, touched by the sight of her daughter overcome with such genuine emotion. "Oh, Hayley, don't despair. I'll be back to visit again, I promise. Just not in the winter. My body is no longer equipped to deal with the cold weather."

"I'm just going to miss you so much . . ."

Sheila threw out her arms and grabbed Hayley, squeezing her tightly. "And you and Bruce are welcome anytime to come down and stay with me in Florida."

Hayley sniffed, trying desperately to get herself under control, but she just couldn't.

Sheila gently patted Hayley on the back. "There, there, I had no idea you'd be this sad to see me leave."

Hayley nodded, not having the heart to tell her mother that she was actually ecstatic over the fact that her mother was finally leaving. No, her grief and sorrow, her endless stream of tears, actually had nothing to do with her mother's departure. But she was not about to admit it, especially with her mother so close to finally walking out the door after three long weeks.

She heard Bruce descending the stairs. He sneezed loudly, causing both Hayley and Sheila to jump. When he reached the bottom and rounded the corner toward the kitchen, he was lugging the cat carrier. Through the wire mesh she could plainly see the wide angry eyes of her cat, Blueberry, glaring at her. He knew something was up but hadn't figured out what it was yet.

Bruce opened his mouth and sneezed again, and then grabbed a dish towel off the kitchen counter to wipe his nose. He set the carrier down on the high-top table in the breakfast nook.

Sheila bent her knees so she was eye to eye with Blueberry, staring at his grumpy face through the carrier. "How about it, Blueberry? Are you ready to go on an adventure with me?"

"I really appreciate you taking him with you, Sheila," Bruce said.

"Consider it my wedding present to you and Hayley," Sheila said, laughing.

Hayley chuckled, pretending to be light-hearted about the whole thing, but inside she was full of sadness. It had not been an easy decision. Bruce had dialed back his insistence that she make a Sophie's choice—the cat went or he did. He knew Blueberry had been around a lot longer than him and he was not about to break his new wife's heart by getting rid of one of her beloved pets. It had been Hayley's idea to ask Sheila if she would consider adopting him and taking him home to Florida with her. Sheila at first appeared surprised that Hayley would give him up, but when Hayley explained how miserable Bruce was with his cat allergies, she quickly warmed to the idea. She needed something to dote on, and an ill-tempered blue Persian cat was the perfect solution. Bruce was more than happy to pay the extra hundred and fifty dollars the airline charged to bring the cat carrier on board, and Hayley had already shipped a box of Blueberry's favorite toys and snacks ahead of time to her mother's house in order to make the adjustment to his new home easier.

But now that the day was here, and it was time to say goodbye to Blueberry, she was a blubbering emotional mess. They had never had an easy relationship, not since the day she had decided to take him in after his previous owner, an elderly local woman named Imogen Tubbs, had been hospitalized following a car accident. The first night in Hayley's house, Blueberry had peed on the living room rug and managed to alienate just about everybody, including Gemma and Dustin, Hayley herself, and especially her dog Leroy, who he habitually terrorized. After Mrs. Tubbs recovered but had to leave town rather unexpectedly, Hayley made the fateful decision to keep Blueberry, for better or worse.

But she had also made the same vow to Bruce, not that she was comparing her new husband to a fat, cantankerous cat, but she knew what she had to do.

Hayley slowly approached the carrier and noticed Leroy sitting in the corner of the kitchen near the door to the basement, smiling, almost joyous, as his little mind was processing that his arch nemesis was leaving on a trip somewhere, and he would finally find a little peace. Hayley could only imagine how he would be running in circles, tickled pink, if he actually knew it was permanent and that the moody cat was never coming back. Hayley lowered her face and smiled at Blueberry, her throat catching as she spoke, but determined not to cry again. "You behave and be a good cat for Mom, okay, Blueberry?"

She knew that was an impossible request, but she didn't want Sheila realizing the difficulty of the job she was taking on and getting any second thoughts.

Blueberry just stared blankly at her, nonplussed. For a moment, she expected him to just shrug and say, "Whatever." But he didn't. He had his usual look of perpetual annoyance, but she did hear him purring. Talk about a complicated feline. She decided to take the soft purring as a compliment, a clear indication that he might have a soft spot for this woman who had cared for him the past seven years. When she poked her finger through the wire mesh to stroke the top of his head between the ears, he reared back and hissed at her.

Nope, he was not going to give her the satisfaction.

He was going to be obstinate until the end.

Bruce turned to Sheila, his eyes watery and his nose stuffed, and said, "Good luck."

Sheila smiled at her new cat through the wire mesh of the carrier. "I have a feeling we're going to be the best of friends."

The front door opened and Carl Flippen ambled inside and headed to the kitchen, where they were all gathered. He pointed at the large baby-blue suitcase next to Sheila. "This the last one?"

"Yes, thank you, Carl," Sheila cooed.

He lifted it effortlessly by the handle and gave Sheila a melt-your-heart smile. "Ready to go?"

Carl had graciously offered to drive Sheila to the airport. Sheila at first demurred, falsely telling him that Hayley would be happy to give her a ride, but Carl wouldn't hear of it.

Sheila slipped her arm through Carl's free one that wasn't holding the suitcase. "Carl is going to come visit me in a few months down in Florida."

"I booked my ticket this morning," he said, beaming.

Sheila looked at him, stunned. "You did?"

"Yup, and I bought us Disney tickets. I've never been and I hear Epcot is a must."

"You *what*?" Sheila said, her mouth dropped open.

"Three weeks in October!" Carl said.

Sheila's eyes nearly popped out of her head. "*Three weeks?*"

Carl nodded, excited. "I was going to stay a month but I just can't take that much time off from work, at least not yet."

Sheila gulped and then said tightly, "I thought we were going to wait until I got home to discuss dates . . ."

"Why wait? You only live once, right? You still want me to come, don't you? How else are we going to know if we're a good fit?"

"Well, I, um, uh . . ." Sheila stammered.

Hayley was loving every minute of this.

"It's just that . . . I mean . . . what if after a few days we get on each other's nerves? What will we do the rest of the time?"

Carl gave her a sweet peck on the cheek. "I think we both know that's not going to happen."

Hayley was growing more fond of Carl with each passing minute. How could she not love a man who made her mother nervous?

Sheila didn't know what to say so she just waved at Hayley and Bruce. "Goodbye and thank you for everything. I'll call you when I get home so you know the plane didn't crash."

"Don't even say that, Mom!" Hayley cried.

"If I say it out loud, the opposite will happen," Sheila said.

"Where do you hear these things?" Hayley asked, shaking her head.

Bruce grabbed the handle of the animal carrier. "I'll help you load up the car, Carl."

"Thanks, Bruce," Carl said.

As Bruce passed him with the carrier and Hayley watched Blueberry's final departure for the sunny climes of the east coast of Florida, her eyes welled up with tears again. She was just about to start sobbing when she was startled by another loud sneeze. Only this time it didn't come from Bruce. It was Carl, who was reaching into his back pocket for a handkerchief.

"You're not coming down with a cold are you, Carl?" Sheila asked.

Carl blew his nose and shook his head. "I don't think so. Must be an allergy."

All eyes focused on the cat carrier Bruce was holding next to Carl. Hayley could see her husband start to panic.

"You two better get going or you'll miss your flight! I'll get the carrier strapped down in the back seat. Say goodbye, Blueberry!"

Bruce flew out the door with the carrier before anyone had a chance to even suggest that Carl was allergic to Blueberry and Sheila might not be the perfect guardian after all, if things eventually worked out between them.

Carl shrugged, still blissfully unaware he was allergic to cat dander, and smiled at Hayley. "See you around town."

"Bye, Carl."

He sneezed again and followed Bruce out the door with Sheila's suitcase.

Hayley turned to her mother. "I like him."

"It's not going to last," Sheila said.

"Mom! Why do you always do that? Give it a chance . . ."

She noticed her mother grinning and then it dawned on her. "Oh, wait. I know what you're doing. 'If you say it out loud, the opposite will happen!' Which means you're hopeful."

"I raised such a smart girl," Sheila said, kissing Hayley and then heading out the door to what Hayley hoped would be, fingers crossed, a bright future.

Island Food & Spirits
BY HAYLEY POWELL

There has been a lot of major drama happening in our small town over the past few weeks—the shocking and untimely deaths of two residents, the very public arrest of salon owner Julio Garcia and his cousin, not to mention all the canceled hair appointments, and of course, the Golden Girls sleuths finally hanging up their detective shields and going back to their normal lives. Things in my life finally seemed to be settling down.

Or so I thought.

Randy and Sergio felt bad that Bruce and I had to postpone our honeymoon cruise to a later unknown date because of the fast unfolding events we had to deal with recently. They were also very much aware that when we took our impromptu wedding vows, we never really had a chance to have any sort of celebration. So out of the goodness of their hearts, the boys decided to throw us a surprise evening wedding barbecue party at their beautiful home on the shore path, with all our friends in attendance along with a couple of extra surprises thrown in for fun.

With the finicky Maine weather gods providing a beautiful warm summer evening, Randy and Sergio spared no expense when it came to the barbecue, which is one of Bruce's all-time favorite meals. If he could, Bruce would scarf down barbecue every day if I didn't change it up with some Italian or Mexican food on occasion.

Mainely Meat BBQ was called in to cater the whole affair with their delicious pulled pork, sausage baked beans, corn on the cob, and tangy coleslaw. And for dessert, Mona enlisted someone she knew who she considered to be "a baking genius" to provide some delicious blueberry tarts. In fact, a lot of people commented that the tarts even rivaled, perhaps tasted even better than Caskie Lemon-Hogg's recipe, God rest her soul.

Which leads me to our next surprise. Apparently, "the baking genius" was my own daughter, Gemma, who with her boyfriend, Conner, had arrived in town a day prior, unbeknownst to me. They had hidden away for the night at Randy and Sergio's house so they could surprise us at the party!

Then, of course, there was my favorite boxed wine and Bruce's preferred canned beers iced down in metal wash tubs. Randy, who always insists on serving a signature cocktail at any party that he hosts, enlisted his friend Dana from college, who also happened to be visiting for the weekend, to whip up her favorite summer cocktail, Thyme for Maine Blueberries. A drink so good Randy said he was going to steal the recipe and serve it at his bar for the rest of the summer.

Yummy food, tasty cocktails, and close friends all gathered at a gorgeous home on the water. What more could anyone ask for?

Well, that's when Randy announced an extra special guest would be attending. A world-famous performer who happened to be a dear old friend of mine was in Portland for a concert. Randy had just called him up and asked him to surprise me and Bruce by showing up at the party. Not only did he accept and break speed records from Portland to Bar Harbor to be there on time, he also offered to be the evening's entertainment and sing for us! Out came Wade Springer, my favorite country singer of all time! Wade and I had met a few years back when he was performing in Bar Harbor and I was hired to cater his meals. We also had managed to get caught up in a murder investigation! But what I prefer to remember about that time together was the blossoming love connection between us, which had caused me a few heart palpitations. But a full-blown romance was not to be. And I got the guy of my dreams in the end anyway when I married Bruce. Wade and I, however, remained good friends and occasionally email back and forth or jump on the phone for a few minutes during holidays.

Well, suffice it to say, the party guests went wild when Wade hopped in front of the microphone and belted out one of his top-ten country hits.

The night was perfect except for one tiny detail.

The guests of honor were a no-show.

That's right. Randy waited until the last moment after all the party plans were in place to call Bruce and me to invite us over for "a simple cocktail on the front porch." Unfortunately, earlier in the day Bruce and I had the crazy idea of getting away for the night, just the two of us. So we packed an overnight bag, called Randy's cell and left a message when he didn't answer that we would be over sometime the next day to visit with Dana, and headed up to Bangor for a night of gambling at the Hollywood Casino.

It was the first time in history that I convinced Bruce that we should go "off the grid" as they say and turn off our cell phones so we would not be disturbed. On our way home the next morning was when we finally turned them back on and heard all of our missed messages from the frantic hosts demanding to know where we were and why we weren't answering our phones! It turned out Randy had not heard my previous voicemail message until after the party because he had put his phone away in the house and he had been using Sergio's to call us nine times.

I must admit my heart skipped a beat when I listened to the last message and heard that deep, slow, Southern drawl I knew belonged to Wade Springer. Wade had said he was sorry to have missed me and my new husband, but the next time he was in our neck of the woods, he would be sure to stop by to say hello. However, he would definitely call first and give plenty of notice as he laughed that deep, intoxicating, manly laugh. Is anyone else feeling a little hot right now?

Well, at least everyone had a great time, and I must say, even though Bruce and I apparently missed the party of the summer, we did enjoy our uninterrupted night alone together in Bangor.

The bonus was when Gemma brought over a plate of blueberry tarts that she had set aside for us, and Conner made Dana's cocktail recipe for us all to enjoy when we finally arrived home.

It's still blueberry season, so I definitely want to share Gemma's delicious blueberry tart recipe and Dana's Thyme for Maine Blueberries Cocktail.

THYME FOR MAINE BLUEBERRIES COCKTAIL

INGREDIENTS
¾ ounce blueberry-thyme syrup
Lemon zest from half a lemon
¾ ounce lemon juice
2½ ounces gin
3 dashes Angostura bitters
Soda water
Ice

In a cocktail shaker add all the above ingredients except the soda and ice. Shake until well blended and pour into cocktail glass with ice and add a splash or two of soda.

BLUEBERRY-THYME SYRUP
INGREDIENTS
1 cup wild Maine blueberries
1 cup sugar
1 cup water
2 tablespoons corn syrup
3 sprigs thyme

Add all the ingredients to a saucepan and bring to a boil, then simmer for three minutes. Turn off the heat and let cool in the pan. Pour through a strainer, pressing the blueberries to get all the syrup and juice. Store in the fridge.

GEMMA'S SUMMER BLUEBERRY TART

CRUST
INGREDIENTS
1 cup all-purpose flour
2 tablespoons sugar
¼ teaspoon salt
½ cup cold butter cut in small cubes
1 tablespoon vinegar

In a bowl combine flour, sugar, and salt; cut in the butter with a pastry cutter or clean fingers until mixture is crumbly. Add the vinegar and mix it in with a fork. Press the mixture into a lightly greased 9-inch tart pan and set aside.

FILLING
INGREDIENTS
4 cups fresh blueberries
⅔ cup sugar
2 tablespoons all-purpose flour
½ teaspoon ground cinnamon
¼ teaspoon ground nutmeg

Pour two cups of the blueberries into a bowl and lightly mash with a fork. Combine the sugar, flour, cinnamon, and nutmeg and mix into the mashed blueberries. Spread mixture evenly into tart crust and sprinkle one cup of the remaining blueberries over the top.

Place filled tart pan on a baking sheet and bake in a preheated oven at 350 degrees F for 40 to 45 minutes until crust is brown and filling is bubbly.

Remove from oven and cool completely on a wire rack. When cool add remaining one cup of blueberries to top of tart. Slice, serve and enjoy!

Index of Recipes